Hi, E

# DEADLY DEEDS

Happy reading —

**Neal Sanders**

*The Hardington Press*

*Deadly Deeds* is a work of fiction. While certain locales and organizations are rooted in fact, the people and events described are entirely the product of the author's imagination.

## Also by Neal Sanders

*Murder Imperfect*
*The Garden Club Gang*
*The Accidental Spy*
*A Murder in the Garden Club*
*Murder for a Worthy Cause*
*Deal Killer*

*"No good deed goes unpunished."*

-- Clare Boothe Luce (1903-1987)
      American Playwright, Politician and Envoy

# DEADLY DEEDS

## Prologue

Al Pokrovsky, Jr. slumped by the side of the car and wondered how it had all come to this.

His father certainly never had these problems. His father, "Smilin' Al" Pokrovsky, apparently never had a problem in his entire, charmed life. But then Smilin' Al had bought his first Toyota dealership for $25,000 back when American cars ruled and Japanese imports were the butt of jokes. Smilin' Al had built an empire selling inexpensive, fuel-efficient Toyotas, Hondas, Hyundais, Kias, Subarus and Mazdas to New Englanders shell-shocked by inexorably rising gasoline prices. Seven years earlier, Smilin' Al had bequeathed that money-minting empire to his son.

And now it had all fallen apart.

It was two in the morning, and surrounding him were eighteen gas-guzzling behemoths; gargantuan vehicles that had cost him $1.2 million. Eight months earlier he had seen the future and it was these autos. The economy was rebounding and America again wanted off-road luxury. The beauty of it all was that instead of squeezing out a few hundred dollars profit from the sale of a $22,000 car, he would earn more than $20,000 in net profits off of each sale. It was the beginning of a new era; one where he would emerge from the shadow of being "Junior" – Smilin' Al's son who inherited his father's tried-and-true playbook and had no new ideas of his own.

Except that it wasn't the future. No one had taken any of these test vehicles for a test drive in months, even as he piled on the incentives and added special advertising. After eight months in inventory, it was clear that no one wanted these obscene cars with their rhino guards and mountaintop suspensions coupled with fine leathers and rare wood trims. He had paid $1.2 million for instant junkers.

He sighed and pulled himself up. It had to be done. If he didn't do it, these cars were going to sink the entire overextended Pokrovsky chain of dealerships that stretched from Rhode Island to New Hampshire.

To save his empire, he had, over a three-week period, quietly sequestered these eighteen vehicles in a remote corner of his Reading dealership. Tonight, he would solve his financial problems with the striking of a match.

The graffiti he had painted on them was a perfect mixture of righteous moral outrage and deeply disturbed environmental extremism. "STOP THE PIPELINE", "THE 1% CAN TAKE THE T", "SHAME", and "FRACKING" with a circle and bar through the word. Some he had spray-painted with his left hand, some with his right. Now, he doused gasoline from the third of the three, five-gallon cans on the last of the vehicles.

With the final ounces of the can's contents, he poured a trail to a safe distance. From his pocket, he pulled out a pack of convenience store matches. He struck the match.

Suddenly there was blinding light from four sources.

A bullhorn blared, "You are under arrest!" A figure with a fire extinguisher and flame-retardant suit appeared out of nowhere, grabbed the matches from Pokrovsky's hand, and began spraying foam over the gasoline trail he had created. Pokrovsky put his hands above his eyes to shield them from the lights. He began to be able to discern activity.

Perhaps fifty feet from him, a state trooper held a bullhorn. A ring of firemen stood by their equipment, apparently ready to put out any flames that Pokrovsky might have managed to start. Two more state troopers held video cameras. They had captured every moment of his intended arson from two angles. How had he missed all those people?

Then, his eyes shifted to a group of five individuals standing off to one side of the law enforcement tableau. He adjusted the shielding of his eyes and squinted. They were women. They were not moving. They just stood there, three of them with their arms crossed, looking back at him.

As he adjusted to the play of light and shadow, he thought he recognized some of them. Was one the old bag who had been temping in accounting for the past two months? If so, what in the hell was she doing here? The thin one looked like the blonde woman who had taken a dozen test drives and spent days in the showroom with some story about buying two dozen cars for her husband's company's salesmen. There was a new runner who dealt with the RMV paperwork. Was she the heavy-set woman on the right?

And then his eyes went to the tall one. A young, African-American woman. This one he definitely knew. It was the goddam insurance investigator who had been all over his case after two of his slow-selling cars had been totaled during test drives – accidents he had carefully arranged – and two trial-run auto torchings attributed to eco-terrorism. Unable to prove his complicity, her company had grudgingly paid the claims. Now, she was smiling. She noticed he was looking in her direction. She uncrossed her arms and waved at him.

Peripheral movement caught his attention and he turned to see. It was one of the state troopers, walking toward him. He carried handcuffs and a gun. The trooper's gun pointed directly at him.

Al Pokrovsky, Jr. suddenly became aware of the warm wetness on his right leg. He had peed his pants.

1.

Alice Beauchamp studied herself in the mirror. *It is a wake, not a funeral*, she reminded herself. Gray seemed to be the proper choice. The silk blouse with its carefully tied bow conveyed respect. The dark gray skirt showed modesty. She wore no jewelry; this was not a time for ostentation. A friend had died and she was paying her respects.

No. Cecelia Davis had been more than just a friend and one-time neighbor. They had been one another's shoulder to cry on, sounding board, and keeper of confidences. Though more than two decades apart in age, they were more like sisters than friends. Cecelia had even called Alice her daughter.

And now, at 93, Cecelia was dead. Dead without warning. A heart attack, they said, likely brought on by mourning the death of her husband, Harry, four months earlier.

*Poor Cecelia*, she thought.

Harry had been the constant in Cecelia's life. He was a successful lawyer, beloved and respected within the community. He chaired a church building committee and was president of the Rotary Club for nearly a decade. He gave generously to community causes, and Cecelia had told Alice – strictly in private – that Harry was also on Hardington's Home Committee, a group of local businessmen who privately helped families in need. His mind remained sharp, and he had kept up his law practice well into his eighties.

Two years ago, Cecelia's world had been upended by Harry's stroke. Six months of rehabilitation had only confirmed the original diagnosis: the right side of her husband's body was permanently paralyzed. He could no longer feed or bathe himself and required far more care than Cecelia could provide.

And so, reluctantly, Cecelia and Harry had sold their home and moved to Cavendish Woods, a 'life care' facility that provided Harry the services he needed. It was, she said, the best option available;

frightfully expensive but, then, Harry had invested wisely through the years.

Alice took one final look in the mirror, applied a light coating of blush to her cheeks and pronounced herself ready to say goodbye to her old friend.

\* \* \* \* \*

Paula Winters felt a sense of satisfaction as she pulled into the parking space in front of Alice's condominium. Six months earlier, Alice had resided in Hardington Gardens, a depressing town-owned housing complex for seniors on limited incomes. Alice's share of "the job" – as they all called it since that day in August when they had robbed the Brookfield Fair and unintentionally walked away with $350,000 of money intended for payoffs – coupled with generous contributions from other members of the Garden Club Gang, had paid for Alice's condominium in Olde Village Square. In the three months since Alice had moved in, the physical and emotional improvement in her friend had been palpable.

But then, all four of their lives had changed. Eleanor's anxiety over the cost of her husband's nursing home care had abated. Jean had taken her cruise and, while she failed to find a husband, she had returned in better spirits, a mood that continued to the present.

And Paula? She inhaled the chilly February air. She was alive. She had come through the surgery and made a full recovery. Four follow-up visits since her rehabilitation each showed no cancerous cells.

And she had Martin Hoffman in her life. He was the single most unexpected outcome of the entire affair. Twice a week – sometimes more often – they would go out for dinner or into Boston. On the nights they did not go out, they talked on the phone. It was intoxicating, and she prayed it would last. He had not yet spent the night, but it was only a matter of time.

Which made hiding her "secret" life all that much more important. When she told Samantha Ayers she couldn't play a role in the Pokrovsky Motors operation, Paula had been honest: Martin was aware that Samantha worked for Mass Casualty because the two had "cooperated" on solving the Brookfield Fair heist (a "solution" that provided a satisfactory set of arrests for law enforcement agencies while leaving the four women completely in the clear). Paula's fear was that, when and if Al Pokrovsky was put on trial, his attorneys would go looking for the "little old ladies" who infiltrated his Reading dealership.

Samantha had understood.   Accordingly, Paula's role became primarily one of an observer.   Nothing would link her to the investigation.  Paula spent dozens of hours at the dealership over a month-long period getting to know the staff under the guise of making a fleet purchase.  While she had made several of the crucial observations that tipped Pokrovsky's plans, Paula was part of no official record.   Moreover, Paula's share of the "bounty" was paid directly to the "GCG Trust".  She was safe.

Paula saw the door open and Alice Beauchamp appear.  Alice's face brightened when she saw her friend.  They had a lot of catching up to do.

* * * * *

Seven months of the year, the entrance to Cavendish Woods was awash in lush flowers and groomed shrubs.  Now, under a coating of snow, the dominant feature was a 15-foot-high statue of Athena, the goddess of wisdom, beside a ten-foot-wide globe.  The objects were likely cast from resin, but the resemblance to marble was unmistakable and likely intentional.

Athena, in turn, was the recurring theme within Cavendish Woods, a thirty-acre development along the Charles River in which the words "nursing home" never appeared.   Instead, this was a "continuing care retirement community" with lifetime education as its noble purpose.  Its residents could pursue non-degree courses with moonlighting professors from nine area colleges and universities.  Cavendish Woods' five-person Education Department organized field trips to museums and excursions to the cradles of civilization around the world.

There was even a small art gallery and a museum on premises, comprised of loans from residents and minor works from museums. When you gave your address as Cavendish Woods, it was understood you had taken up residence at an exclusive college catering to those seventy and over.

As she had done every time she entered the property, Alice marveled at the meticulous attention to detail. The individual units for those of means who were ambulatory and needed only occasional medical care looked like lakeside cottages. And, indeed, many of those cottages were on two small ponds, now ice-covered. Closer to the center of "the village" was "The Overlook", an elegant, low-rise apartment block with spacious balconies and terraces. It was here that Cecelia and Harry had moved, and where Cecelia had remained after her husband's health began its terminal decline four months before his death.

At the village center was the Great Lodge, a collection of restaurant-style dining rooms, conference rooms and classrooms, a theater, boutiques and conversation areas. In warm weather, a terrace overlooking the Charles River hosted concerts.

Paula pulled into a visitor's space by the entrance to the Great Lodge. Though she had been here only once before; to attend an Ikebana demonstration a year earlier, her own practiced eye looked beyond the veneer of the pursuit of late-in-life education and peeled away the façade to discern the ultimate reality.

She knew that off to one side of the Great Lodge, behind dense shrubbery and tall evergreens, would be the skilled nursing facility where those too mentally or physically frail to care for themselves lived out their last months. The facility's location – or even its existence – was not marked on any of the dozens of fingerpost signs they had passed during the half-mile meandering drive past the main entrance. Mortality was one thing; a person could face the reality that their lifespan was finite. Helplessness was something completely different, and Cavendish Woods did not want to remind its residents that the end of their lives might be spent in a thicket of tubes and machines.

Cecelia had been Paula's friend as well. Twenty years earlier, when she was a shy, thirty-two-year-old newcomer to Hardington, Paula had attended a meeting of the town's garden club. Five minutes after entering the room, the spry, seventy-three-year-old Cecelia Davis had taken Paula under a protective wing. Cecelia introduced her to every club member under the age of forty, and sat with her during a presentation on vegetable gardening, offering *sotto voce* asides on what she thought was right and wrong with the presentation. Paula joined the Hardington Garden Club that day.

Their four-decade age difference was too great to allow a close bond to form. Paula's life was consumed with juggling the demands of two children and her husband's new business, while Cecelia already had grandchildren who were teenagers. But Cecelia was a pleasure to talk to, even if her stock-in-trade was gossip about people who Paula barely knew. More than anything, Paula appreciated Cecelia's sunny outlook on life and enjoyment of the everyday. Though not as close as Alice, Paula counted Cecelia as someone about whom she cared, and the news of her sudden death had been accompanied by a strong sense of loss.

Inside the main entrance to the Great Lodge was a poster-size photo of Cecelia and an arrow pointing to the complex of meeting rooms. Nearby, an electronic message board listed half a dozen activities: Thai food preparation, intermediate German, Course 303 of European History, web page development, a rehearsal for an unnamed play, and "Davis Wake" in the Mountain Laurel suite.

* * * * *

They entered a large room that already hosted at least thirty attendees. A few were men in suits and women in dresses but most wore slacks and sweaters. To Alice, informal clothing conveyed a lack of respect for someone who had been a pillar of the community for more than half a century. A number of children were in the room – probably Cecelia's great-grandchildren to judge by their age.

There was a guest register which she signed, and then Alice

joined the line to pay her respects to the family. As she waited, she assessed those to whom sympathies were being expressed. At the head of the receiving line was a man her own age. That would be Rudy, Cecelia's oldest. He had aged visibly in the last few years; his hair was white and reduced to a fringe around his ears and the back of his head. He had also grown fat, his belly extending over his belt and jowls that shook as he spoke. At his side was Donna, also white-haired and twenty pounds heavier than Alice remembered.

Next to Donna was Cecelia's middle son, Pete. Pete had to be in his mid-sixties, but his hair was brown, until Alice looked more carefully and determined it was a toupee. Also, Pete's wife, Clarice, was not part of the receiving line. Alice knew – because Cecelia had told her two months earlier – that Pete and Clarice had separated. But didn't respect for your mother-in-law and the grandmother of your children trump personal discord? Pete had an earnest expression on his face as he spoke or listened to each person in line, as though trying to find some hidden subtext in their condolences.

Next to Pete was what Cecelia had always jokingly called her "one for the road" child. Alex would be in his late fifties now. He looked much younger than his brothers and still had an athletic build. He was the son who was still at home when Alice and her late husband, John, moved to Hardington and purchased the home across the street from the Davises. Alice did not recognize the woman standing next to him. While Rudy and Pete lived in the Boston area, Alex had moved to California after college. One of Cecelia's continuing laments had been that she saw too much of her older sons and not enough of Alex.

Beyond Alex was a gaggle of men and women ranging in age from their thirties to late forties, only two of whom Alice recognized. These would be a cross-section of the grandchildren, few of whom showed any emotion as they quickly greeted and shuttled along the line of mourners.

Alice reached the head of the line and was greeted by name by Rudy, who grasped both her hands in his. "I was hoping the gang from the neighborhood would turn out," he said. Then, repeating a line he had spoken to her the previous November, when Alice had stood in a different receiving line for the death of Harry Davis, Rudy cocked his head and said "I heard you had moved to Florida…"

"Just for a few years," Alice said, forcing a smile. "I'm back. This will always be my home." Then added, "I've just moved to Olde Village Square." She wasn't certain why she felt the need to establish that her address was a 'good' one, but then relegating her to being just part of 'the gang from the neighborhood' was a hurtful thing to say. Alice, after all, considered Cecelia one of her closest friends.

"Mother lived a very long and full life," Rudy said, patting Alice's hand. "We were all proud of her." To Alice, it sounded like a trite and unfeeling statement.

Alice exchanged a few perfunctory words of condolence with Donna Davis, whose attention appeared to be focused on the young children playing nearby. Alice turned her attention to Pete. Yes, it was a toupee. A good one, too, though she did not consider herself an expert on such things.

Pete gave a smile of recognition. "Hello, Alice," he said. "So good of you to come. Mom told me the two of you still had lunch almost every week. That was very kind of you."

*Yes,* Alice thought, *I was the person closest to her.* They met every week, sometimes just taking a seat on the terrace and drinking tea Alice brought in a Thermos from home. It was at one of these alfresco luncheons that Cecelia had said, "I always wanted to have a daughter. Then, I realized, I do. You are the daughter I wanted." Those were the kindest words any friend had ever spoken.

Alice was tempted to ask after Clarice, but good manners prevailed. If Pete wished to explain his wife's absence, it was his option to do so. He said nothing further and so Alice moved down the line to the youngest son, Alex.

"Hello, Mrs. Beauchamp," Alex said. It had been four decades since he was the teenager across the street. He might be in his late fifties, but the habit of calling a neighbor by her formal name, even one just a decade and a half his senior, was still ingrained. Alice thought it in good taste.

After Alice expressed her condolences, Alex introduced her to "my friend, Holly". If Alex was approaching sixty, Holly, at least, was over fifty; not one of those youthful, athletic women that older, successful men seemed to have on their arms. Cecelia had alluded to her son's serial relationships. She said she could never fully grasp that one of her children saw no need to wed and wondered if the lack of commitment was her fault. To Alice, that Alex had placed Holly in the receiving line was curious for someone who otherwise seemed sensitive to proper protocol.

Alice gave a brief smile and greeting, and moved on to the line of grandchildren. Only one greeted her with any warmth. Marilyn, one of Pete and Clarice's children. "Children", of course, was relative. Marilyn was in her mid-thirties, already with a few wisps of grey in her hair.

Marilyn grasped Alice's hands tightly. "I had hoped you would be here," she said. "I was going to give you a call. You had lunch regularly with Grandmother, didn't you?"

Alice nodded. "About once a week."

Marilyn gave a small sigh. "She thought the world of you. When things quiet down here, can we speak privately for a few minutes?"

"Of course, dear," Alice said. The way Marilyn had held Alice's hand made it clear that the conversation was not going to be a light one.

\* \* \* \* \*

Paula was several people behind Alice. She introduced herself as a "friend from the garden club" and so exchanged only brief words with most of the family. Of the oldest son, though, she asked the question that had puzzled her since word went round of Cecelia's death: why was the wake being held here, at Cavendish Woods?

Rudy provided the answer. "Mom had a lot of friends in the

complex, and getting to a funeral home or a church would be difficult for them."

The answer seemed reasonable, though Paula recognized most of the wake-goers as Hardington residents. She had seen the same group at Harry's funeral four months earlier. That service has been held in the Unitarian Church in Hardington.

"We didn't see a notice for the funeral," Paula said.

Rudy nodded. "Mom asked to be cremated. We'll have a memorial service in the spring."

Paula passed into the main room, where a photo montage of Cecelia Davis' life played on a large-screen television. A light classical piece played as background, largely drowned out by the din of people speaking.

She caught a strain of conversation of two men standing behind her.

"...supposed to have been a traditional declining contract, but Rudy says his paperwork makes reference to an eighty percent refund because of her age," the first man said.

"Even after eighteen months? That's highly unusual," said the second man.

"She was already ninety-two when she moved in," the first man said. "The actuarial tables were against her from the day they signed the agreement. Rudy said he got a rider based on her age. Cavendish says..." The rest of his explanation was spoken low enough that Paula could not make out the words.

"...eight hundred thousand is a chunk of change," the first man said.

"They're counting on it," the second man responded. "If they don't get it, watch out."

The second man did not explain who "they" were, though it sounded ominous. *Who are these men?* Paula thought. They were in dark suits and ties; to the best of her knowledge, they were not part of Hardington's business community.

Paula casually slipped her phone out of her purse and, while appearing to tap in a telephone number, she took their picture.

\* \* \* \* \*

It was Alice who spotted Eleanor Strong and Jean Sullivan as soon as they came into the room. Like Paula, they had been welcomed into the Hardington Garden Club by Cecelia when they ventured into their first meeting decades earlier.

And, like Paula and Alice, they had participated in "the job" at the Brookfield Fair the previous August, and, over the past two months, "the car thing" at Pokrovsky Motors. It was, Eleanor had said at the private, celebratory dinner ten days earlier, "like having a secret identity."

"We don't dare tell anyone what we've done," Eleanor has said. "We'd all go to jail for what we did in Brookfield, and we'd blow our chance to do it again if we talked about what we did to Al Pokrovsky. Sometimes, it just doesn't seem fair."

The fifth participant at that dinner, Samantha Ayers, the insurance investigator who had deduced their role in the Brookfield Fair Heist and then recruited them to take down Pokrovsky, had said she understood because she, too, was sworn to secrecy. "You are Wonder Woman times four," she told the group. "Each of you is – what was Wonder Woman's secret identity? – Diana Prince until you hear the call."

"I was beginning to think of us as Charlie's Angels," Paula had said.

"No, we're still the Garden Club Gang," Eleanor said. "Besides, I could never identify with Farrah Fawcett-Majors. I never jiggled. Not even a little. At least not in the right places."

The three women hugged. Alice indicated who was who in the receiving line.

Eleanor, though, pointed at an object in the back of the room. "What's that?" she asked.

Alice looked around; her eyes fell on a painting in a gilt frame being admired by several people. "That was Cecelia's pride and joy," she said. "Henri Fantin-Latour. *White Roses*. She and Harry bought it when they were on vacation in France. It was in their bedroom in Hardington; Cecelia brought it here when they moved; it was her reminder of home."

"It looks very expensive," Jean said.

"Not when they bought it, Alice said. "Cecelia saw it in a gallery in Nice and said it cost less than a thousand dollars – not that a thousand dollars wasn't a lot of money in 1954 – and that Harry just said, 'happy anniversary'."

"How can you be so certain of the date?" Jean asked.

Alice nodded. "Cecelia said they were filming *To Catch a Thief* in Nice and Cannes while they were there. She saw Grace Kelly and Cary Grant several times. I think the painting was as much a souvenir of seeing two movie stars as it was an anniversary present. They certainly never bought anything that extravagant again."

"It's beautiful," Eleanor said. "I would have loved to have something like that."

Eleanor was poised to say more when Paula joined them. Their friend seemed quite excited and barely said hello before asking the group to look at two men who were now standing by a buffet table, eating shrimp.

"Do any of you know either of those two men?" Paula asked.

Each of the women peered and, one by one, shook their heads.

"I caught a fragment of a conversation," Paula said in a low voice. "They were talking about Cecelia and Rudy and money. Please don't ask me to explain, but I didn't like the tone of that conversation. I'm asking a lot, but could we take turns staying by them to see if they pick up that conversation?"

"I remember your asking us to rob a fair," Eleanor said. "This sounds like child's play compared to that. I don't really know the family, so I'll skip the receiving line and take the first shift." And, with that, Eleanor walked over to the buffet table, picked up a cracker, placed a wedge of brie on it, and stood within earshot of the two men.

The two men took no notice of Eleanor, but neither did they

appear to be talking.  From twenty feet away, Jean said to Paula, "I used to resent being invisible.  Now, I'm beginning to love it."

* * * * *

A half an hour later, Marilyn – Alice was not certain of the granddaughter's married name – asked if they could speak in a private place.  An adjacent meeting room was unoccupied.  Marilyn closed the door and found two chairs.

"My grandmother said you and she were very close friends," Marilyn said. She was a striking and confident-looking woman.  Her hair was glossy black and worn shoulder length.  She wore a charcoal-color suit and a dark blue blouse.

"We used to sit in her kitchen and talk for hours," Alice said, uncertain how much detail to provide.  "When she and Harry moved here, I made a point of coming out at least once a week."

"She trusted you.  She could be completely honest with you," Marilyn said.  It was not phrased as a question, but seemed to call for a response.

"I believe so," Alice replied.

"Tell me about the last few times you saw her.  What did she talk about?"

Alice knew that she could, at this point, have asked the purpose of this young lady's questions, but she felt that it was not yet the time to do so.  "She still missed Harry every day, but she accepted the loss," Alice said.  "She had two years to come to terms with the reality that his life would be foreshortened because of the stroke.  But she also knew that it did not mean that *her* life was over.  She was looking forward to seeing her family."

"Did she have any concerns about her health?"

Alice thought for a moment.  "She expressed some surprise.  She said, 'I am continually amazed that I am in my nineties.  All around me are people ten years younger and they are in poor health.' Cecelia's mind was perfectly clear; she walked without a cane.  She took care of herself."

Marilyn nodded as Alice spoke, absorbing her words.  "Was

there anything troubling her?"

"If there was anything," Alice replied, "it was that she was *here*. As long as Harry needed care, she recognized the need to be in Cavendish Woods or someplace like it. But she disliked everything about the environment, and especially about being billed for everything…"

Marilyn broke in. "She and I also had that conversation several times. One of the staff would call her and say, 'Hey, we're going to the mall; would you like to go?' She would go, and then learn that she had been billed thirty-five dollars for 'transportation'. She hated being nickeled and dimed at every turn."

Alice added, "She told me she wanted to move. About three months ago, I moved into Olde Village Square in Hardington. Cecelia said she could live there, hire a housekeeper, walk into town, take taxis for everything else, and still save a bundle of money."

Marilyn listened, nodding. Then she asked, in a soft voice, "Do you have any reason to believe that my grandmother's death was not of natural causes?

2.

The question took Alice's breath away. "Didn't she die of a heart attack?" was all she could think to say.

"My grandmother's heart was in excellent condition according to her latest physical," Marilyn said. "I checked. She didn't even have a cardiologist. It had never been flagged as a risk factor…"

"Are you a doctor?" Alice asked, sudden wondering why Marilyn knew so much about things like hearts.

Marilyn shook her head. "I teach science and health to middle school students. I've spent the past few days educating myself."

"Have you told this to your father or your uncles?"

Marilyn closed her eyes. Alice saw a welling of moisture around her eyelids. "I have never seen two men – my father and Uncle Rudy – who were less concerned with the circumstances of a parent's death. I haven't spoken with Uncle Alex. He just flew in yesterday, and I haven't seen him since Grandfather's funeral."

"You could go to the police."

Marilyn looked at Alice. "I did. The head of Cavendish Wood's medical staff signed the death certificate. As far as the Town of Cavendish police are concerned, that's the end of the discussion unless I 'have persuasive evidence that the death certificate was signed in error'. I got the sense that the police hear, 'someone poisoned grandma' a lot. All I have is a feeling. Someone who is in good physical and mental health and no history of arrhythmia isn't supposed to keel over and die of a heart attack just because they're ninety-three."

"So, what do you do?" Alice asked.

"I'm trying to talk to everyone who might be able to shed light," Marilyn responded. "You're the third person I've spoken with. If you had told me that Grandmother said she was feeling poorly or was depressed, that might have been enough. Instead, she told you just what she told me and two other people: that she was getting past

Grandfather's death and asking when I can bring the kids to see her."

"The kids?"

Marilyn smiled. "I have a one-year-old and a three-year-old. It's why I've taken a sabbatical from teaching."

Alice thought about the fragment of conversation Paula had relayed. "There are two men in the next room. A friend of mine overheard a snippet of their conversation about your Uncle Rudy and money. Does that mean anything to you?"

"Uncle Rudy is obsessed with money. Could you point them out to me?"

Alice and Marilyn went back into the Mountain Laurel suite. Alice did not see the two men but did see Paula. She was making introductions and stumbled after saying "Marilyn".

"It's Davis. I kept my maiden name. Mrs. Beauchamp said you overheard two men talking about my Uncle Rudy and money."

Paula glanced over at Alice, who gave an imperceptible nod of approval. Paula pulled her phone from her purse and held up the display. "Do you know either of these two men?"

Marilyn shook her head. "They don't look at all familiar."

Paula pursed her lips. "They left a few minutes ago; Jean got both of their license plate numbers. They were talking about paperwork and a refund. Something was supposed to have been a traditional declining contract but Rudy's paperwork referenced an eighty percent refund."

Marilyn again shook her head. "I'm sorry. That doesn't mean a thing to me."

Paula continued. "One man said the actuarial tables were against your grandmother from the first day. Your Uncle Rudy apparently had some kind of contract rider, based on her age, promising the larger refund, which the other man said was unusual. I lost the rest of the explanation except that there is a large amount of money at stake – eight hundred thousand dollars."

Marilyn mouthed the words, "eight hundred thousand".

"But then I heard one last comment. I'll try to repeat it as much word for word as I can. 'They're counting on it. If they don't get it, watch out.' I have no idea who the 'they' is."

Marilyn shook her head. "That's over my head. Uncle Rudy…" Then, she paused and looked quizzically at Paula. "You took those men's picture. And you said someone got their license plate numbers. Why did you do that?"

Paula did not answer for a moment as she tried out explanations in her head. She finally settled on, "I didn't like the sound of the conversation. It sounded… menacing. When I mentioned it to Jean…"

"And you also mentioned it to Mrs. Beauchamp," Marilyn said. "That's two people…"

"We're natural busybodies," Alice interjected. "We didn't mean any harm."

"No," Marilyn said. "What you did was incredible. It's like you were thinking the same thing as me. Thank you. And, who is Jean?"

"Jean is Jean Sullivan," Paula said. "We're all members of the Hardington Garden Club, which your grandmother was also a member of. And what I said about the conversation being menacing was true. I wanted to know who those men were. Jean said she would keep an eye on them. But you were talking about Uncle Rudy and 'contract riders'."

Marilyn appeared to consider the explanation. "As my grandparents got older, Uncle Rudy apparently tried to insinuate himself into their finances. Until his stroke, Grandfather had the mental acuity of someone half his age. I saw it played out at family events like Thanksgiving and anniversaries. Grandfather told Uncle Rudy to 'go to hell' on more than one occasion."

"I'm sorry to ask," Paula said. "I don't know your Uncle Rudy. What makes him competent to run his parents' finances?"

"Uncle Rudy was a dentist," Marilyn said. He retired from his practice seven or eight years ago. He has no special financial skills that I'm aware of, and my father has said in a couple of unguarded moments that Uncle Rudy made some terrible money decisions a couple of years ago."

"Then why would your Uncle Rudy have some kind of a contract rider with Cavendish Woods?" Paula asked.

"I have absolutely no idea."

"Could he have become your grandparents' guardian after they moved here?" Paula asked.

Marilyn again shook her head.

"Someone has to have financial liability," Alice said. "We could ask Eleanor. She'd know."

"Who's Eleanor?" Marilyn asked.

"I think we all need to go back next door," Alice said. "I don't want to attract attention."

* * * * *

"So there are four of you?" Marilyn said after introduction had been made. "The four of you took it on yourselves to follow those two men, take their photo, and record their license plates and car descriptions."

"We're very thorough busybodies," Alice said. "Eleanor was about to tell us about financial liability."

"My husband, Phil, is seventy-three and has late-stage Alzheimer's," Eleanor explained, speaking to Marilyn. "He went into a nursing home a little over a year ago. We have nursing home insurance and he is a private-pay patient." Her voice began to quaver. "I've seen what some nursing homes do with Medicaid patients. They just warehouse them. It's horrible."

Eleanor paused and regained her composure. "I cover what the insurance doesn't pay. Phil's nursing home is nothing like this one, but the financial disclosures they required before they would take Phil as a patient were downright scary. They know the value of our home and its contents to the dollar. They know how much money we have and what I spend each month."

Eleanor continued. "I am financially responsible for Phil's nursing home bills right up until the time I completely run out of assets. And, by 'run out of assets', that means I have sold my home, drained my bank accounts, and disposed of every other asset I have. Excuse me. I'm allowed to keep my wedding ring. I'll have to sell my engagement ring, but I can keep my wedding ring as long as it is below a certain value." Perhaps unconsciously, the fingers of Eleanor's right hand reached to protect the wedding band and engagement ring on her left hand.

"When it became apparent that Phil was getting worse, I looked at some less-fancy versions of this place. I never got past the initial interview. They don't want Alzheimer's patients, and they certainly don't want someone who might become a Medicaid patient."

"Why not?" Marilyn asked.

"Because Medicaid reimbursement to a nursing home is about a third of what that nursing home charges a 'private pay' patient," Eleanor said. "And, once you're in a nursing home, you can't be thrown out. So, CCRCs – excuse me – continuing care retirement communities – demand huge upfront payments. The ones I looked at wanted a few hundred thousand, and I would have still been responsible for several thousand dollars a month beyond what his insurance would pay. And, of course, they wouldn't take him anyway."

Paula held up a hand. "If I said 'traditional declining contract', would that mean anything to you?

Eleanor nodded. "That has to do with getting back part of that upfront payment. Each month you stay, the percentage you get back goes down by about two percent, plus some processing fee. Harry died – what? -- about fourteen months after he and Cecelia moved here, and Cecelia was here about eighteen months. Depending on how a contract was structured, the family would be entitled to a refund of about sixty percent of the upfront payment."

"If I understand correctly, that one man talked about Rudy expecting to get back eighty percent or eight hundred thousand dollars," Alice said. "That implies the upfront payment was a million dollars. Could it possibly be that high?"

"It would depend on the level of care expected," Eleanor replied. "Harry had a stroke and needed round-the-clock care. Yes, Cavendish Woods might have asked for a million dollars up front."

Paula picked up the conversation. "So, someone in the family was responsible for the bills. The question is, who?"

Eleanor held up a finger. "There's one other option. You hear those ads on the radio about 'protecting your assets from the nursing home'."

"I hear them," Alice said. "I hate them."

"Your assets go into trusts," Eleanor explained. "In theory, you have no control over those assets so they're out of reach of those nursing home financial disclosure forms. Most people use it as a way around Medicaid's look-back rules…"

"I'm sorry," Alice said. "Look-back rules?"

"If you've given away money to anyone – church, children, charity – in the five years before you apply to a nursing home, the government assumes you did so to avoid paying for nursing home care," Eleanor said. "They want it back. When I was investigating options for Phil, I went to one of those seminars advertised on the radio. I felt like I was being dropped into a shark tank."

"Why?" Marilyn asked.

Eleanor waved her hand dismissively. "It's lawyers and accountants looking for a way to extract money – and I mean lots of money – from elderly people, or else greedy kids trying to keep hold of more of mom and dad's estate, without any thought of what kind of hell-hole it might consign mom and dad to."

Eleanor realized what she was saying. She looked at Marilyn and added, "Phil and I never had children. So, I'm allowed to say things like that out loud."

"But you're apparently willing to spend every dollar you have to keep your husband in a 'good' nursing home," Marilyn said. "I can't think of anything more noble than that."

"Oh, I've put aside a little something for my old age that they don't know about," Eleanor said, and gave a very slight smile.

"So," Paula said. "Marilyn, we've told you what we know. Does it help?"

Marilyn looked around the room at the four women. "Yes, it helps. And I'm still trying to figure you out. Mrs. Beauchamp, you knew my grandmother well, and she thought the world of you. She loved it that you came to see her all the time, just to talk and to keep her up to date on things back in Hardington."

Marilyn paused, then addressed Alice directly. "She also said something that is starting to make sense. She told me that, when you moved back from Florida, you were very depressed. She said she spent as much time cheering you up as you did keeping up her spirits. But something happened last summer. Grandmother said it was as though you had a new lease on life. She thought you might have won the lottery. But you wouldn't share whatever it was, and Grandmother wasn't one to pry. She was thrilled for you. And, looking at you now, I have a sense it had something to do with these other women."

Alice said nothing. The others shifted uncomfortably.

"I'm not completely certain why, but I think the four of you may be able to help me. I really don't know how to proceed on this, but I want to know if my grandmother's death was from natural causes, or if someone killed her. And, if they did, I want to know why, and I want them to be punished."

There was a silence in the room for many seconds. Then, Paula said quietly, "I have a friend who may be able to help."

3.

Samantha Ayers looked over her meticulous notes, backed up by the digital recorder on the table. Marilyn had told her story. Now the questions began.

"Who has the will?" Samantha asked.

"I don't even know if there *is* a will," Marilyn said. "My family very seldom talks about money."

"Well, your first responsibility is to find out what it says," Samantha responded, keeping an urgent tone in her voice. "Who are the beneficiaries and who is the executor? Who gets that painting you talked about? That thing ought to be worth a small fortune."

"Uncle Rudy took it home with him after the wake," Marilyn said. "Maybe it was left to him."

Samantha looked across at Marilyn, exasperated. "We can't deal with 'maybes'. And time is not on our side. That scene you see on television where everyone gathers in the library for the reading of the will? That doesn't happen. You can be absolutely certain that the executor is already hard at work figuring out how to distribute the estate. If it is a family member, it will happen quickly. If the executor is an attorney, it will go even faster. The best case for us would be if your grandmother effectively died intestate because your grandparents left everything to one another and your grandmother never updated her will after his death."

Marilyn was bewildered by this conversation and its circumstances. It was taking place in Paula Winters' large home, in an enormous "great room" with a massive stone hearth in which a fire blazed. The six women sat in a circle on comfortable chairs and sofas but, so far, Marilyn and Samantha had done all of the talking.

One of the uncomfortable things was Samantha. Not that she was African-American. That was no issue; the principal and vice-principal of her school were black. Rather, it was that she looked so *young* – barely out of her teens. That youthful look was accentuated by her clothing: blue jeans, a tank top and plaid wool shirt that would not have looked out of place on one of her students. Samantha had assured Marilyn that she was a senior investigator for a major insurance company and had been one for several years and that, before becoming an investigator, she had been a police officer.

Another uncomfortable thing was that the five women interacted in a way that indicated this kind of thing had been done before. They were all on a first-name basis. They knew Samantha wanted a steady stream of Diet Cokes. And Samantha, in turn, clearly respected their judgment.

"Is the will the only thing you need?" Marilyn asked.

"The will is just the tip of the iceberg," Samantha said, taking a swallow of her drink. "It will establish the pecking order of things. Ultimately, the will has to be filed with a probate court, but that can be months from now, and we need to know *now* who is in charge in the family."

"You seem to assume that someone in my family is responsible."

"Not at all," Samantha said. "That's just one angle; although, if the police were investigating this, that's where they'd start. We also need to know what kind of financial trouble your Uncle Rudy got into. I can check court filings but it may not have gotten that far. I also need the name of your uncle's former dental practice."

Samantha addressed the group as a whole. "Thanks to the license plates, I can track down the two men. That was very good thinking on everyone's part. And now, we turn to Cavendish Woods. You may want to fortify yourselves."

Wine was poured into many glasses.

"I only had an hour, but Cavendish Woods appears to have a clean record," Samantha said. "They're fully certified by the state and have no outstanding complaints. Their profits are buried inside a parent company and that parent company is privately held, but I have some sources."

"The key thing I'm looking at is deaths," she continued. "Cavendish Woods has 464 residents, and the facility had eighteen deaths reported last year.  By nursing home standards, that's low, and it speaks to Cavendish's targeting a healthy older customer.  What caught my attention is that six of those deaths were heart attacks.  The number isn't off-the-charts suspicious, but once someone has an M.O. that works, they stick with it.  That's human nature."

Samantha knew she had her audience's attention.  It was time to spring her plan.  "If we're going to find out if someone inside of Cavendish Woods did this – and that assumes that there is a 'this' in the first place – you're going to have to go inside."

Samantha looked around the room.  She saw neither fear nor surprise, which was excellent.  "Drink up, ladies.  You're about to get your assignments."

Five glasses went to five sets of lips.

"Paula, you told me you were a nurse once upon a time," Samantha said.

"It's been nearly twenty years," Paula said.  "You have to renew your license every two years, and my accreditation is a couple of decades out of step."

Samantha shook her head.  "We need someone on the inside.  They're going to look at you and see, 'bored, empty nester getting back into the work place', which means they think they can get you for less than the going rate.  They're going to make you an offer on the spot."

Samantha turned to Jean.  "Are your cleaning skills still up to snuff?"

Jean gave a look of mock incense.  "Is that my lot in life?  Cleaning lady?  I can do more, you know."  But then Jean smiled.  "Yes, my skills have not atrophied in the past two months."

"I'll find out who their contractor is, and I'll give them a call."  Samantha returned the smile.  "It's just that you're perfect."

"Alice, you're going into a nursing home," Samantha said.  "A one-month trial visit to see if you can adjust to the Cavendish Woods lifestyle.  I'm guessing the freight is about ten thousand."

"She'll need a sponsor," Eleanor said.  "They won't let her in the door without a guarantor."

Samantha nodded. "Paula will be the sponsor, but it should be just the one visit. Being able to write a check works wonders with these people. They remember your money, not your face."

"What about me?" Eleanor asked.

"I want to find out who those two men were. Then, I'll give you your assignment."

As Marilyn listened to the handing out of assignments, she comprehended that this had happened before. These women had done something like this, and it had been in the last few months, based on the comment about Jean Sullivan having been part of a cleaning crew.

Who *were* these people?

And then another thought intruded: *money*. Ten thousand for a month's stay at Cavendish Woods.

"Who's paying for this?" Marilyn asked. "Am I?"

Samantha smiled. "No, dear. You're not expected to pay for this although, if after it's over and you want to contribute, you're welcome to. You have a problem. You asked for assistance. I think we can help although, if you can't get the information I asked for, it will be a lot harder and perhaps impossible."

"Then who are you?" Marilyn asked, trying to comprehend the evening's events.

It was Alice who answered. "We're the Garden Club Gang."

4.

At that same hour in a seaside home in Marblehead Neck, a very different conversation was taking place. Earlier in the evening, it had been mostly profanity-laced screaming between two of the three participants. Now, after nearly an hour of venting, a sense of purpose if not calm, was settling in.

"We can beat it. The question is how far we're prepared to go."

The speaker was Al Pokrovsky, Senior. At eighty, he was nominally the retired patriarch of The Pokrovsky Motors Group; spending winters in Florida and summers on Cape Cod. He was, by reputation, a doer of good deeds, a soft touch for charities, and a three-handicap golfer who was not averse to wagering five hundred dollars on a single hole.

He was a wiry man, an inch under six feet who still stood erect even after eight decades. His face was tanned and leathery, his hair a fringe of white. His sole concession to age was a pair of thick, frameless glasses.

Al Pokrovsky, Senior was also a ruthless businessman who had survived the gasoline crises of 1973-74 and 1979, three recessions, and decades of government policies that seemed intent – in his eyes – on driving automobile dealers out of business. He had parlayed a used car lot and a single Toyota franchise into a sales colossus. That he had done so frequently with bribes and intimidation was – again, in his eyes – immaterial. He had succeeded. That was his legacy.

Just as it was not germane that, when he wagered that five hundred on a hole of golf, he tilted the odds in his direction by nicking his opponent's ball with a razor blade. He played to win. That was also his legacy.

Al Senior had a few other character blemishes that, in his mind, were also not germane. The largest of these was a side business importing cheap and poorly manufactured Chinese auto parts that came boxed with "Genuine Toyota" or "Genuine Honda" imprints.

Some of these parts were sold through Pokrovsky dealerships but most went to independent garages. The growth of this side business had been the driving force in Al Senior's decision to turn the Pokrovsky Motors Group over to his son.

And now, his imbecile son was intent upon losing everything he had worked to build.

Two weeks earlier, he had gotten the news of his son's arrest not from his own family but, rather, from watching the morning news programs in Florida, where three networks took delight in showing a video of his son, captured via night-vision photography and released by the Massachusetts State Police, spray-painting graffiti on cars, pouring gasoline on them, and then striking a match. Anchors whom he had admired made jokes about the Massachusetts car dealer who intended to solve his financial woes through arson, and then wet his pants when caught in the act.

He had not watched those news programs since.

He had made one immediate phone call, to his family attorney in Boston, to ensure that the attorney placed a gag in his son's mouth – whether a metaphorical one or a physical one did not matter – to prevent him from self-incrimination.

He had then flown north to begin the process of preserving the empire he had spent his life building. The first step, painful but absolutely necessary, was to erase the Pokrovsky name from that empire. In less than a week, "a proud member of the Pokrovsky family" had been replaced by the generic "Mazda of Belmont" and "Honda of Beverly". Every scrap of literature had been reprinted, every form and business card replaced. The name Pokrovsky had been erased from the face of the business world as thoroughly as any Egyptian pharaoh had chiseled out the cartouche of a despised predecessor.

It had not been enough to save the Reading dealership where the arson took place, but the seventeen other franchises survived. As a result of the publicity, sales had dipped. With the Pokrovsky name removed, those sales were already recovering. The bleeding had been staunched. Now, it was time to cauterize the wound and begin the healing process.

The conversation was taking place in his son's ostentatious home, a three-story replica of a sea captain's mansion; and in a room on the top floor that expressed what some interior decorator had decreed that a sea captain would have wanted to return to after a long voyage. Except that this sea captain had run his ship straight into rocky shoals, and now needed to be rescued.

The bitter taste in the mouth of Al Pokrovsky, Senior, was that the first step of rescuing his worthless son was erasing his own name from the business he had built.

"Gerry, tell us what you know," Pokrovsky Senior said.

Gerald Turow – long since inured to jokes about sharing the surname of a lawyer-turned-author – cleared his throat.

"The weakest element of the state's case is causation," Turow said. "Junior didn't actually torch those cars. The *actus reus…*"

"Skip the Latin, Gerry," Pokrovsky Senior instructed.

"Junior never lit the cars on fire," Turow said. "He spray-painted them, he doused them with gasoline, and he struck a match, but he never burned a single car. And, moreover, he *owned* those cars. Even if he had torched them, his offense was failure to have a burn permit."

Turow cleared his throat again and adjusted his glasses. "The state will argue that, even though no destruction of property took place, arson applies – plus intent to defraud – because of the incidents last September. They'll compare the spray paint and the 'handwriting' as it were, and attempt to prove that Junior did it twice before and was about to do it again on a larger scale. If an insurance company paid once, they would pay again."

Pokrovsky Senior glared at his son.

"The handwriting is a tough hurdle," Turow continued. "Many of the words were the same so the police have a direct comparison available. Their experts will say it's a one hundred percent match."

"What we're left with for a defense is diminished capacity," the lawyer said, adjusting his glasses yet again. "We can argue medication. We can argue that Junior is not guilty by reason of disease or mental defect."

"No!" Pokrovsky Senior shouted. Then, more softly, he said, "We will not argue anything of the kind. We will stop this before trial."

"By pleading out?" Turow asked.

Al Pokrovsky Senior glared at Turow, and then at his son.

"The state police came to be at the Reading dealership on a particular night because they had inside information," Pokrovsky Senior said. "They obtained that information through subterfuge. They *stole* it. I know this because my son recognized the Mass Casualty woman that night. She even waved at him. *She* knew what was going to happen. Al says there were four other women. I believe they were Mass Casualty plants inside the dealership."

Turow said, "So we depose the Mass Casualty woman. She will have to divulge the names…"

"No," Pokrovsky Senior said. "We do not depose anyone. We never let on that we suspect there was inside information. We find those four women on our own."

"But they're part of the chain of informational custody." Turow said. "They're critical to the State's case…"

"Exactly." And, for the first time that evening, Al Pokrovsky Senior smiled. "We break the chain of informational custody. They go away, and so does the State's case."

5.


Samantha Ayers took a bite of microwaved pizza and idly wondered just how old this particular slice might be. There were three boxes in her apartment's refrigerator, each the product of a spur-of-the-moment stop at a Pizza Hut or other chain on her way to or from an assignment. Each box had three pieces missing and each was mushroom and sausage.

*You are in a rut, girl,* she thought.

But if it was a rut, it was the most exhilarating one she had ever been in. She had taken down Al Pokrovsky. Mass Casualty had already filed suit against Pokrovsky Motors to recover the claims paid out by the insurer over the eight years they had covered the dealerships. Samantha was in line to receive fifteen percent of the hefty proceeds if the suit was successful.

She had already received a bonus or, rather, GCG Trust had received funds paid by Mass Casualty. Her employer did not know about Paula, Eleanor, Jean and Alice; nor did they want to know. Samantha was free to use "independent contacts and resources" as she saw fit in the recovery of claims believed to have been paid fraudulently. She did not need the bonus and the women had certainly earned it.

Six months earlier, good detective work had led her to the four women. They had explained how they had used their invisibility to their advantage at the Brookfield Fair. It had been a revelation to Samantha who, by dint of her African-American heritage, height, and age made her stand out in every crowd.

If Samantha could not go anywhere without being noticed, these women could escape attention under almost any circumstance. And so, after careful thought, she had devised a plan that allowed her to "see" inside Pokrovsky's Reading dealership, where the earlier frauds had been perpetuated.

Like any greed-driven business, Pokrovsky Motors never

hesitated to pay below-market wages and so Alice, with her banking skills, quickly found employment in the dealership's back office accounting department. Paying just twelve dollars an hour, the job had been on Craigslist for months with no takers. There, while handling accounts payable and receivable, Alice carefully kept track of how long cars sat unsold in inventory. Samantha initially expected another "accident" involving a test drive and expected to find evidence of a payoff, but Alice's reports suggested something more ominous: a large number of one model vehicle that simply refused to move.

Alice also found irregularities in time sheets, commission statements and expense reports. All of these were collected and organized for greater scrutiny by Samantha.

In the meantime, Eleanor found work as one of the dealership's registry runners: making trips back and forth between the dealership and the Registry of Motor Vehicles. This was one of any auto dealer's high-margin sidelines. Pokrovsky added a $299 "document preparation fee" to the sale of every vehicle. Like other runners, Eleanor was paid twenty-five dollars for each car she registered, regardless of whether it took half an hour or (more likely, with interminable RMV lines) three hours.

It was Alice's discovery that one hundred dollars of every document preparation fee transaction never made it into the accounting system. Instead, it was diverted into an "incentive account". The sole signatory on the account was Al Pokrovsky, Jr. The Internal Revenue Service paid finders' fees for information like this. Samantha would disclose it when the time was right.

Jean had drawn the unenviable task of becoming part of the nightly cleaning crew at the dealership. This was one part of the plan where Samantha had needed to call in a favor. Organizations like Pokrovsky Motors scrimped everywhere they could, and benefits like health and vacations were avoided wherever possible. Alice received no benefits because she worked only thirty hours a week. Eleanor was an independent contractor responsible for her own medical insurance and savings plan.

Non-critical functions were farmed out to service contractors, giving Pokrovsky Motors deniability about immigration status, working conditions and pay of the employees who did these jobs. Samantha found the name of the contractor who supplied Pokrovsky's janitorial services. Though she had never worked with the firm, she contacted a friend at a similar organization. A call was made and, in a matter of two days, Jean had a job: five hours per evening, six days a week, eight dollars an hour.

Every night, Jean would carefully segregate and bag the garbage from Al Pokrovsky's Reading office. Pokrovsky purportedly kept an office at three of his dealerships, but Reading was the closest to his Marblehead home and so was used most frequently.

Samantha could never decide whether Pokrovsky was simply careless or profoundly stupid. Every dealership presumably had a shredder at the ready for the disposal of sensitive material, but the one in Pokrovsky's office was never used. So, over a two-month period, Samantha pieced together the paper trail of a desperate man. There was Pokrovsky the gambling addict who could lose $30,000 in a single weekend at Mohegan Sun. There was Pokrovsky the philanderer who showered one Dee Simonson with jewelry from Tiffany and paid for her waterfront condo in Revere. There was Pokrovsky the incompetent businessman who threw away invoices and beseeched his father for more counterfeit parts to bolster his profits. And there was Pokrovsky the thief, who drained the incentive account and then tapped every other source of cash available within the network of dealerships.

The net result of this colossal mismanagement was an empire on the brink of collapse. Pokrovsky borrowed or stole at every turn, depending on steady auto sales to hide the cash drain. In most automotive dealerships, such a kleptocracy would have been detected by bank auditors watching over the health of the credit line they extended to the company. But the Pokrovsky Group had no credit line and boasted in its advertising that, because it paid cash for its cars, savings were passed along to consumers (an untrue statement: any savings went directly into Pokrovsky's pockets). The eighteen unsold luxury vehicles, paid for in cash, were a weight that the Pokrovsky Group could not withstand.

Samantha was uncertain how much of this archive was admissible in court. It was a gray area of the law. Had the trash been personally bagged and placed by Pokrovsky in an outdoor rubbish bin, it would have neatly fit into a pocket of jurisprudence that permitted the police to seize as evidence anything thrown out by a suspect. But these papers had made it only as far as a wastepaper basket in Pokrovsky's office. Acting on Samantha's specific instructions, Pokrovsky's trash was placed in a yellow bag and thrown in the dealership's dumpsters. Samantha retrieved it each evening, brought it back to her Framingham apartment, and organized it by degree of larceny.

It had been the discovery of Pokrovsky's precarious finances that led Samantha to coax Paula into the scheme. Paula's "cover" was as a prospective buyer of a fleet of vehicles for an imaginary company owned by an imaginary husband. For weeks she spent time shopping, test driving, negotiating, and then starting over when her "husband" deemed the chosen car "too plain" or "too conspicuous". All the while, Paula watched the automotive inventory on the lot for telltale changes. She was the first to see the pattern of the unsold behemoths accumulating in a distant corner of the lot. She even accurately predicted the day that the arson would take place.

But if Paula was the one infiltrator who never collected evidence except what she could see with her own eyes, she was also, in a sense, the most vulnerable. While all four women worked at or visited the dealership under false identities, it was Paula who had worked with half a dozen people on the sales staff, each of whom would have taken stock of her to assure themselves she was a serious buyer. Over a period of weeks, she might have said something to one of them that could be traced back to the "real" Paula Winters.

Samantha had come to respect and admire these four women,

but it was Paula who had saved her life one night in Framingham six months earlier.  When Enrico "Boz" Boscales attacked her, Paula had not hesitated for even a moment.  The woman weighed probably 120 pounds but had fearlessly gone after Boz with a baseball bat, breaking his hand and shoulder.  Had Paula obeyed Samantha's instructions to stay in the car and leave if there was trouble, Samantha had no doubt that she would have been killed.

That debt could never be repaid.  It was the largest single reason why, when Paula had called Samantha two days earlier and outlined a granddaughter's suspicions about the death of a very elderly woman in a nursing home, Samantha agreed to hear the story and propose a plan of action.

Well, that, and it sounded like fun.

Mass Casualty did not provide insurance for nursing homes so there was no conflict of interest to worry about.  And Marilyn's tale had been compellingly told by someone who was both passionate and intelligent.

Could they prove there had been a murder and identify the perpetrator?  They were stepping on no one's feet because there was no investigation.  Samantha had called the Cavendish police and been told that a death certificate was signed by the head of Cavendish Woods' medical staff within an hour of the discovery of Cecelia Davis' body, and filed with the state the following day.  Because Davis was in a nursing home (by whatever name) and under the continuing care of its staff, there was not even a *pro forma* intervention by the Medical Examiner's office.  A very old woman had died.  End of story.

Was there a police report?  Samantha had asked.  No, there was no report of any kind.  A hearse had been called to take the body to a funeral home.  Twenty-four hours later, the body had been cremated in accordance with the deceased's written wishes.

At which point the until-that-time-helpful person on the other end of the line at the Cavendish police asked what connection Samantha Ayers was to the deceased?

*Lie or truth?* Samantha had thought. "A relative asked me to check," she had said, and then added, "That's everything I need."

One part truth, one part lie.

She also had her first piece of independent intelligence. Tracking down the two license plates had taken just minutes, and the information was intriguing. Both cars were leased to the same firm: Liss and Swann, LLC, a firm specializing in 'eldercare' law and estate planning. A quick perusal of the firm's website showed that Liss and Swann actively recruited clients via "protect your savings" seminars heavily advertised on radio and television. Samantha's visceral reaction to hearing such ads had always been to find another radio station or hit the 'mute' switch on her TV.

Their profession explained the snippet of conversation overheard by Paula, but did not shed any light on their possible connection to Cecelia Davis. Had she been a client? Were they working for one of Davis' children?

Also, who exactly were the two men? The website photos of Liss and Swann showed one was a woman and the other a man in his sixties. The two men in Paula's cell phone photo appeared to be in their thirties.

Samantha took another bite of her now-cold pizza and a swallow of Diet Coke, and decided that Eleanor was going to go hear about how to protect her savings from those evil nursing homes.

6.

The day after the wake, Rudolph Franklin Davis, DDS (Retired) sat in stunned silence. The pained look on his face was palpable.

The man across the table in the small conference room of a Boston-based auction house had seen such a look before; in fact, many times. He repeated his verdict in soothing tones.

"It's a copy," he said. "There are half a dozen telltale signs. The biggest flag is the absence of re-work. Fantin-Latour painted rapidly and with confidence but, even on his most minor works, he would re-think the placement of a flower or shape of a vase. That re-working shows, especially after more than a century. This painting was executed, perhaps from the original but more likely from a photograph, with knowledge of the completed composition already in mind."

"But my parents bought it at a reputable art gallery…" Davis said, pointing to the yellowed bill of sale on the table between them.

The man nodded. "Galerie Carlton was associated with the Hotel Carlton and it catered to a tourist trade, not serious art collectors, and they closed in 1968 leaving few records. There's no record of their being engaged in art fraud, but it doesn't mean it wouldn't have happened, especially with American tourists on that 'trip of a lifetime'."

Davis clenched his fists under the table. This was too important to let go of without a fight. "You said there were other signs."

The man nodded again. "There is a gallery stamp on the back for F. and J. Tempelaere, a Paris dealer that would have ostensibly handled the painting at an earlier time. The stamp is hand drawn. We considered that fact fairly well conclusive in determining that the painting was a copy."

"But the frame…" Davis said.

"The frame *is* nineteenth century," the man said. "In selling copies, it often helped to place the painting in a frame authentic to the period of the work being represented."

"And it *looks* old…"

"There are many techniques that can make even a freshly painted canvas look centuries old."

"How much would it have been worth… if it were genuine?" Davis asked, an acknowledgment of defeat in his voice.

"It doesn't help to dwell on such things," the man said. "This painting has no auction value because of the forged name. It is a keepsake from your parents' trip to France in the 1950s. That is the only way you can treat it."

"Humor me," Davis said. "I accept that the painting isn't a Fantin-Latour. But, if it was, what would it sell for?"

The man tapped a pencil on the table for a few moments. "Fantin-Latour occupies an unusual place in the art world. Today, because of his group portraits, he is associated with the Impressionists but his painting style was essentially Romantic and much more conservative than a Monet or Renoir. That is why his paintings sold so well in his lifetime, especially to Britons visiting the continent. A Fantin-Latour required no appreciation for the avant-garde. It was a beautiful painting of exceptional quality that could grace any reception room."

He tapped his pencil several more times. "But Fantin-Latour was also prolific; almost promiscuously so. He may have executed as many as a thousand paintings, six hundred or more that still exist. His work comes up for auction with some regularity. Small florals can sell for around… a hundred thousand. Large pieces like the one of which yours is a copy, can reach into the low seven figures."

*More than a million dollars*, Davis thought.

"I know what you're thinking," the man said. "You can take the painting down to New York, but you'll be told the same thing. The painting in your possession is not a genuine Fantin-Latour. It is a copy. Fairly well executed, to be sure, but a copy nonetheless. I acknowledge that ours was a fairly cursory examination. The gallery stamp raised a red flag, the absence of re-work confirmed it. There are consultants who can examine the painting, its canvas and frame more closely and can pinpoint its age and maybe even its origin, but it will not change the conclusion."

The man rose, signaling an end to the meeting. He offered his hand.

Davis, not wanting to, but forced by circumstances and upbringing, extended his own.

"I'm sorry," the man said. "So very sorry."

* * * * *

Once out of the auction house, Rudy Davis buried his head against the steering wheel of his car. Tragedies were supposed to come in threes. This was, by his count, number four or maybe five. The first shock had been the 11 p.m. call from Cavendish Woods five days earlier informing him of his mother's death. That one, he could get over with in time.

The second shock had been the call from Liss and Swann early the following morning, asking for a meeting to "discuss your mother's estate and last wishes". He had never heard of Liss and Swann, then realized this was some law firm that pitched its services on cable television.

"I don't need any help," he told the caller, and started to hang up.

"Wait!" the caller said. "You may not know it, but we've represented your mother since a few weeks after your father's death."

*What the hell?* He thought. "I have power of attorney in my mother's affairs. She couldn't do anything like that without my approval."

"You have durable power of attorney in health issues," the man countered. "There is no extant general power of attorney document that predates your father's death."

"But I have her will," Rudy said. "That's..."

"You have her *old* will," the man said. "She made a new one after your father died. That's why we need to meet."

Rudy was speechless. His mouth hung open. No thoughts went through his head.

"I strongly suggest today," the man said.

"But my brothers and I are supposed to be making funeral arrangements…"

"I suggest you postpone that meeting. You and I definitely need to meet as soon as possible," the man said. "For one thing, your mother specifically asked to be cremated."

\* \* \* \* \*

Liss and Swann, LLC occupied most of the first floor of a new-looking building in an office park in Burlington. Rudy gave his name to one of two receptionists and took a seat in a crowded waiting area. After less than five minutes, a man of about thirty-five came out, spoke briefly to the receptionist, who discreetly pointed to Rudy.

The man came over and held out his hand. "I'm Steve Turner," he said. "We spoke on the phone this morning."

Rudy was led into a small conference room; it had barely space for a table and four chairs. He turned down an offer of coffee and sat nervously while Turner assembled file folders and documents on the table.

"Your mother was a dear woman and I'm deeply sorry for your loss," Turner said. "We got to know one another pretty well over the past few months, and she spoke very highly of you and your brothers."

"Yet she never mentioned you," Rudy said.

Turner did not respond directly. "The elderly approach their finances in many ways. Some are quite open, some are extremely secretive. Some have complete confidence in their families and some want an independent perspective."

"You're saying my mother didn't trust her family," Rudy said.

Turner took a sip of his coffee. "Your mother had complete confidence in your father who was, of course, an attorney. In their original will – the one you have – they left their estate to one another and, in the event that both died, to their children. After your father's stroke, your mother's confidence was quite shaken. I believe you helped her with the decision to move to Cavendish Woods."

"She made her own decision," Rudy said. "She could no longer care for my father at home. A place like Cavendish Woods could provide…"

"Were you aware of your mother's disappointment that neither you nor Peter offered to provide part of that care?" Turner asked.

"You mean pay for it?"

"No," Turner shook his head. "She said both of you were retired. She had hoped you could take a few hours a day to relieve her. She would have much preferred to stay in her home."

The answer took Rudy aback. "She never asked."

"It was something she hoped you would volunteer to do without being asked."

Rudy did not like the direction of this conversation. "So she made a new will."

"She said she gave it a great deal of thought," Turner said. "She had many pages of notes with questions and ideas, which we have retained. We listened. Liss and Swann didn't even agree to take her on as a client initially. Usually, people in their nineties have some level of cognitive impairment. Testing proved your mother…"

"You had my mother tested?" Rudy said, alarmed.

"She had *herself* tested," Turner said, sliding out a thick document from a folder. "She wanted to prove to *us* that she was quite capable of deciding what she wanted for herself. She resented having been pressured into turning over a sizeable part of her and her husband's savings to get into Cavendish Woods. A million dollars is a lot of money."

*And an estate residue of nearly two million plus eighty percent of her entry fee to the nursing home*, he thought. "It guaranteed that she and my father would receive topnotch care," was what Rudy said.

"Her care was excellent," Turner said. "But your mother was also deeply troubled that you and Peter were pushing decisions on her that, well, benefitted the two of you. She was also very concerned that Cavendish Woods would get its hands on more of her and your father's savings. She wanted protection against that possibility, especially as she hoped to move out of Cavendish Woods and into a private residence, with full-time assistance. You see, your mother expected to live to a very old age." Turner smiled.

"What are you telling me?" Rudy said, now getting angry.

Turner finished his coffee. "You mother established an irrevocable trust with the preponderance of her liquid assets. When we established that trust five months ago, we – your mother and Liss and Swann – thought the proceeds would provide her care well beyond the age of a hundred. Instead, because of her untimely death, the trust reverts to the trustees for disposal in line with her wishes."

"And what were her wishes?" Rudy was gritting his teeth.

"It's all in the will," Turner said, sliding out another document.

"Why don't you give me the highlights?" Rudy snapped.

Turner did not hesitate in his answer. "Most of the trust goes to charities she designated. I think you'll approve of them; they were all causes she and your father supported."

"And what about her three children, five grandchildren and five great-grandchildren?"

Turner smiled. "Your mother believed that her three sons were living comfortably and had put away sufficient funds for their own needs and the education of their children."

"So, there are no bequests in her will?"

Turner gently pushed the document across the table. "It is all spelled out in here. It should be read carefully. I suspect that the two things that are most financially relevant are that you and your brothers share her personal property and funds not in the trust at the time of her death. That would include any entry fees returned from Cavendish Woods. It would also, of course, include the Fantin-Latour painting, which I gather is quite valuable. I would add that her hope, as expressed in the will, are that the three of you will donate the painting to a museum of your choosing, though it is not a requirement."

"And what if I or one of my brothers chooses to question whether my mother was coerced into signing these agreements?"

Turner nodded. "You could, of course, pursue that option. But your mother's specific instructions – which are spelled out in documents that are part of the trust and the will – are that the cost of any challenges to the will is to be subtracted from the estate's corpus."

Rudy felt his blood pressure rising and his face reddening.

"You seem to have thought of everything," he said.

"Your *mother* tried to think of all eventualities," Turner said. "Including that she didn't want a funeral. She thought your father's service and burial was – and these are her words – 'something of a circus' and she wanted nothing like that for herself. Just a wake and, if her death was during the cold-weather months, a memorial service in the spring. Let me walk you through her thoughts on music…"

* * * * *

The morning after the meeting at Liss and Swann, Rudy left the arrangements for their mother's cremation to his brother Peter. Rudy went to Cavendish Woods and headed directly for the Financial Affairs office. While he did not expect to walk away with a check, he was at least confident he could learn the amount that would be returned.

With him, he took both a copy of his mother's will – stipulating that funds not held in trust at the time of her death be divided among her three sons – and the paperwork from his mother and father's original admission to Cavendish Woods eighteen months earlier.

The heart of that paperwork was a document that explained the "traditional declining contract" her mother had signed. Her admission fee was one million dollars. For the payment of that sum, Cecelia and Harry Davis were guaranteed care for the rest of their lives. They also paid a fairly modest rent for their three-room apartment – $3,500 a month – which included meals. At the time of the surviving spouse's death, the admission payment would be refunded, less reasonable and necessary expenses accrued during their stay. The refund would be reduced by two percent per month of residence, plus a four percent processing fee.

Because his mother had lived there a total of eighteen months, the returned fee would have been sixty percent of a million dollars. But Rudy had obtained a separate document that raised the return to "up to eighty percent" because of his parents' advanced age. Eight hundred thousand, even divided three ways, would solve a lot of problems in his life.

But his meeting at Cavendish Woods lasted just long enough for Rudy to be told that his visit was at least a week premature.

"We have just started to gather your mother's expenses." The speaker was a young, red-haired woman in her early twenties. She was attempting to look older by wearing large, black-framed glasses and a severe suit. But Rudy could spot someone who was just a few years out of college. He was being lectured to by someone a third of his age.

"Then, how long will it take?" Rudy asked. He allowed his voice to show some of the irritation he was feeling. Part of that irritation was that the woman's name badge identified her as Senior Finance Manager. How could she be 'senior' after being on the job for a year? Or, was "senior" just a throwaway title, like all those make-believe "vice presidents" at his local bank.

"It will be a week at least," the woman said. Her name tag said Tiffany. How could anyone take anyone with the name Tiffany seriously? Moreover, the woman had this perky, sing-song voice and her head bobbed as she spoke. "When we give you a final accounting, we want to make certain that we've included everything." Then she added, "Once the final accounting is done, you can be sure we'll cut a check to the estate that same day."

It didn't make "a week at least" any easier to take, but it gave a finality to the process. At least that was something.

Tiffany saw the look of disappointment on his face. "Let me

ask: your mother's death notice wasn't in the newspaper this morning. Do you plan a wake for her?"

Rudy nodded. "My mother asked to be cremated. We thought we would have a wake at the funeral home in Hardington."

"You mother had a lot of friends here at Cavendish Woods," Tiffany said. "If you would like to hold the wake here, we'll absorb all of that expense. It's the least we can do."

Rudy thought to himself for a moment. While his mother's will had been specific about where her ashes were to be scattered, it had been silent on the subject of a wake, except that it be "dignified". That morning, he and his brothers had agreed to hold a wake at the funeral home. But that agreement was just hours old and the public notice was still being prepared. Here, at last, was an opportunity to save some money. He could sell the idea to his brothers on the basis that Cavendish Woods had large rooms and that she had friends here for whom getting to Hardington would be difficult.

"That is a very generous offer," Rudy said.

"When had you discussed holding the wake?" Tiffany asked.

"The day after tomorrow," Rudy replied. "Is that too soon for you?"

"Not at all," Tiffany said, reassuringly. "We'll use one of our larger function rooms. There's almost always one available."

"My mother's will asked that her wake be 'dignified'."

"I can promise you it will be," Tiffany said, smiling broadly. "We loved your mother as part of our family. It's our gift to you and your family." They shook hands.

"One more thing, Mr. Davis," Tiffany said. "The sooner your mother's apartment is cleared of furniture and her personal effects, the sooner we can complete that financial accounting. I don't want to put any pressure on you…"

"I understand," Rudy said. "In fact, I was going up there now."

Tiffany nodded. "You'll want to take the painting home, of course."

\* \* \* \* \*

He went to his mother's apartment in The Overlook and, after asking for a key from the central nurse's station, went inside. He had not been inside these rooms since his father had gone into the skilled nursing facility. He had met his mother for lunch every two weeks, but always in the Grand Lodge.

*Why not here? What did I have against these rooms?* The furniture was familiar; pieces selected from his parents' home. The Early American chairs, sofa and tables all sat in much the same arrangement as they had in the 1950s. For his parents, this must have represented comfort and continuity. For him, it was… what? A reminder of what had been expected of him. A hint of the silent disappointment that his father conveyed with just a glance.

Well, he had made his own life. He was a dentist and, if his father didn't think that was as good as being a "real" doctor or a lawyer, then screw him. Rudy was seventy-one; his practice had been successful until the walk-in dental clinics, HMOs and falling Medicare reimbursements cratered the profitability of the profession and made his practice essentially worthless.

Then he went into the apartment's bedroom and looked at the painting on the wall. *White Roses.* That painting was his ace in the hole. He had followed the sales of Fantin-Latours on the internet. The painting was worth at least a million; maybe two. Yes, he would have to divide the proceeds with his brothers but, even so, this was his secure retirement.

He removed the painting from the wall, found a bed sheet in the linen closet, and wrapped it carefully.

There were other paintings in the apartment, none of them valuable. In fact, there was nothing else in these three rooms that he ever wanted to see again. He would call his brothers and tell them that if they or their children wanted any of the contents of the apartment, they should claim them at the wake.

Rudy returned the key to the nurse's station and followed the corridors back to the Great Lodge. He thought about getting something to eat at one of the restaurants but the idea was too depressing; a reminder of those meals he had with his mother over the past two years.

He saw the sign for the art gallery – "The Cavendish Collection" – and, on a whim, went inside, the painting under his arm. He and his mother had spent time here after their lunches. She had even loaned *White Roses* to the gallery for two of its shows, and had beamed when it garnered a place of honor amid works by comparable artists.

The Cavendish Collection's "curator" – a woman named Jillian if he remembered correctly – approached him when he entered. She saw that he carried something rectangular under his arm and smiled sympathetically.

"We were all so saddened to hear of your mother's death," she said, touching him on his arm. "She was a delightful lady. I had hoped she would be with us for many years."

Rudy mumbled his thanks. Jillian's nametag said her last name was Connolly and she was, indeed, according to the nametag, the Curator. She was in her forties, thin with straight, blonde hair which contrasted her black suit.

"We are putting together a spring show," Connolly said. "One of our new residents has a small Homer, and another has agreed to loan us her Corot and Millet. It would have been quite a sight: magnificent paintings by four outstanding artists." She again touched him on his arm. "I assume you are taking the painting home."

"It seems like the right time," he said.

"When is your mother's service?" Connolly asked. "I would very much like to pay my last respects to her."

"She didn't want a funeral," Rudy replied. "But her wake will be here. A young lady in your financial office made the suggestion. That will be the day after tomorrow."

Connolly's face brightened. "I have an idea. Would you mind displaying *White Roses* one last time? Your mother was so proud of the painting. I can make certain it is lighted dramatically yet safely out of touching range. I think it would a wonderful gesture."

"Are you suggesting I leave the painting with you?" Rudy involuntarily held the painting more tightly with his arm.

"Of course not," she smiled. "Just bring it with you to the wake. And, rather than carrying it around in that sheet, I have a packing box in my office that might be a little more appropriate."

\* \* \* \* \*

Rudy lifted his head from the steering wheel. He looked at the painting on the passenger seat beside him. Until a few minutes ago, the path had been so clear: put the painting up for auction through Christie's or Sotheby's, collect his share of the proceeds from the rest of the estate, and then coast through retirement.

Now, that was all gone. There was still his share of the returned entrance fee, but the more he read the Cavendish Woods contract, the more he feared that the "reasonable and necessary expenses" that could be deducted from the fee might mean something different that he thought. Fine print had never been his strong suit. There were twenty pages of dense type in the contract. He could not make sense of them and had stopped trying.

The beneficiaries of the trust were just as depressing. The Nature Conservancy, the Audubon Society, the Garden Conservancy, the World Wildlife Federation. They were the same organizations to which his mother and father had written end-of-year checks for decades. Except that instead of a few hundred dollars, each organization was going to get a windfall of half a million dollars. His inheritance was going to charity.

He realized that he had to tell people about this. His wife, Donna, needed to be first. She would be livid, of course. It wasn't his fault. It wasn't *anyone's* fault but it would re-open fault lines that he thought had been patched over by the promise of a major cash infusion into the family's finances.

Then, he would have to tell his brothers. Alex wouldn't care. Alex was apparently rich, though he never shared anything about his finances with the family and barely spoke about his job, which he would only say was something in life sciences. Alex was staying in Boston at the Four Seasons with his girlfriend. But Pete would be devastated. Like Rudy, Pete needed this money. Pete hadn't worked in a year. Pete's wife had walked out on him for reasons that seemed to change with every telling of the story. Pete was going to be a problem.

It was strange how Donna had reacted to the phone call with the news of his mother's death. The call had come at 11 p.m., when they were already in bed. A call that late was never good news and he lifted the phone from its cradle hesitantly. He listened as the head of Cavendish Woods' medical unit explained that his mother had gone for an early dinner but had not been seen since seven o'clock. As was the staff policy, a "wellness check" call had been placed at ten o'clock and, when there was no answer, an aide was dispatched to make a visual check.

His mother's lifeless body was found slumped in a chair with the television on. All signs pointed to a heart attack. She had been taken to the nursing home's critical care unit but, based on body temperature, it was determined she had died at about eight o'clock. Resuscitation was pointless. Because he had his mother's health care proxy, Rudy was being contacted first as a courtesy, and to determine if he wanted to make the calls to other family members.

Lying next to Rudy in bed, Donna could hear his side of the conversation and so certainly knew what the call was about. But, when he hung up the phone after speaking with Cavendish Woods for ten minutes, she asked, "Who was that?," pretending she had heard nothing. Donna then cried, going on about what a terrible loss his mother's death was. In life, Donna considered his mother and father to be congenitally unable to accept her as a "good match" for their son, and she was always to blame when anything went wrong.

It made no sense. Had Donna said, "Good riddance," Rudy would have been hurt, but accepted his wife's honesty. Had she offered a tempered condolence, it would have been along the lines of what he expected. Her outburst of mourning seemed almost staged.

He did not understand his wife.

Defeated and depressed, Rudy turned the ignition in his car. His life had come completely unraveled in just a few short days. And there was nothing he could do about it.

7.

Marilyn Davis had always believed that using a direct approach when dealing with difficult subjects rarely brought honest answers. In teaching, the true depth of a student's knowledge was ascertained only through gentle probing. Asking a student to expand on one answer brought out a second drop of accurate information which became a trickle and then a torrent. *Never be satisfied with the first answer* was the mantra she had learned from the most experienced faculty members.

It was also her way of dealing with her father.

Her father, Pete, had lied to her all her life, it seemed. Most of his lies were petty but some were unforgiveable. He lied about his smoking when his clothes reeked of tobacco. He lied about his drinking when his speech was slurred and his eyes bloodshot. He lied about working when it was evident that he no longer had a place of employment. And he lied at Christmas when he said, "Your mom and I have decided to take some time apart."

Getting the truth out of him required all of her teaching skills.

Marilyn started by cooking dinner for her father at his home the night after her meeting with the five women – an event that Marilyn was confident she would never forget as long as she lived. She had tried to begin by drawing out an elliptical strand of veracity.

"Do you miss Grandmother?" she asked.

"Of course I do, Sweetie," he replied. She had been "Sweetie" all her life, while her brothers were "Ray" and "Cal".

"What do you miss most?"

He thought about the answer; a hopeful sign. A quick answer was always a lie. A pause before answering could also be time to prepare a lie, but it could also be time to think and tell the truth.

"I miss that she could predict exactly what your grandfather was going to say before he said it. I'd be in the kitchen with her and she'd hear his car pulling into the garage. She would listen to how he closed the car door and say, 'he's going to walk in here and say, 'I hope you had a better day than I did' or 'what's that great smell coming out of the oven' and she'd always be right."

It was the correct approach. She encouraged him to reminisce. She had broiled a steak with mashed potatoes, always his favorite meal. He devoured it. He obviously wasn't eating well. "Shondra" or "Sandra", or whatever her name was, was apparently not a cook.

It took an hour to work around to the questions she needed to ask. Everything had to be phrased in a non-threatening way so as not to raise her father's defenses. Eventually, though, she heard the story, or at least one part of the story that had the ring of truth, albeit tinged with pathos.

"Your grandmother and grandfather had a good sized estate," he said. "Before your grandfather died, their money would have come down to us. But, sometime after your grandfather died, your grandmother changed her will and put almost everything into a trust that is supposed to go to charities. Maybe it was your grandmother's idea or maybe she was talked into it. Your Uncle Rudy talked to the lawyer and, the day before the wake, Rudy gave us each a copy of the will."

He continued. "The saddest part is that the painting your grandparents loved so much turned out to be just a copy. It's worthless. Rudy took it to an auction house yesterday. The auction house said we could pay for experts, but they'd tell us the same thing. For nearly sixty years, your grandparents treasured a painting that was supposed to be by a famous artist. Instead, it was just something passed off as authentic to a couple of American tourist suckers."

Marilyn held her breath. *Now or never.* "Do you still have the will?" she asked.

Her father's face showed a momentary flash of caution. Then he closed his eyes; emotional collapse evident in his countenance. "It's on the table in the bedroom."

Marilyn went into the only bedroom still in use in the house.

Her father had moved out of the master bedroom and into the one once occupied by her brother, Ray. The room still featured the basketball trophies and ribbons won at Hardington High. The will was on a chest of drawers in the room, and Marilyn quickly photographed each of its eight pages with her phone.

She brought it back into the dining room. "This seems awfully thick," Marilyn said. "Aren't most wills just a few pages?"

Her father shrugged. "It's mostly about the trusts."

Marilyn flipped through a few pages, then folded the document and handed it to her father. "Well, it's none of my business."

They spent the balance of the evening talking about her brothers. The important issues – the questions that mattered – were left un-asked and un-discussed. They did not talk about who was the Shondra or Sandra that Marilyn's mother had sneeringly referenced a few weeks earlier, or why her father continued to maintain the fiction that he was still employed. Marilyn did not comment on her father's acquisition of a toupee, nor did he ask her opinion of it. And, she did not raise the most important question of all: whether her father thought someone in the family might have had a hand in Cecelia Davis' death.

Marilyn was tired of the lies.

\* \* \* \* \*

The next day, Marilyn took the train into Boston. She was no stranger to the city, having gotten both her Middle and High School Education B.A. and M.A. degrees at Simmons College. She missed the city life, but she wanted to raise her children in the kind of quasi-country environment that both she and her husband, Trey, had grown up in.

Trey had spent his childhood in Duxbury; Marilyn in Hardington. Neither town was affordable to a couple in their thirties living on one income, so they had settled in Ashland, where an older Cape on half an acre of land was within their price range.

Her Uncle Alex had offered to meet her for lunch in the Bristol Lounge at the Four Seasons. Everything about the restaurant looked expensive yet her uncle looked quite comfortable in these surroundings. Her father must be correct: Uncle Alex was doing very well out in California. He was tanned and athletically built, and his dark hair flopped down boyishly over his forehead and eyebrows. He looked a decade younger than she knew him to be.

"I really haven't been part of this family for thirty years," Alex said. "I talked with Mom and Dad every couple of weeks, but it was never about anything of substance. They'd fill me in on some of the drama, but it mostly went in one ear and out the other."

"Grandmother told me that she wished she saw more of you," Marilyn said. "She used to tell me she saw too much of Dad and Uncle Rudy and not enough of you."

Alex laughed. "I can see how those two could make a nuisance of themselves. But then, for them, it was – and you'll have to pardon me for being blunt – as much about checking up on their inheritance as being good sons."

Marilyn sensed she had the opening she needed. "You've heard about the new will."

Alex nodded. "Rudy, your father and I had a long discussion a couple of days ago. It's a piece of work. I offered to send it to my attorney for review, but I told them that what they'd likely learn is that Mom was of sound mind when it was written." He shrugged. "The money goes to charity. End of story."

"What if her death wasn't an accident?" Marilyn asked.

Alex's brow furrowed. "You'll have to explain that one to me."

Marilyn leaned across the table. "Grandmother had no history of heart trouble. She was amazingly healthy for her age. Yet, out of the blue, she had a heart attack, and she wasn't found for several hours. Who would benefit by her death?"

"You're serious?" Alex asked.

Marilyn nodded. "I saw her every week. She was moving past Grandfather's death. She wanted to move out of Cavendish Woods. She hated the place. And then she died. I have an uncomfortable feeling that her death was not of natural causes."

Alex drummed his fingers on the table. He kept his eyes on his niece. "Let's start with my own thoughts and a reality check: after about age eighty-five, you're living by the grace of whatever deity you happen to believe in. Both your grandmother and grandfather – my mom and dad – made it to ninety-three. That is a long, long time. And, just because Mom didn't have a *diagnosed* heart condition doesn't mean she didn't have one."

He continued. "And, just to underscore this discussion, everyone's body wears out in a way that is fundamentally unpredictable. You teach health; you understand that. But you're also a granddaughter to a wonderful woman, and part of you wants to believe that she would have lived past a hundred. To that end, you're predisposed to suspect foul play."

He pressed his fingertips together, palms resting on the table. "With that said, I'll answer your question in as serious a manner as I can. You really have two questions on the table. The first is 'who benefits from her death based on what we know right now'. The second is, 'who might have *thought* they were going to benefit based on what they *believed* to be true when she died'."

Marilyn cocked her head. "I don't think I understand…"

Alex held up two fingers of one hand and began ticking them off. "Since Mom died, we've learned a couple of things – or at least I have. We've learned that her assets are going to charity, not to her family. And, we've learned that a painting everyone assumed was very valuable is a copy. In short, a group of people who were expecting an inheritance isn't going to get one."

"You think someone in the family may have done something to her?" Marilyn asked.

"I have no idea," Alex said. "What I do know is that some people in this family have been living the past few years on an expectation…" He paused, looking for the right words. "…That there was a financial windfall right around the corner."

Alex continued. "From what I understand, Rudy had a very good dental practice for a very long time. But he didn't see that the world was shifting under his feet. The prosperous independent dentist on the second floor of an office building went out with the *Bob Newhart Show*. He didn't adapt while he could. It meant that, instead of being his nest egg to sell to some eager young dentist looking to buy into an established practice, Rudy just locked the door and sold off his equipment. And, to complicate matters, Rudy made some really bad investments with the money he had in his pension account."

"What about my father?" Marilyn asked.

Alex shook his head. "I don't want to go there. I think you already have the pieces of that puzzle. And, besides, I don't really know…"

"Then tell me what you think," Marilyn asked. "I'm not fifteen."

Alex drummed his fingers again. After a long pause, he said, "Your father did everything right for most of his life. He worked his way up the corporate ladder and raised a great family. Then, about two years ago, Pete screwed up big time. Pete's division got a special audit, and it uncovered some accounting issues in expense reports."

Alex looked at Marilyn directly and spoke carefully. "I only know Pete's side of the story. He admits he fudged his travel and entertainment reports to the tune of a few thousand dollars. He offered to make restitution, but the company said 'no'. He filed an EEOC claim saying the whole thing was just age discrimination; trying to get him and his big salary out of the way to make room for younger, less expensive managers. I can believe that part, by the way. At sixty-two, unless you're a company officer, you have a big red bull's eye on your back every day."

Alex continued. "Pete says the company backed off the expense report claim but wanted him out. He was in the midst of negotiating a package when one more issue surfaced…"

"Sandra," Marilyn said.

Alex nodded. "Actually, I think it's Shondra, although I've never met her. It was a direct violation of company policy. Pete was her immediate manager's boss. The EEOC option went by the boards.

His company gave him a year's salary along with twelve months of outplacement. I think that ended about two months ago."

"Which is when Mom moved out," Marilyn said.

Alex nodded. "I'm very sorry, Marilyn," he said. "In theory, Pete ought to have a big retirement fund stashed away plus money from stock options. They paid him a lot of money for a long time and the company was doing well."

"Did he ask you for money?" Marilyn asked.

Alex paused, then shook his head. "That question is over the line. I told him that no... relationship... was worth breaking up his family."

"I think the breaking up part is pretty much a done deal," Marilyn said, bitterness in her voice.

"Let's keep to the real issue," Alex said. "You think someone had a hand in your grandmother's death and asked me who would benefit. Here's my answer: based on the way her will is written today and the way things turned out with the painting, no one in the family benefits – unless someone is so desperate for money that they think their share of the returned entry fee to that nursing home is worth doing something that's going to be front and center of your conscience every waking minute for the rest of your life."

Alex continued. "But go back a week and things might have looked different. Rudy and your father were both counting on an inheritance. And, if you want to cast the net a little wider, so were Clarice and your Aunt Donna." Alex saw a look of horror come over Marilyn's face. "You asked me to speculate," he said. "I can either give you honest answers or I can sugarcoat them. You've always struck me as someone who wanted the truth."

"You think my mother or father could be capable of murder?" Marilyn asked.

Alex shook his head. "You asked me who would have benefitted. That's not the same as being capable of killing someone. But let's talk about who *would* have benefitted given the way your grandmother's will was actually written. Would the nursing home have gotten more money? No, I don't think so. They were making money hand over fist off that 'buy-in' provision. But what about that Liss and Swann outfit? Some of those outfits really skate on the edge of the law. They make a ton of money when they sign you up as a client, and another ton of money liquidating your estate. In between, unless there are trustee fees, it's just paperwork in a file. Do I think they're going to benefit? I'm sure of it."

Alex paused, pondering whether to give voice to his thought. "You're well read," he said. "Last year, I saw this report on *60 Minutes* about a male nurse…"

"The guy who worked at all those nursing homes in New Jersey," Marilyn said. "I saw the segment. He admits he killed forty people. He may have killed four hundred…"

Alex nodded. "He went for years without being detected and, even when hospitals and nursing homes suspected, they just told him to move on. Could there be someone like that at Cavendish Woods?"

"That would be horrible," Marilyn said.

"If you truly think that your grandmother's death wasn't just a heart attack, you have to look at all the possibilities," Alex said, taking his niece's hands in his own. "Do you really want to go rooting into that kind of muck?"

"Some friends have offered to help," Marilyn said. "They may not come up with an answer. But I know that if I do nothing, it will haunt me all my life."

Alex again nodded. "Then I understand what you have to do. And, when I get back to California, I'll have my attorneys go over the will and codicils. I'll call you if they turn up anything interesting."

8.

Leonard Swann's voice fell to nearly a whisper, which made the audience of nearly a hundred lean toward him to catch every word.

"They're vultures," he hissed. "They're vultures and proud of it, so you have to think of yourselves as their would-be prey. They want every last dollar and, when they've got it, they'll peck the carcass some more to see if there's anything else that's salable."

Now, his voice rose in strength. "Are you going to let them do that?"

*No!* the crowd roared.

"Are you going to *keep* what you've worked so *hard* for?"

*Yes!* said the crowd.

"They've got everything going for them," Swann said, shouting now. "They've got the IRS in their back pocket. They've got Congress wrapped around their little pinkie. They snap their fingers and senators and congressmen say, 'How much more do want us to collect?'."

There was silence in the room. He broke it with another whisper. "Well, we've got a few tricks up *our* sleeve, too, my friends. And, before the IRS and Congress make it illegal for you to keep any part of your nest egg – that nest egg you've worked your whole life for – you need to act. You need to plan…"

Eleanor Strong had been listening to Leonard Swann for nearly an hour. Her Cobb salad sat untouched, her coffee had grown cold.

*Why didn't I do this?* she thought. As soon as Phil started to exhibit signs of Alzheimer's, why hadn't she gone to see a firm like this?

"It isn't too late," Swann said, offering salvation with his smile. "How many of you already have a loved one in a nursing home? Let me see a show of hands?"

Eleanor tentatively raised her hand.

Swann walked over to one woman of about seventy. "Tell me,

Dear," he said. "How much is that nursing home charging you every month?"

The woman whispered a number.

"Don't be ashamed," Swann said. "We're all in this together."

A youngish man with a cordless microphone appeared from the side of the room and held it in front of the woman.

"Thirteen thousand, two hundred dollars a month," the woman said.

There were nods of agreement around the room.

"Thirteen thousand, two hundred dollars each and every month," Swann repeated. "That's more than one hundred fifty thousand dollars a year. That one hundred fifty thousand dollars that you can't live on, and one hundred fifty thousand dollars that you can't leave for your grandchildren's education. That's one hundred fifty thousand dollars that is going into the voracious money machine that is the nursing home industry. An industry that made more than fifty *billion* dollars last year. Fifty *billion!*"

Swann's voice fell back to a whisper. "Let us help you. Let us show you the way to keep those vultures away. Keep them away *legally*. Keep them away *permanently*. Keep them away so that your grandchildren will smile and hug you when they see you. Let us *help* you."

"Thank you," Swann said, his voice humble with gratitude.

Everyone rose to their feet, applauding. Eleanor felt tears in her eyes.

She felt a touch on her arm. It came from a young man at her table, neatly attired in a suit and tie. He glanced at Eleanor's name tag. "Mrs. Strong," he said. "I'm Steve Turner. I work with Mr. Swann. I noticed you raised your hand when he asked if you had a loved one already in a nursing home."

"My husband, Phil," Eleanor said. "It's been a year now."

"And you're starting to understand the financial pressure."

"Yes," Eleanor said. Out of the corner of her eye, she could see other such pairings taking place. In that audience of more than ninety in the private dining room of the Café Beauclair in Needham, apparently a third of the attendees were men and women whose job was to corral those who had come for the informational seminar and convert them to clients.

"You didn't raise your hand when he asked how many of us had children," Turner said.

"No," Eleanor said. "It has always been just Phil and me."

Samantha had prepped Eleanor for this conversation. Two days earlier, Eleanor had registered for the Liss and Swann "Protect Your Assets" seminar. Samantha told her that, as soon as she registered, her name immediately went through a credit check and all public records were searched to determine, as close as possible, just how many assets Philip and Eleanor Strong had to protect. That her husband was already in a nursing home was known as was the nursing home's fee and her insurance company's payment.

In essence, her attendance at the seminar was merely a signal that she was ready to have "the discussion". Steve Turner had already been assigned to her; he had taken his seat only after she was at the table, her nametag in place. He would have reviewed a printout with all the salient facts that could be gleaned from those records. That Eleanor raised her hand in the appropriate places served two functions. First, to prove to Liss and Swann that she was not here under some subterfuge and, second, to provide the necessary cover so that Turner could begin a conversation without letting on that he already possessed far more information about Eleanor Strong that he had any right to know.

In return for a Cobb salad and a cup of coffee that cost Liss and Swann less than ten dollars per attendee, these seminars produced a stream of what the industry called, "self-qualified leads". Liss and Swann's goal was to convert that ten-dollar investment (plus extensive radio and cable TV advertising) into a payoff that could prospectively be measured in the tens of thousands of dollars.

Leonard Swann's talk, seemingly fifty minutes of off-the-cuff remarks, was in fact a carefully crafted pitch that had been refined over seven years; distilled into an emotional roller coaster designed to lower the guard of those who heard it. And, despite being told all of this in advance, Eleanor had, by the end, succumbed to its appeal. It was only the touch on her arm – which Samantha had said would come within thirty seconds of the talk's conclusion – that snapped Eleanor back to reality.

"Perhaps we could sit here for a moment and talk," Turner said.

*Agree with whatever he says*, Samantha had urged her.

"Only if I can get my coffee warmed up," Eleanor said, smiling.

Turner motioned with his hand to someone on the other side of the room. He made a coffee-cup-tipping sign with his fingers.

"You said your husband – Phil? – has been in a nursing home about a year?"

"Just about a year," Eleanor said. "He has Alzheimer's. I took care of him at home as long as I could."

Turner nodded at each comment. "I imagine he's in one of the good facilities. Fortunately, Boston has some of the best in the country. Does insurance cover any part of it?"

Samantha had told Eleanor that the person who approached her at the seminar would already know the answers to the questions he or she asked, and that Eleanor should be forthright. "Insurance covers about four thousand dollar a month," she said.

"Leaving you with, probably, eight thousand out of pocket," he said.

"Eighty-two hundred," Eleanor said.

Turner let out a low whistle. "Every month," he said. "And the costs will just go up from here while the insurance payment stays the same."

Eleanor nodded.

Turner looked Eleanor directly in her eyes. "What if I said you may not have to pay that anymore? What if I said you could legally end those payments to the nursing home and that your husband's care would remain exactly the same? What if I said you could keep your savings so that you have the money *you* need to live on?"

Eleanor paused. Samantha had given her the answer Turner would most want to hear. "I would say that is wonderful. I would also say that it sounds too good to be true."

"Eleanor – may I call you Eleanor? – it *is* true. The nursing home wants your money, and you've signed paperwork that says you'll keep paying that money until there isn't any more. And, after that, they'll make you sell your house and everything in it so that they can keep getting paid." Turner paused. "But you don't have to keep paying them. And I can show you how."

"And his care will be the same?" Eleanor asked.

"I swear," Turner said.

Which is how Eleanor knew he was lying. She had already seen what happened at Phil's nursing home when families either could no longer pay or adopted "asset protection" strategies. Legally, the nursing home could not evict a patient. Medicaid took over the financial responsibility, paying the nursing home a flat fee that was a fraction of what was paid by a private patient. Care was cut back to exactly that prescribed by Medicaid guidelines. The usual impact was that residents' physical and mental health declined at an accelerating rate. Samantha had shown her the articles and the studies on which the articles were based.

Eleanor knew one other truth that Steve Turner could not possibly know. In her heart of hearts, she acknowledged Phil had only a short time to live. Her husband, once so mentally and physically active, was now a shell of himself. He did not know her. He did not engage in conversation. But somewhere, deep inside of him, that once-sharp mind had given a final set of orders to his body: *shut down.* She saw it progressing every month. The nursing home could make Phil comfortable for his remaining weeks or months, something Eleanor had become unable to do at home, but they could not instill in Phil a will to live when his life had, effectively, been taken away from him by Alzheimer's.

It was this truth that allowed Eleanor to go through with the charade she had volunteered to perform. Otherwise, that deliberate lie told by Turner would have caused Eleanor to slap the smiling young man's face. She could not abide liars. And she was in the presence of one who was not only a liar, but a thief as well. What she had to find out was whether this man – or someone else in his firm – was capable of murder.

9.

Martin Hoffman was so stunned that he dropped his fork.

"You're going back to work?" he said, not certain he had heard Paula correctly.

"Just for a month or two," Paula said. She shrugged. "It's February. There's no gardening. I thought I'd give it a try."

"The night shift?" Hoffman said. "At a nursing home?"

Paula nodded. "Four nights a week. That's all. I just want to see what it's like. You don't mind, do you?" She gave him her brightest smile.

Hoffman was caught off guard. "I can't tell you, you know, what to do with your time... but it's just so.... out of the blue."

"I know," Paula said. "And it's out of character and, no, I don't need the money. I just... thought about it and decided that it would be... interesting."

A thought crossed Hoffman's mind. "This doesn't have anything to do with, you know, your recuperation?"

Paula laughed and took his hand across the table. "No, that's fine. Over and done with." But an idea occurred to her as well. "But maybe that was the catalyst," she said. "I spent a lot of time around a lot of very caring people. I mean, nurses who genuinely cared about me. Not because they were being paid to do so; they genuinely wanted me to recover and they were pulling for me every step of the way. Maybe what I want to do is to give something back."

"By being on the night shift at Cavendish Woods?," Hoffman said. His voice still evinced doubt, but he was coming around.

"Yes," Paula said. "For a month – maybe two – I'm going to be a night nurse. It's light duty, but maybe I can help someone. And, when that's over, I'll go back to being predictable me."

The conversation was taking place over dinner at Zenith, the upscale bistro in the center of Hardington where the two of them dined at least once every other week. Paula had chosen this place because it was part of their routine and she did not want Martin in unfamiliar surroundings when she broke her news. She did not want him to be either suspicious or upset and, so far, he was neither.

There were, in fact, only two people outside the Garden Club Gang whom she felt any obligation to tell. She told Julie during a long mother-daughter phone conversation the previous evening. Julie seemed thrilled by the idea. "Good for you, Mom," she has said.

But with Martin there was body language to contend with as well as one other undeniable fact: she was falling in love with this man. No, that was untrue. She was already in love with him even if she had never spoken those words.

Martin was straightforward, handsome, funny, caring, shy, intelligent and un-self-conscious. He was not only the antidote to Dan, her ex-husband who had traded Paula in for a woman just a few years older than Julie; he was the man she wished she had met thirty years ago.

She knew that Martin was also "damaged goods" – a term that he had used to describe himself. He had called Paula after the arrests were made in the Brookfield Fair robbery to propose lunch, only to learn that Paula was recuperating from surgery. It had taken almost three months to arrange that first "date" (a term neither one of them would acknowledge, though it was an apt description). At that first lunch, Martin had told Paula that his wife had died four years earlier in a senseless auto accident. He had mourned Kelly for three years, leaving the Cambridge home they had lived in most of their married life.

He had started fresh; retiring from the Cambridge Police where he had been a senior detective and had taken a job in Brookfield as the town's lone detective on a six-man force. He had moved into a vast apartment community in Framingham. Slowly, gradually, grief yielded to acceptance. "You wouldn't have wanted to know me two years ago," he told her.

"And you wouldn't have wanted to know me," Paula had replied, thinking back on the rage and bitterness she felt.

Now, her goal was to walk a fine line: to tell Martin as much of the truth as she dared, and to not have him draw the conclusion that she was somehow distancing herself from him.

"It's a seven-to-seven shift," she said, reassuringly. "I even get a two hour nap break. And, I get three days a week when I don't have to think about work at all. I figure that by the middle of April, the garden will be calling me. I'll have it out of my system."

The look on Martin's face still showed doubt.

Paula's right foot found one of Martin's under the table and she rubbed his shin. "I'll tell you what," she said. "You circle April 15 on your calendar, and then you draw a line through the week after that. You tell the Board of Selectmen that you're going to be unavailable for duty for that week."

"I thought you said your garden would be calling by the middle of April," Martin said.

"I let some calls go to voicemail," Paula said, with just the hint of a grin.

10.

Alice Beauchamp felt the mattress in her apartment with her fingertips. *A little too firm*, she worried.

But the rest of the surroundings were beautiful. Yes, it was only two furnished rooms and her new condo had five. But here on the fourth floor of "The Overlook", she had thirty feet of a glass wall, beyond which was a terrace and, beyond that, a view of the park-like grounds that surrounded the entrance to the building. The room décor was bright and cheerful; the furnishings appeared new and expensive.

The lone concession to the notion that she was in an "independent/assisted living facility" was that against each wall of her apartment was a bright red, three-inch-wide button. Pushing any of those buttons would produce, in under a minute, a nurse. Pressing one of the buttons for more than ten seconds would summon EMTs.

That she was here at all was a pleasant surprise. It all seemed so easy. She and Paula had driven here four days after Cecelia's wake. Paula explained to the Cavendish Woods admissions director that, as Alice's "goddaughter" and Alice having no relatives living nearby, that there was some question of whether Alice could or should remain alone in her home. Alice had resisted the idea of a "nursing home". Cavendish Woods offered one-month trial "experiences" for prospective residents. Could one be arranged for her godmother?

Without being prompted, Paula had produced a financial statement in a leather binder. The admission director had studied it for about two minutes. She had left the room for five minutes with the statement and returned smiling. Cavendish Woods would be pleased to make room for Alice Beauchamp for a period of thirty to sixty days, after which Alice could make the decision to remain or return to her home.

On the drive home, Alice had asked what such a stay would cost.

"This is an investment in finding out who killed Cecelia Davis," Paula said tersely. "You need to be there, following in Cecelia's footsteps, meeting the same people, taking the same classes. More than anyone else, you're in a position to find out what happened to her. Don't be concerned with the cost. Be concerned with who might have had a reason to kill her."

It did not stop Alice from performing a lengthy internet search that evening. When she found the information, she gasped.

*Cavendish Woods offers pre-enrollment visits of up to sixty days to prospective members. Your loved one will experience all the benefits of the Cavendish Woods lifestyle including all meals and services. Each thirty-day period is priced at $15,000 to $20,000 depending upon accommodation ands view.*

Alice kept those figures in mind as she unpacked her three suitcases. She wasn't here for a vacation. She was here to find out who murdered her friend.

11.

Jean Sullivan caught sight of herself in the reflection of a glassed-office wall and frowned. The dark blue "uniform" she wore as a member of the cleaning crew was a disaster. Her pants were too baggy, her sweatshirt made her look frumpy, and the lanyard with her security badge hung down nearly to her waist. Her hair was misshapen under a Red Sox cap.

*And I get stuck with garbage duty*, she thought.

No, that wasn't the case. At Pokrovsky Motors, she would bag the contents of "Al Junior's" trash can every evening. By noon the next day, Samantha would be on the phone to her, thanking her profusely for what she had found. Every few days Jean would drive to Samantha's apartment where the two would sort the handwritten notes, memos, receipts and other papers into a series of coherent story lines. Collectively, they formed what Samantha said was both "the paper trail to hang the bastard with his own stupidity" and one she called "our insurance policy".

"I know you've got the crappy job," Samantha told her. "But you're bringing home dynamite. Everything else is circumstantial. This is the stuff that sends people to prison."

To Jean, it was at least some small compensation for the letdown she had felt following "the Job". She had collected her share of the $350,000 and earmarked $10,000 for a luxury cruise; the beginning, she hoped, of a new life.

Jean had researched cruises carefully, looking for ones that attracted middle-aged single men. She read cruise reviews and joined online forums and discussion groups that offered frank advice about finding marriage-minded men on ships. Two weeks before her departure, Jean purchased an appropriate wardrobe; her first new clothes in two years.

In early October she flew to Ft. Lauderdale and boarded a 500-passenger cruise ship paying ports of call in seven Caribbean locales over ten days. She had booked a suite that was just below the top price level because, she had learned through research, men paid careful attention to such things. A suite on the Emerald Deck meant the woman was wealthy and therefore the target of gold-diggers. A shared room on the three lowest decks meant she was on a tight budget.

At the end of ten days, Jean had learned three expensive, bitter lessons: the first was that attractive single men on cruise ships were looking for sex, not marriage. The second was that men automatically eliminated from consideration any women who were not at least ten years their junior. The forty-something divorcees got to pick and choose from the available supply of men. Everyone else went to bed alone. The third was that men over the age of sixty-five who expressed interest in a post-cruise relationship were looking for a nurse, not a wife. When one elderly man casually inquired over lunch in St. Croix if Jean had experience in giving insulin injections, she had to repress the urge to get up from the table, excuse herself, and take a taxi to the local airport and board the first flight back to the mainland.

Jean's lone fond memories of the cruise were the late night, boozy talks with other women on the last days of trip. They would gather at large tables in the otherwise deserted dining room and dissect both the men on the cruise and their own lives.

What Jean discovered was that she was not alone and her situation was not unique. Al Sullivan, her bastard, controlling husband, was not the only monster in the world. Half of the women she met on the cruise had been married to such men. Most had outlived their spouses and those who did freely confessed that becoming a widow ranked as one of the happiest days of their lives. The ones who had won their freedom through divorce considered themselves released from prison.

On the last night of the cruise, Jean shared her story of coming in from working in the garden and finding her emphysema-debilitated husband dead in front of the television. She told of waiting an hour to call the paramedics, just to be certain there was no chance of reviving him. She got many nods of recognition. "I waited three hours," one woman said. "And after the ambulance left, I opened the best bottle of wine in the house."

One very good thing came out of the cruise. When Jean explained to the late-night group the financial straitjacket her husband had left her in with his will and its various trusts, one woman looked at her oddly. As the group was breaking up, the woman – an attorney from Atlanta – asked why Jean had never challenged the conditions of the will, especially given the length of her marriage.

"I couldn't afford to," Jean said.

"But you're on this cruise, which would have more than paid for a court challenge," the woman said.

"I won a small lottery and took the cash payout," Jean lied.

"Well, if there's anything left from that lottery, you go get yourself an attorney who specializes in wills and trusts," the woman said. "Not some hometown friend who does real estate; a real specialist." The woman reeled off the names of several Boston firms that Jean could contact.

A week after returning home, Jean had called two of the firms. One declined because the size of the estate fell below the firm's minimum. After a meeting with the second firm, though, the attorney took her hand and said, "Ms. Sullivan, I think you've suffered long enough."

That had been in early November. Paperwork had been filed and a court hearing was scheduled for next month. It was possible – just possible – that by spring, Jean could never have to think about Al Sullivan again for as long as she lived.

In the meantime, though, her job was undercover cleaning woman.

Samantha had warned her that there was no single suspect. "This isn't a repeat of Pokrovsky Motors," she said. "There, we knew who the boss was and we figured out early on that he was stupid.   At Cavendish Woods, we're not certain what we're looking for.   Your job is to blend in, keep your eyes open, and look at what people are throwing away.   Ninety-nine percent of it is going to be worthless.   You have to be able to recognize that one percent that will be gold."

Jean took another look at her reflection in the glass wall.   On second thought, the baggy pants made her look no different from the other women on the cleaning crew.   The sweatshirt hid her figure, which was for the best as she did not want to attract the attention of the security detail or evening medical staff.

She hefted a trash can and put its contents into the plastic garbage bag she pushed from room to room.   She noted the kind of papers the trash can had contained and began mentally cataloging the source of the printouts, Xeroxes and memoranda those trash cans contained.

*One room at a time.   One night at a time*, she thought.   *The pattern will show itself.*

12.


Alice was winded from the *t'ai chi* class. For an exercise that appeared to be all about slow-motion aerobics and meditation, the bending and stretching was anything but simple and relaxing. She was normally sedentary in the winter months. In March, she would start building up her flexibility for working her vegetable plot in Hardington's community garden. By later April and May, she would be as limber as a teenager, or as limber as anyone her age had a right to be. But asking muscles that had been dormant since October to suddenly stretch in unusual ways was an unexpected strain.

"Let's go get a smoothie," her *t'ai chi* partner, Gwendolyn, said. Gwendolyn Durham was a vigorous eighty. She was also someone about whom Cecelia had spoken warmly.

Alice had devoted several hours to putting down on paper every activity Cecelia talked about participating in at Cavendish Woods, and every person she called a friend here. On this, her first full day of residence, Alice had met with a "life stages counselor" and provided a list of educational and recreational activities that, as close as possible, mirrored the ones Cecelia had been involved in during the last months of her life.

Gwendolyn led Alice into one of the restaurants in the Great Lodge, went to a counter and ordered a banana-strawberry-melon smoothie. Gwendolyn turned to Alice. "What are you having?"

"Oh, that sounds good," Alice said. She had heard of smoothies but had never tasted one in her life.

The order taker behind the counter recognized Gwendolyn and tapped something into a computer tablet. The person looked at Alice quizzically. "Guest or resident?"

"Resident," Alice said. "Brand new, today."

"And your name?"

"Alice Beauchamp. B-E-A-U…"

"Got it," the order taker said and tapped something into the computer tablet. "I'll remember next time," she said, smiling brightly.

This is what Cecelia had railed against while the two of them had brown-bag lunches on the plaza outside the Great Lodge. *"They say, 'meals included' but everything is a 'special order' whether it's a second cup of tea or a slice of cake instead of the pudding. Nothing has prices on it. They just tap their little computers and it all shows up on the monthly bill. It's the one thing I hate most about this place."* Cecelia rarely lost her temper, but Cavendish Woods' determination of what was and was not covered under "meals and lodging" was a continuing point of contention.

The order taker produced two greenish frozen concoctions in plastic cups. Alice took hers and wondered what kind of charge would show up at the end of the month. She would certainly want to reimburse Paula for extravagances like this.

Gwendolyn led Alice to a table, set as though in a Parisian café. A card on the table provided other suggestions for mid-morning snacks: "health-nut brownies", biscotti, cappuccino or espresso, and kiwi sorbet. Of course, there were no prices on the card. Just names and beautiful photographs of the food and beverages.

For ten minutes, the two women exchanged the kind of pleasantries that people of their age were prone to fall back on when first meeting someone: children, grandchildren, hometowns. Then, Gwendolyn said, "You looked a little stiff out there. You know, there's also a beginner's class."

"Cecelia said she picked it up very quickly," Alice said. "I don't get nearly enough exercise in the winter."

Gwendolyn shook her head. "She was a great lady. I miss her every day."

"I do too," Alice said. "Maybe it's why I'm here." She took a sip of her smoothie. It tasted sweet and mostly of banana. What could it cost? Two dollars? Three dollars?

"What do you mean, it's why you're here?" Gwendolyn asked.

"She was so healthy; so full of life," Alice said. "She never spoke of any heart condition."

"And I never thought I had any problem with my bones until I fell off a ladder," Gwendolyn said. "Now, I think half my right leg is titanium. So you're investigating Cecelia's death?"

"I didn't say that," Alice said defensively.

"You said, 'I do, too. Maybe it's why I'm here'," Gwendolyn said, holding up finger quotes. "I have an excellent memory. That statement would have made sense if you moved in while Cecelia was alive. It *doesn't* make sense ten days after she died."

"I'm not convinced Cecelia died of natural causes," Alice said softly.

"Well then, why didn't you say so?" Gwendolyn asked. "The way she died has been bothering me every since I heard the news. I just don't have any way to do anything about it. Are you a private investigator? Did the family hire you?"

Alice stated to shake her head and say "no". Then, she reconsidered. "Not exactly a private investigator," she said. "More like someone who is helping someone else who *is* an investigator by occasionally going undercover."

Gwendolyn looked at Alice with a new appreciation.

"I'm following in Cecelia's footsteps," Alice said. "I'm trying to see the world in the same way she saw it those last few months."

"Including moving into Cavendish Woods," Gwendolyn said.

Alice gave a dismissive wave of her hand. "I can afford it." The lie sounded so natural that Alice surprised herself. "The important thing is to do the same activities and meet the same people." Alice paused. "I'm risking a lot by telling you this. No one else knows about this."

"And I won't say anything to anyone," Gwendolyn said. "But, if you're looking for ideas, there's a group of Cecelia's friends who get together a couple of times a week. We play cards and we read mysteries. Probably more mysteries than is good for us because we all have overly active imaginations. None of them have said anything to me about Cecelia not passing away of natural causes, but they might have some ideas worth listening to."

Alice felt her heart beating faster. "This group," she said. "Could I meet them?"

"Hell, yes," Gwendolyn said. "I have just two questions: do you play bridge and how much can you afford to lose?"

* * * * *

At two o'clock, Alice reported to one of the meeting rooms for Art Appreciation. Eight other residents sat in chairs arranged in a semi-circle. All had notebooks and pens. Alice had arrived empty-handed. Though she was on time, the class seemed already to have started.

A blonde, forty-ish woman stood at the head of the semi-circle. She stopped talking when Alice came in. The woman smiled. "You must be Alice." Turning to the others in the group, she said, "Everyone, this is Alice Beauchamp" The woman pronounced it "Bow-champ".

"It's pronounced 'Beechum'," Alice said. There was an empty seat in the semi-circle and Alice took it.

"And I'm Jillian Connolly," the woman said. "We're delighted you're joining us, even in mid-course. Our topic this month is the Pre-Raphaelite Brotherhood. Do you have any foundation on that school of painting?"

Alice thought for a second. Art history had been one of her favorite subjects in college. "British. Nineteenth century. Millais, Rossetti, Burne-Jones. Swapping mistresses and high on opium most of the time."

The last comment drew a laugh from the group.

Connolly laughed, too, though Alice thought it a bit forced. "Well, I'm not so certain that the last part is *completely* accurate. But it's obvious that you have a grounding on the topic."

For the next ninety minutes, Alice listened as Connolly delved into the background of Sir John Elliot Millais' *Ophelia*: its origins in Shakespeare's *Hamlet*, the model Elizabeth Siddal, and the symbolism of the flowers that populate the canvas.

Connolly spoke of what she called the "politics" of the painting:

that Siddal was, by all accounts, as gifted an artist in her own right as the men for whom she posed, but that women artists in nineteen-century Britain found neither encouragement of nor markets for their art.

Alice decided that Connolly was knowledgeable about her topic and genuinely interested in sharing that information with her "students". Cecelia had also spoken highly of Connolly and her passion for art.

At the end of the tutorial, Alice briefly thought of broaching her concerns about Cecelia's death with Connolly. But the instructor kept looking at her watch through the question and answer period and began packing her books and materials as the clock showed three-thirty. So instead, Alice simply said, "I think I'm going to enjoy this class."

Connolly smiled. "It's good to have another person in here who isn't just looking for something to fill their afternoon. And, you're right about the opium. But talking about drugs in this particular environment violates several finicky state laws so I just leave that part out."

With that, Connolly was gone. And Alice was left to wonder if Cecelia had been the other person who wasn't "just looking for something to fill their afternoon".

\* \* \* \* \*

Alice wandered the Great Lodge, marveling at its cleanliness and sleek lines. Everywhere was color: displays of quilts and paintings, pottery and antique maps. There was nothing in the Great Lodge that hinted this was a nursing home. There were shops, restaurants and public spaces. A movie theater's marquee announced the showing of a Claudette Colbert festival with *The Egg and I* starting in five minutes.

Alice went into the darkened room. To call it a movie theater was perhaps an overstatement. It held perhaps thirty seats and the screen was an oversized flat-screen television. Eight of the seats were taken, and no one asked her name, so this was apparently a free activity.

The film began and Alice was quickly caught up in Betty MacDonald's humorous plight of being a newlywed with a city-reared husband intent upon making a go of an abandoned chicken ranch. Fred MacMurray's cluelessness about the realities of operating such an enterprise was at once funny and heartbreaking.

MacMurray's Bob MacDonald was in so many ways a portrait of Alice's late husband, John. Like Bob MacDonald, John Beauchamp had been at heart a good man – a wonderful, loving man – but he had no head for business and especially no comprehension of finance. Through thirty-six years of marriage, he insisted that the stock market was no place for their savings and that mutual funds were designed to part investors from their money. And so, year after year, he placed their paltry savings in certificates of deposit and low-yielding bank accounts.

When he died – now seventeen years ago – the combination of the expenses of his final hospital stay and the corrosive effects of inflation on their savings left Alice with too little to live on. Until "the Job", Alice had been heading into a poverty that was both humiliating and private. Now, through the grace of her friends, she had restored her financial equilibrium. She had vowed to herself that she would find a way to "pay forward" what she received from "the Job". Pokrovsky Motors had been her first payment.

Betty MacDonald's eccentric neighbors turned out to be wonderful people, helping the MacDonalds rebuild after a disastrous fire. Cecelia Davis had been such a neighbor for Alice, warmly welcoming her to the neighborhood in Hardington and lending a sympathetic ear at every turn. Now, Alice had a second opportunity to pay forward the kindnesses that Cecelia had shown her through the years. By the end of the film, Alice had tears streaming down her face.

*Somewhere, here in Cavendish Woods, is a person who may have taken your life*, Alice thought. *Through the grace of God, I am here to help find that person.*

\* \* \* \* \*

"An excess dose of digitalis, a shot of insulin, curare, or even an air bubble injected into the bloodstream." Celie Sturtevant held up four fingers. "Any one of them can give a person a heart attack. There are also some veterinary drugs that will work, though I'm not certain of their names." She declined to increase the number of fingers on display.

"And exactly where is someone going to come up with curare?" asked Marge Constantine. "Doesn't that come from the Amazon? Should we be on the lookout for some native with a blowgun?"

Alice looked around with a combination of awe and bewilderment. She was one of eight women at two card tables. The women were all residents of Cavendish Woods and ranged in age from about seventy to more than ninety. Some had physical infirmities but all were mentally sharp. She knew the latter was true both because of the nature of the discussions around her and the fact that she was down, at ten cents a point, more than eleven dollars. Alice considered herself a decent bridge player. She was playing with sharks.

But it was the surroundings that were the true eye-opener. When Gwendolyn said "bridge with friends at seven", Alice assumed they would be playing in one of the common rooms in the Great Lodge. Instead, she was told to take one of the shuttle carts to "The Moorings" and ask to be let off at "Number Six".

The Moorings turned out to be the most luxurious of the private villa clusters at Cavendish Woods. Number Six, according to the brass nameplate at the gate, was the residence of Priscilla and Alan Clurman. Their cottage fronted on a small pond ringed with white lights and was as lavish and well-appointed as a penthouse. Alan Clurman, Alice learned, was not in residence at the moment. He had flown down to Florida for the week to play golf. Priscilla appeared to be well into her eighties. The photos of the man at her side were certainly not of someone younger than Priscilla.

The Clurmans could afford to move into Cavendish Woods with

its steep up-front payments. They could afford to live in an opulent cottage. They could afford to jet off to Florida to play golf.

The Clurmans, Alice quickly deduced, were loaded.

Yet this evening was the exact opposite of her horrid nine months in Delray Beach, where it was like being back in high school with its snotty cliques and stage-whispered putdowns. There, she had been continually judged (and found wanting) based on the jewelry and clothes she wore. She was never once invited to a private get-together in Century Village. Here, she had been instantly accepted even though she showed up in a simple dress and a well-worn sweater. But then, that is how all the other women were dressed. None wore jewelry. Priscilla Clurman's pink sweater had a noticeable rent in its left elbow.

There must be, she thought, some unseen threshold that she had crossed. By being able to *afford* Cavendish Woods, Alice had established some pedigree. By being known as a friend of Cecelia Davis, she had proven she was worth knowing. (That she was here by the grace of Paula Winters' checkbook was something that the group could not know and she had no intention of volunteering.)

Call it Yankee frugality, Alice concluded. A bunch of rich women (herself excluded) sitting around in comfortable clothes on a cold, February evening, playing bridge at ten cents a point.

The conversation had come back around to things that could trigger a heart attack. Alice had said she wanted to write a mystery about an elderly male patient being killed, and the murderer making it look like heart failure. "Potassium chloride," added Celie Sturtevant. "That's another one I read about. The body needs it in small quantities but, give someone a high dose and *wham* – it will stop your heart. In fact, it's the third drug used in lethal injections." Then she added, "I bid two spades."

"So, someone just goes into a patient's room and says, 'drink this'?" The question came from Gwendolyn. "If someone did that to me, I'd tell them to drink it first."

"Even if it was a doctor?" asked Maureen Fry, who was seated at

Alice's table.

"One of the nurses says, 'it's time for your shot.'" Gwendolyn said. "Do you ask what drug he or she is giving you? I have a pill regimen. I have a shot regimen. If someone – anyone – changes the order of things, I want to know why."

There was a general murmur of agreement.

"Let's acknowledge that my story couldn't happen at a place like this," Alice said.

"I'm not so certain," said Hermoine Kleeves. "Unless the person lives right by the nurse's station, I can get to anyone's room in The Overlook without ever being seen, just by using the stairs. This place was designed to give us a sense of privacy."

"But aren't there cameras?" Priscilla asked.

"Only in the public areas," Hermoine replied. "I wouldn't want to live some place where there were cameras everywhere, in every corridor."

"So, someone intent upon committing a murder can get to a room unseen," Maureen Fry said. "That's just the beginning. They can't break down the door; that would be too noisy. I keep my door locked. I don't want someone from the staff walking in on me. So, the murderer would have to know his victim. That's the key."

Seven heads nodded in agreement. Play momentarily stopped while Maureen continued. "But if you think you're in danger, just go to one of the red buttons."

More nodding heads. Several of the women looked around the large room in the Clurman's cottage where the tables were set up. There were four of the red buttons in this one room.

"In my story, I guess we assume there are no red buttons," Alice said.

"Not so fast," Maureen said. "If the victim knows and *trusts* the person, he isn't going to lunge for the red button. It could be a friend, a staff member, or someone from the outside who knew where he lives and had visited enough to observe how to avoid going by the nurses' station."

Maureen finished her statement and smiled, which Alice thought somewhat macabre.

"It would also have to be someone who has access to drugs," Celie said. "And, presumably, a syringe, since I don't think anyone but an idiot would willingly consume something offered to him. And, unless you're on the medical staff, getting hold of a syringe is next to impossible."

Hermoine Kleeves added, "I think we can rule out anything administered as food or drink. The body would have to absorb it through the stomach. There's a good chance the victim would gag before a poison could work."

"So, we're back to a syringe and someone who has access to one of those drugs Celie talked about," Priscilla said. She then turned to Alice and said, "What do you think?"

Alice had been listening intently and absorbing what the other women said. She was unprepared to be asked for her own opinion. She paused before speaking.

"This is all fascinating," Alice said. "But I want to focus on motive in my story. The person I have in mind is someone who doesn't have enemies. Everyone likes him. He's a nice guy. The person who is going to kill him has something to gain. And, when I say 'gain', inevitably that seems to always come down to money."

Alice noted that every set of eyes were on her.

"For example, let's say he had some new firm advising him on estate planning after his wife dies," Alice said. "Those people collect a lot of fees for setting up trusts, and then they collect a lot more fees when someone dies. Is that a motive?"

Alice paused, hoping someone would add something. After a few moments, Priscilla cleared her throat.

"It reminds me of a few conversations Cecelia and I had after Harry passed away," Priscilla said, choosing her words carefully. "She asked how she thought her three sons would react if she changed her will to give most of her money to charities instead of keeping it in the family. I told her to do what she thought best but, if she did change the will, not to say anything to her sons because they'd try to talk her out of it."

"We also talked about estate administration," Priscilla said. "Harry had always handled all of their legal affairs, and Cecelia said the firm she was speaking with gave her a fee proposal that she thought was quite high. I told her that lawyers and accountants were a fact of life and so were their fees. None of the accountants I know are homicidal, but she didn't say what firm she was speaking with. All in all, I'd say that was a dead end."

"I have a nephew who would bump me off in a heartbeat if he thought he could get away with it," Hermoine offered. "When I do go to meet my maker, he's going to get a big, fat, unpleasant surprise coming to him."

\* \* \* \* \*

Riding back in the cart to the Great Lodge, Gwendolyn leaned over to Alice and whispered, "Something you said tonight got me to thinking. Cecelia told me that she was weary of her sons coming around to show what dutiful progeny they were. And then their wives would make the same trip a few days later to show her endless photos of grandchildren who all needed to be in private schools."

The last statement caught Alice's attention.

"Donna and Clarice came here?" Alice asked.

"Is that their names?" Gwendolyn asked. "The wife of the son who was a dentist was the real pest. She would just show up – she knew that if she called ahead she would never get an invitation – and say that it wasn't fair that Cecelia still had all this money tied up after Harry died while she and her husband were going into debt to cover private schools for their grandkids."

"Cecelia never told me any of that," Alice said, truly perplexed.

"Well, the reason I knew was that this white-haired, hefty woman…"

"That would be Donna; Rudy's wife," Alice said excitedly.

"All right, Donna was waiting for Cecelia outside of the *t'ai chi* class just after Christmas, and Donna was in a royal snit because

Cecelia had sent everyone Christmas cards with – and I'm using Donna's words – 'these insulting checks'. Donna said, 'These are your grandchildren and you're robbing them of their future by being such a miser.'"

"What did Cecelia say to Donna?" Alice asked.

"Cecelia just looked right past her and went to the reception desk," Gwendolyn said. "The receptionist made a phone call. I gather Donna got the hint that Security had been summoned because she made a few more choice comments and then left before she could be dragged out of the place."

'What did Cecelia say afterward?" Alice asked.

Gwendolyn thought for a moment. "She said, 'That woman has disliked me for nearly fifty years. It's only now that she's finally finding the courage to say it to my face and, even now, she's couching it in terms of helping out her grandchildren'."

Gwendolyn saw the look on Alice's face. "Alice, you said were looking for someone who had a motive. I think I just gave you one."

"You certainly did," Alice said, softly.

"Then I need to tell you the other daughter-in-law wasn't exactly an angel," Gwendolyn said.

"What do you mean?"

"She would come around essentially begging for money," Gwendolyn said. "Her husband was out of work. It was tearing her marriage apart – that sort of thing. This woman…"

"Clarice," Alice offered.

"Clarice," Gwendolyn repeated, "laid on the guilt trips. Cecelia wouldn't take her calls so Clarice camped out here, hoping to catch her. We'd be walking through the Great Lodge. If Cecelia spotted Clarice first, Cecelia would grab my arm and say, 'just turn around and keep walking.' If Clarice saw Cecelia, she'd rush over and say, 'Oh, I'm glad I caught you. Could I have just a minute of your time?' And Cecelia would get this look on her face. She'd come back five minutes later gritting her teeth. She'd say, 'That woman thinks she is going to wear me down. Well, she's wrong.'"

"This didn't just happen once," Gwendolyn added. "I was with her on at least two occasions when she got ambushed. She told me about a couple of others. She was visibly upset by those encounters."

"What a horrid thing to have to go through," Alice said, shaking her head. "Cecelia was a good, kind woman."

13.

"We got the first one, Al."

Al Pokrovsky, Senior, leaned back in his chaise and put his hands behind his head. He had grown bored studying the sailboats in Green Pond trying to navigate the jetty to get out into Vineyard Sound.

Mike McDonough, a beefy man of about fifty with no discernible neck, stood, hands behind his back, grinning from ear to ear, waiting to be asked to elaborate.

"So tell me," Pokrovsky asked. As he did, he motioned that Mike should have a seat. Good news merited the opportunity to tell a story in relative comfort.

"We figured the social security number for the accounting lady was a phony and it was," McDonough said "The broad always parked at the farthest end of the lot but we kept going through security footage until we got some of her leaving. She only slipped up twice but we got a full plate. It's a 'greenie' and not a very legible one, but we kept enhancing the photo."

A "greenie" was a pre-1988 Massachusetts green-on-white license plate and a badge of pride for residents who disdained the red, white and blue "Spirit of America" plates that had replaced them. Motorists could retain their old plates so long as they were in continuous use. One of the benefits was that only the rear plate was required. The absence of a front license plate had made identifying the woman's car that much more difficult.

"The car is registered to Alice Beauchamp," McDonough spelled the name. "The registration address is senior citizen's housing in Hardington."

"Hardington," Pokrovsky said, trying to place the name. "That's where they start the Marathon."

"I'm pretty sure that's Hopkinton," McDonough said. "Hardington's big claim to fame is that Tom Snipes lives there."

"Hero of two AFC Championship games; goat of two Super Bowls," Pokrovsky said. "I lost ten thousand bucks because of that guy. Already I don't like this town."

"Problem is," McDonough said, "her car ain't there. We asked around…"

"You did this very, very quietly," Pokrovsky said, looking in McDonough's face for evidence that he had not followed specific instructions.

McDonough nodded. "We know we got to be under the radar on this one. What we found out is that she moved a couple of months ago to someplace else in town…"

Pokrovsky started ticking off ideas on his fingers. "She's getting her mail forwarded, she changed over her electric, she told the AARP she has a new address, or you can just look for the car."

"We're following every lead – off the radar. We'll find her." McDonough's voice left no room for doubt.

"What about the others?"

"Junior said he saw four women plus the insurance broad," McDonough said. "I talked to three salesmen who are writing down everything the skinny one said while she was supposedly shopping for a fleet. They don't know why they're writing it down, but they know their careers depend on it. They say she was talkative but she was also vague. We'll come up with something. They always slip up."

McDonough continued. "Junior said one of the others might have been a Registry runner, and we pay them in cash. We've got nothing on security cameras, but we've got friends at the Registry. They photograph everything. I'm owed a couple of favors. I'm calling them in."

"Turow says we've got three weeks until the preliminary hearing," Pokrovsky said. "If we're going to bury this thing before that illustrious District Attorney can get his ducks in a row and start leaking everything to the press, we really have two weeks. If those four ladies are still walking around and capable of talking, we got a problem."

"You're not going to have a problem," McDonough said, breaking into a sly grin. "I know what I'm doing and so do my guys. Two weeks is enough time to make the problem go away."

14.

Paula Winters studied the Area-Of-Responsibility chart, trying to memorize the names and departments within the Cavendish Woods Medical Group. At the top was Dr. William Downey. It was Downey who had signed Cecelia Davis' death certificate within two hours of the discovery of her body.

Underneath Downey were seven doctors: physicians, geriatricians, physiatrists, psychiatrists, and clinicians. Except for Downey, none of the senior medical staff worked full-time at Cavendish Woods. Rather, they maintained a practice within the facility and kept office hours there two or three days a week. The chart also showed multiple nurse practitioners including two with titles that indicated specialization in geriatrics.

There were eight "floor stations" in the complex. Two were in the skilled nursing building that was both physically and psychologically removed from the rest of the complex. Five of the other six were like the one Paula now occupied: comfortable alcoves where two nurses sat, with access to an array of computer screens. The last floor station served the cottages and villas and was located in a small service building.

The arrangement's goal was to ensure that all residents were within a one minute walk (or cart ride) from one of the floor stations. Line-of-sight views of rooms were not deemed important and, indeed, Paula could see only four doors out of the thirty-six on her floor. Someone could easily have gone to Cecelia's room without being seen.

But Paula was not especially interested – at least not for the present – in outsiders sneaking into rooms. Her assignment from Samantha was to look for someone inside the organization who might have either had a reason to kill Cecelia Davis or who killed because they had a twisted mind.

On the surface, it was a preposterous notion that a nursing

home might harbor a serial killer. But the revelations about a nurse named Charles Cullen – who floated through multiple hospitals and nursing homes, killing at random – meant that the notion could not be dismissed. Moreover, Cullen was just the most recent and widely written about such person. Paula's cursory research showed names like Orville Lynn Majors, who was convicted for killing six patients in Indiana and who likely killed many more. In Massachusetts in 2001, Kristen Gilbert, a nurse working at a VA Hospital was convicted of killing at least four patients.

Paula's hiring had been surprisingly easy. She had presented herself at the personnel office of Cavendish Woods, neatly dressed with newly renewed license and résumé in hand. She explained she had not been actively in nursing since leaving the work force to raise her children. Now divorced and, frankly, bored, she was seeking to see if a return to nursing was an antidote. She preferred to work nights. Two interviews later, Paula was offered the seven-to-seven shift.

Paula also carried with her a printout supplied three days earlier by Samantha. The single sheet of paper contained the names of the six Cavendish Woods residents that had died of heart attacks during the previous twelve months. Was there any pattern to the six? Did they tie in any way to Cecelia?

The advantage of working the overnight shift was that a nurse's primary responsibility was to respond to resident requests and emergencies. After ten o'clock, most residents were asleep and, in this "independent living" area, emergencies were few. It would give Paula the opportunity to research the staff, the residents and those other employees who had access to the residents.

If, of course, she could break free of Leslie. Leslie Brown was the other nurse at the station and apparently saw Paula's arrival as the most fascinating thing to have happened at Cavendish Woods in the three months Leslie had been there. Newly graduated from nursing school, living at home, and unable to find "real" nursing work, Leslie had accepted this overnight shift in a nursing home to start repaying her student loans. Paula learned all of this – plus the biography of the boyfriend Leslie was able to see only three nights a week – in her first hour on the job.

Paula would provide either cursory or noncommittal answers to Leslie's questions, hoping it would cause the young woman to go back to the romance novel splayed open on her side of the counter.

Instead, those answers apparently only deepened the intrigue because Leslie would keep coming back with new lines of inquiry. When Paula excused herself to use the bathroom, Leslie took advantage of the absence to use Google Maps to find Paula's home and take an aerial and street tour of it.

"The house is *huge*," Leslie exclaimed. "How could you ever want to leave it? And, do you really live there alone?"

"It is too large," Paula said. "But I can't think of where I'd move to and so I stay." She added, "Inertia, I guess," and smiled, hoping it would draw and end to the interrogation."

"But you could move to France," Leslie said. "Or New Zealand. Everyone says New Zealand is way cool…"

It was obvious to Paula that on this, her first day on the job, little was going to get done toward finding Cecelia's killer.

As she composed a reasonable answer as to why she did not want to move to New Zealand, a figure came down the hallway, pushing a cart. The cart and the person pushing it stopped at their station.

"Hello, Ladies," said a short woman in baggy pants and a dark blue, equally baggy sweatshirt. "Anything to empty?"

It took Paula a moment to realize that the stooped woman with the tired voice was Jean Sullivan.

Leslie picked up the wastebasket behind the desk and held it out for Jean to take.

Paula stared; transfixed by how thoroughly Jean had transformed herself into an invisible member of a nocturnal cleaning crew.

"Thank you, Ladies," Jean said, handing back the wastebasket. She gave Paula a quick, sideways glance that had a hint of a smile.

Then, she continued pushed her cart down the hall.

* * * * *

It was midnight when Leslie left for her two-hour break. There were three beds in the infirmary where nurses on long shifts were encouraged to sleep, and Paula hoped her partner would take full advantage of the allotted time. From her purse she took the sheet of paper with the names of the six residents that had died of heart attacks.

When Leslie had been gone two minutes, Paula turned on the computer in front of her and found a "Local Records" tab. She tapped it and a table appeared with the header "The Overlook – Third Floor". Below it was a grid with the room numbers and names of the forty residents under her care. By tapping the highlighted name, she could see medication schedules and care history for each person on the floor.

*OK*, she thought. *Now let's look at the six heart attack victims.*

Next to "Local Records" was another tab marked "All Medical Records". She tapped it. A screen appeared with a red box with the words, "Secure Area". Beneath that were two lines and form boxes. The first read, "Password"; the second "Security Code".

Paula wanted to bang the desk in frustration.

15.

Samantha Ayers' office at the Massachusetts Casualty Insurance Company – or "Mass Casualty" as it was known to everyone in the industry – was little more than an 'L'-shaped desk in an open area of the third floor of the company's Worcester headquarters. Samantha preferred to work from home and, in any event, her field work would have kept her away from the office three or four days each week.

She typically came into the headquarters office on Friday afternoons where she would sort through snail-mail correspondence and meet with her supervisor if such a meeting was warranted.

The stack of mail on Samantha's desk was small and she dealt with it quickly. She was getting ready to leave when a thought struck her. She got up and went to a glass-walled office some fifty feet from her desk. Inside the office, Desiree Henley was staring at a computer screen. Samantha tapped on the glass. Desiree looked up and motioned Samantha in.

"I don't see a deposition schedule for Pokrovsky," Samantha said. "Do you have it?"

Henley considered the question, cocked her head, and turned to her computer screen. She tapped a series of keys, waited several seconds, and then said, "Huh."

"They haven't made the request yet," she said. "Or, if they have, it's not in the system."

"The preliminary hearing is in three weeks," Samantha said. "They're cutting it kind of close, don't you think?"

Henley nodded. She tapped some more keys. "Counsel of record is one Gerald Turow of the illustrious firm of Herr and Turow, LLC, of Lynn, Massachusetts. Should I give them a call?"

Samantha pondered the question. By all rights, the Pokrovsky Motor Group ought to be represented by WilmerHale or Ropes & Gray or some other big-name firm. And, by now, there ought to have been at least one day of depositions attended by a partner and a gaggle of associates. At the very least, that deposition ought to have been scheduled.

Pokrovsky Motors had suffered a huge loss of reputation as a result of the arson arrest. One dealership had been closed and the others "re-flagged" to downplay the Pokrovsky name. A conviction in the arson case could cause irreparable damage. Yet the company's legal fate was in the hands of a firm she had never heard of.

It made no sense.

"Have the state police been deposed?" Samantha asked.

More tapping of keys. "Last week," Henley said.

The state police deposition would have shown that the stakeout and arrest was because of a tip from Mass Casualty. If asked, the state police would be compelled to say that Samantha was the person who provided the information. The logical next step should be to depose her and learn everything there was to be known about how Samantha had gathered her knowledge.

Was this incompetence? Or was it some shrewd legal maneuver?

"Let's call Gus at the state police," Samantha said. "And let's make it off the record." Samantha pulled a notebook out of her purse and found a cell phone number.

Agustín Ramirez answered on the third ring.

"It was right out of the textbook," Ramirez said. "Turow is good. He asked all the right questions. The state police lawyer found almost nothing to object to."

"And they asked about Mass Casualty and Samantha," Henley asked.

"We spent the better part of an hour on that subject," Ramirez said. "I gave it to them straight."

"Did they ask what you knew about my sources or investigation?" Samantha asked.

"They didn't even go near it," Ramirez said. "It would have been hearsay, and the state police lawyer had already instructed me not to say anything other than what I knew for certain."

"Lawyers always push the boundary," Samantha said. "Their guy didn't try to get you to say something, even if it was inadmissible?"

"Not even close," Ramirez replied. "If anything, it was weird; like they didn't want to know anything about your investigation. I figured they'd grill you after they deposed me."

The conversation with the state police trooper ended with an exchange of cordialities. Henley said she would let Samantha know as soon as a deposition request came in.

Samantha, though, went out to her car and, despite the sub-freezing temperatures, sat with the engine off.

*Everything about this is wrong,* she thought. *Pokrovsky's attorneys should be all over me and all over Mass Casualty. They should be making me reveal my sources and telling them what we found. Yet, they're not doing a damn thing.*

Samantha sat bolt upright. *Because they already know. Or, if they don't know, they want to find out on their own. And, if and when they do, God help us.*

16.

Eleanor noted the change in the tone of the meeting even before she sat down. For one thing, instead of the small conference room where she and Steve Turner had now met twice, she was led to a spacious office with a view of a small, tree-filled park. For another, she was served coffee in a gold-rimmed china cup and saucer.

"I have a surprise for you," Turner said, trying not to sound excited. An aide brought in a plate of warm, chocolate chip cookies.

The conference table at which they were seated would not have looked out of place in a Jane Austen novel, Eleanor thought. The three chairs were ergonomically suited to make her feel comfortable. Even the coffee was rich and aromatic.

All of which, of course, put her on her guard.

The desk in the room and the credenza behind it contained little more than an inbox and, in the inbox, two newspapers. There were no file folders, no computer; not even a telephone. This office was strictly for show.

The door opened and Leonard Swann entered. There was a quick exchange of eye contact and a nod on Turner's part. Swann's smile became expansive.

"I thought I might sit in for a few minutes," he said. "Mrs. Strong, it is a pleasure to see you again." He took her hand with both of his own; a comforting gesture that also conveyed strength. Eleanor found the use of "again" somewhat puzzling as she had not been introduced to him earlier.

Swann, attired in a conservative, three-piece suit, took the third chair and settled back into it, facing Eleanor. For all intents and purposes, Turner was not part of this conversation.

"Mrs. Strong," he began, "we have a crisis on our hands." He waited for a reaction. Eleanor showed him the one he expected: fear.

He continued. "Steve brought me your paperwork yesterday. I

went through it last night and I crunched some numbers. For an accountant, Steve's math skills are as good as anyone's. The problem is that Steve has been looking at just figures – numbers on a page. He forgot to look at the underlying assumptions about those numbers. Sometimes, that very difficult job falls to me."

Eleanor made a mental note that augmented what the activated digital recorder in her purse was capturing. There was no Certified Public Accountant registered in Massachusetts by the name of Steve Turner. Research by Samantha showed that the man with whom she had had been working possessed a BA in Communications from Southern New Hampshire University.

"I totaled up your assets," Swann said. "Not just the way you and Steve figured them, but the way the nursing home calculates them. They say you have less than a year."

Eleanor put her hands to her mouth and gasped.

"Take that insurance policy your husband has. It's for half a million dollars and should keep you comfortable for many years. You see it as your security for your old age. The nursing home sees it as a recoverable asset. It's whole life and is fully paid up. Is that right?"

Eleanor nodded.

"The problem is that the policy has what is called a 'surrender value'," Swann said. "Do you know what that is?"

"We have the right to turn it back into the insurance company and receive money in an emergency," Eleanor said. "We can also borrow against it."

Swann's face suddenly went dark. "Mrs. Strong, the nursing home has the right to surrender that policy the minute you're late on a payment. And, when they do, the proceeds aren't going to be half a million dollars. They're going to be… Mrs. Strong, you better brace yourself. They could be as little as twenty thousand dollars. That's less than two months of the cost of your husband's nursing home care."

While Eleanor's face showed the appropriate shock, she was

disappointed that Swann had slipped in the "weasel words" – qualifying language that made his statement legally meaningless. "Could be as little as" did not mean they *would* be. The twenty thousand dollar figure was plucked from thin air. It was a scare tactic.

"And then there's your home," Swann continued. It's fully paid off and that's wonderful. But when the life insurance proceeds are gone and you are even a day delinquent on that monthly bill, the nursing home has the right to force the sale of your home. And, when they do, they're not going to wait four of five months for a broker to bring you the best offer. They're going to invite in one of those companies that can write a check on the spot."

Swann leaned forward. "You and Steve looked through comparable sales in Hardington and determined that in the current market, your house would sell for about $520,000, which would be a marvelous cushion for your later years."

"But I did my own research. There was a 'quick sale' in Hardington three months ago. The homeowners had been asking $480,000. Do you know what those people got?"

Eleanor shook her head.

"Ninety thousand dollars. Less about ten thousand in fees. Do you know how long seventy thousand dollars will keep your husband in that nursing home? Five months." Swann slowly shook his head. "They're ruthless, Mrs. Strong. They just don't care."

Eleanor noted that Swann had arbitrarily deducted yet another ten thousand dollars from the proceeds. She chose not to correct him. But she also made a mental note to have Samantha go over Hardington home sales over the past few months to find the source of Swann's story.

And then his voice fell to almost a whisper. "And then there's the cap on your insurance. You were very, very smart to buy a long-term care policy for your husband. But they don't pay forever. In fact, if my numbers are right, they could stop paying in April or May."

Eleanor knew her policy covered three years of nursing home care. The policy had started paying benefits thirteen months earlier. Those benefits had nearly two years to run.

"Why do you say that?" Eleanor said, adding a touch of concern to her voice. "The benefits don't run out for nearly two more years."

Swann shook his head again. "They're not interested in your husband's care and comfort," he said. "They're interested in their bottom line. You're one of those cases where the premiums you paid to the insurance company are substantially less than what they're paying out. They *hate* that. And so sometimes they use what they call 'full market value' in their calculation of what they tell you they've *really* paid."

"What does that mean?" Eleanor asked.

"It means that your nursing home sends you an invoice for $9,200 every month, which reflects a co-payment of three thousand dollars by the insurance company. Except that from the *insurance company's* point of view, they may well believe that they negotiated down that cost by – let's say – another five thousand a month. In other words, if they can find someone who is paying $17,200 a month for the same care, they give themselves credit for a co-payment of not *three* thousand dollars a month, but *eight* thousand. And that goes against their payment cap. So, instead of paying out a hundred thousand dollars over three years, they figure they're going to pay it out over fifteen months. Of course, they won't tell you that until it's too late."

It was, of course, more weasel words. The example was purely hypothetical, all couched in "may', "might" and "could". But if someone wasn't listening for those words, Swann's calculations were frightening. It was intended to scare someone into taking action.

"Do you know that's what the insurance company is going to do?" Eleanor asked, hoping the recorder was picking up every nuanced word.

Swann shook his head ruefully. "They keep their cards to

themselves. Remember: I am their worst enemy. If you think nursing homes use my picture as a dartboard, you don't want to know how insurance companies talk about me. But I've seen horrible things happen to decent people like you. That's why I know we're in a crisis situation. If we don't address it now, we're almost certainly going to regret it."

Eleanor noticed the shift to "we'. Liss and Swann were in that lifeboat with her.

"What should I do?" she asked.

"Protect what we can now," he said, the broad smile returning to his face. "Show those greedy people that you're just as smart as they are. Maybe even smarter." He reached out and took her hand, patting it gently. "I'm so glad you came to us when you did. I wish you had come a year ago. We could have protected more. But we can still get you through this crisis."

Swann looked at his watch. "My executive committee meeting calls me away," he said. "I'm going to have to trust Steve to take you through the details." Swann wagged a finger at Turner. "I've taken a personal interest in Mrs. Strong's case, Steve. I'm going to go over every detail of it and make certain that everything is to her benefit."

"I promise you that you won't be disappointed, Mr. Swann," Turner said. They were the only words Turner spoke while Swann was in the room.

When Swann closed the door behind him, Turner took out a file folder from his briefcase. "Let start going over the specifics of our proposal…"

While Turner spoke, Eleanor realized that Swann had been in the room less than fifteen minutes. Armed with an index card full of facts, Swann could deliver this talk four times an hour, thirty times a day. Swann was the "closer", like Kyra Sedgwick on that old TV show, except that instead of getting criminals to confess, Swann got elderly people to rush into doing things they wouldn't otherwise do.

In Massachusetts, conversations recorded without the consent of both parties were inadmissible in court proceedings. Still, every meeting Eleanor had with Turner had been recorded, and Samantha had all of the digital files. When the time was right, Samantha would know how to use them.

The interesting part was that, while Liss and Swann thought their dealings with Eleanor were wrapping up, she knew they were just beginning. And, if Liss and Swann had played any role in Cecelia's death, Eleanor was going to be the person who could point the finger and produce the facts.

* * * * *

Following her meeting at Liss and Swann, Eleanor made her daily drive to the nursing home where her husband, Phil, resided.

Through thirty-five years of marriage, Phil had been Eleanor's rock; a man who was decisive, caring and supportive. He was an engineer by training and a manager by temperament. He was the proverbial "good provider" and they had made up for not having children by travelling extensively and seeing to the educational financing needs of several nieces and nephews.

Less than a year after Phil's retirement – just as they were planning an extended trip to Italy – Eleanor began to notice uncharacteristic slips in Phil's demeanor and, especially, in his language. She at first took those changes as relaxation on the part of a man who had always been called upon to make quick decisions and adapt to fast-moving situations.

But within eighteen months, it was clear that Phil was not himself. He would sleep late, be confused as to the day of the week, and be unable to remember events from a few days earlier. Medical tests showed nothing physically wrong. But an extensive battery of examinations designed to assess his mental health showed unmistakable evidence of dementia.

Even though the diagnosis was almost a foregone conclusion, Eleanor felt that she, herself, was the one who had been found gravely ill. *How will I cope?* was the question that was on her mind for days afterward.

But cope she did. At first alone, and then with the help of an aide and a few hours each day of "adult day care" at Hardington's Senior Center. As the disease progressed, Phil became more irascible and given to tantrums.

Then, one night she awakened to find Phil gone. He was not in the house or in the yard. After three hours of searching by the police he was found a mile away, wearing only his pajamas on a November night that was near to freezing. Two days later, she was told by the Senior Center that they could no longer deal with Phil. He had to be forcibly restrained after he struck another day care resident.

Two weeks later, Phil entered this nursing home. It was the most wrenching decision Eleanor had ever made and one that still filled her with feelings of inadequacy. She *should* have been able to care for Phil at home. With better organization, she *could* have managed.

The reality, she knew, was that she had managed for four years and had done everything that was humanly possible to keep Phil at home. Reality, though, did not ease her self-doubt.

Counselors told her to be aware that, when Phil went into his new surroundings, his cognitive abilities would decline, then stabilize at a lower level. That had happened. And for several months, Phil appeared to find an equilibrium.

Then, Phil began a new descent. He was docile, carrying on conversations with himself that seemed to be from his childhood. Phil no longer recognized Eleanor, much less friends or relatives.

It was just before Christmas, on Phil's seventh-third birthday, that Eleanor saw what she thought of as 'the final decision' from within whatever part of Phil's mind that still functioned. He seemed to be at peace. A few days after Christmas, the home's executive director pulled her aside.

Jane Cronin was Eleanor's age. They had attended the same church for the better part of two decades though they had only a nodding acquaintance until Eleanor began her search for a nursing home that would take on a then-intermediate-stage Alzheimer's patient. Since that anxiety- and guilt-filled time, the two had become friends. For the most part, Jane was a compassionate listener who would always make fifteen minutes to hear Eleanor's concerns. In addition to solace, Jane also offered an honest appraisal of Phil condition. It was Jane who had, two months earlier, confirmed Eleanor's belief that Phil had made that "final decision" about his own life.

"With your permission, and on your schedule, we'd like to move Phil into palliative care," Jane had said on that post-Christmas visit. "You'll need to start thinking about what kind of end-of-life measures you're prepared to take. It isn't a this-week or next-week thing, but we're talking just a few months…"

"Palliative care" was a humane way of saying that the nursing home would no longer administer drugs or physical therapy designed to keep up muscle tone. "End of life measures" meant feeding tubes. Did Eleanor want Phil kept alive by forced feeding after his swallowing reflex began to falter?

This day when she entered the nursing home, Eleanor went to Jane's office. She carried with her a manila envelope with two documents.

"I have everything here," Eleanor said.

Jane nodded. "I think it is time," she said.

Eleanor pulled out the contents of the envelope and handed then to the director. "This is the updated health care proxy," Eleanor said. "It strengthens the 'DNR' to include a prohibition against feeding tubes or intravenous nutrition. When Phil's body says that the fight is over, no one should intervene."

Jane leafed through the document and nodded as she read the language.

"The second document specifies that no one can be empowered to make decisions on Phil's behalf except me."

Jane looked confused. "You already have a durable power of attorney on file," she said. "That should cover all contingencies."

Eleanor nodded. "I guess I ought to explain. Some things have happened over the past few weeks. I am helping out some friends who are looking into the circumstances of the death of very elderly friend of ours who passed away in another nursing home. My part in the investigation has been to go through the motions of engaging the same 'asset-protection' service as was used by our late friend. I am not going to sign any papers, and that is going to create some very hard feelings, and I want to make certain they don't try anything."

"One of those firms on cable TV?" Jane asked.

Eleanor nodded.

"Which would explain several calls I've received in the past week," Jane said. "A lawyer – or at least a person representing himself as a lawyer -- wanting to confirm that Phil is a resident here. Then someone else called wanting his diagnosis. I told that person to put his request in writing on his firm's letterhead. I haven't received anything."

"Then I should have warned you earlier," Eleanor said.

"What a world we live in, Eleanor," Jane said. "Eldercare has been through so many ups and downs and every time we recover from one thing, something else flies up in our face." She paused and looked Eleanor squarely in the face. "May I say something in complete honesty?"

Surprised, Eleanor said, "Of course."

"I mean, not just in honesty, but also in privacy; as two people who have gotten to know one another fairly well, and who respect one another," Jane said.

"You have my word that nothing you say goes beyond this room," Eleanor replied, not knowing what was about to be said.

"I'm going to retire at the end of next month," Jane said. "The clarity of that decision has taken a lot of day-to-day pressure off of me and given me the chance to put my job in perspective. With that perspective has come honesty about the choices I make here every day on behalf of our residents. I realize that the essential lie that these 'asset protection' people tell is the same lie that we in nursing homes cannot admit to. Both we and the asset protection people are in businesses built on falsehoods that neither of us can acknowledge."

The director leaned forward in her chair. "Their whole pitch is built around making people believe that if Grandma goes on Medicaid in her nursing home, nothing is going to change except that the taxpayers foot the bill. And they can point to laws that back them up. By law, we cannot treat patients differently. By law, we cannot tell our staff which beds are Medicaid and which are private pay."

"The underlying problem for us is that it is all a lie. We break that law every day. Twenty years ago, some nursing homes were able to scam the system by billing for services they never provided to residents that sometimes never even existed. Those that didn't get caught got rich. Those that got caught went to jail. But, as a result of that abuse, the system changed to what amounts to flat-rate reimbursements and those reimbursements don't even begin to cover what it costs to keep a resident. And so the word goes out that Mary and John are in Medicaid beds. They get basic care, but they don't get what your husband gets. It gnaws at us, but it is how we stay in business. We lie."

"And, by law, we cannot turn a patient out when their family stops being able to pay. There was a time a decade ago when some nursing homes would send Medicaid patients to the nearest emergency room on a Friday evening – after all the patient advocates had gone home – with some dire, made-up condition. Come Monday morning, the Medicaid patient's bed would have been filled, and the problem would have been shifted to the hospital and social services. That scam got some nursing home operators sent to jail."

"We swear on a bible that Mary and John are getting exactly the same care for four thousand dollars a month as our other patients are getting for twelve thousand. And no one asks us how we do it because everyone is in on the lie. The private-pay patients subsidize the Medicaid patients, but that goes only so far. Sometimes, I think this whole, terrible system is headed over a cliff…"

She stopped herself, shook her head and gave a rueful smile. "I know I went too far. I am upset that we're losing Phil. I saw the two of you in church all those years but never took the time to get acquainted with either of you. I would have liked to have known Phil ten years ago because he seems like he must have been a truly wonderful man. I would have liked to have had a drug that could have arrested his decline or, better yet reversed it."

Jane stopped and choked back what could have been the start of a cry. "That's why I know it's time to step down. Fourteen years now. It seems like an eternity."

The two women stood and embraced. Within a few moments, they were both crying.

Afterward, Eleanor sat by her husband's bed. He did not appear to react to her words or even her presence. His eyes would periodically open but, apart from the rhythmic rise and fall of his chest, there was no sign of life.

"Go in peace, my love," Eleanor whispered.

17.

By her third night on the job, Jean had discovered where the gold was. In a world of computer files, emails and online document mark-ups, the need for printed copies of anything was rapidly dwindling.

But not everyone had gotten the word that the world was going paperless. Cavendish Woods' purchasing and supplies manager was a compulsive printer. Christine Jortberg – a woman in her late fifties to judge by the family photos on her desk – appeared incapable of reading anything from a screen. Instead, she hit CTRL+P on everything from emails to cartoons, sometimes hand-writing out replies on the printouts that she would then type into the system.

And everything went into Jortberg's wastebasket.

Most of the sheets were dross, but there were copies of memos marked "Confidential" and "Senior Staff Only". After a quick glance, Jean would take those that appeared to hold promise and put them into a small bin at the rear of her cart.

She did not allot herself much time to look through Christine Jortberg's accumulation of paper, but this evening, one marked "Confidential" caught her attention, perhaps because of its brevity:

*Chris,*

*Per our mtg this a.m., please pull all reqs initiated or approved by Mandy Ojumbua since 1/1. Please prepare a full drug count charged to his ID# since 1/1. Urgent you forward to me by EOB today.*

*Gretel*

Below the note, in pen, Jortberg had written out five numbers, each beginning with an '03'. These, presumably, were the "requisitions initiated or approved" by the person. Below that was a list of twenty drugs, some with as few as a single dose and three with more than a hundred.

The terse note gave no indication of the subject of that morning's meeting but, clearly, "Mandy Ojumbua" was under suspicion by Cavendish Woods' management for something to do with drugs.

In Jean's mind, a scenario unfolded of a rogue nurse or nursing assistant surreptitiously administering drugs to unsuspecting patients. Perhaps Cecelia had been one of his victims. This memo needed to go to Samantha, but it was also possible that Paula had access to employee records at her nursing station.

There was a copier in the administrative office. When she was certain no other member of the cleaning staff was around, she made two duplicates.

An hour later, pushing her cart past the nurses' station on the third floor of The Overlook, Jean said, "Good evening, Ladies," just as she had done on each of the previous five nights.

Leslie, the young nurse who worked with Paula gave a wave and a smile, then reached under the counter to produce a wastepaper basket. Jean took the basket, emptied its contents, and replaced the liner. As she did, she slipped a copy of the memo into the basket underneath the liner.

"Special delivery," Jean said, handing back the basket to Leslie, who placed it back underneath the desk.

The odd phrase meant nothing to the young nurse. To Paula, it was a signal. It took more than an hour of chatting before Leslie agreed to take her break. Paula then retrieved the single sheet of paper. She read it, focusing on the drugs Mandy Ojumbua had retrieved from the nursing home's dispensary.

In her few days at Cavendish Woods so far, the most tangible change in the world of nursing Paula saw was the change in the way drugs were handled. Even in her final year of hospital nursing – more than twenty years earlier – pills were still taken from large bottles and needle-administered drugs were drawn from vials. Now, almost all pills – even as simple as Tylenol – were dispensed in blister packs. Most fluid drugs were in pre-filled syringes that were, in turn, also in plastic sleeves. Everything was bar-coded.

When a resident received his or her drugs, three bar code

readings were required: one from the drug package, one for the staff member providing the drug, and one for the resident. The resident saw only the pills being taken from a blister pack; the three readings were done either at the drug dispensary or else at the nurses' station.

The stated reason for these changes was patient safety – protecting patients against incorrect dosing. The unstated reason was to protect hospitals and nursing homes from lawsuits and to stop pilferage by employees. For every drug dispensed there was a time-stamped record of what drug was administered to whom by which staff member.

As any viewer of *Nurse Jackie* knew, such precautions were not foolproof. Pills, vials, drip bags and syringes went missing. Pharmaceutical controls could only make theft more difficult and sometimes provide a trail back to the person responsible for the theft. The urgency of the memo meant that someone named Mandy Ojumbua had been flagged.

The drugs on the list indicated to Paula that Ojumbua worked in the skilled nursing building. Aricept, a drug associated with treatment for dementia and Alzheimer's, represented the highest number of doses. There were also drugs indicating the residents Ujumbua worked with had bedsores and relied on feeding tubes; all symptomatic of late-stage Alzheimer's cases.

When Leslie returned, Paula asked her if she had ever considered working in the skilled nursing building.

Leslie shook her head. "I don't think I could do that," she said. "I love this place and these people – it's what I hope my parents get to do when they retire. But, except for people who are post-operative for a few days, skilled nursing here comes down to taking care of people who are never going to get back to where they were. It's not the kind of nursing I want to do."

"Does the name Mandy Ojumbua mean anything to you?" Paula asked.

"Oh, sure," Leslie replied. "Everybody knows Mandy. He's one of the handful of people who love it over there. Very nice guy. He's from some place in Africa. Has this very clipped English accent. Charms the old ladies no end. Do you know him?"

"No," Paula said quickly. "It's just someone's name I heard."

18.

Marilyn Davis received the news that her mother had been to Cavendish Woods to beseech Cecelia to open her purse strings with open-mouthed astonishment.

"My mother wouldn't do that," Marilyn said. "She just wouldn't."

"One of your grandmother's friends saw it happen on several occasions," Alice said, gently. "Your mother would wait around places where she knew Cecelia was taking classes. She told Cecelia that her husband was out of work and that it was tearing the family apart."

"That couldn't be her," Marilyn said.

"Cecelia's friend said your mother was trying to wear Cecelia down, laying on guilt trips." Alice was still trying to be gentle, but also to use the same words Gwendolyn had used just a few days earlier.

The six women were gathered at Paula's home on a Thursday afternoon. A week had gone by since they put their plan in motion. As each woman reported what she had found, the facts and suppositions were linked to other things each had heard individually.

Alice knew she could have mentioned only Donna Davis's uninvited appearance at Cavendish Woods – and Gwendolyn had made it clear that it was Donna who was both the more frequent intruder and more insistent pleader – but Alice also wanted to impress on Marilyn that no one was immune from scrutiny or suspicion.

"Guilt trips are something my mother specializes in," Marilyn conceded.

Samantha kept the discussion on topic. "The big question we have to ask ourselves is whether we think *someone* killed Cecelia. We don't need to start settling on suspects. We're just trying to look at the big picture."

Samantha looked around the room. "Let me tell you what I think. From an insurance company's point of view, there's smoke but no fire. From a *police* point of view, there's not even smoke."

"Our goal isn't to catch a killer," she continued. "It's to find credible evidence that a crime was committed. We will then turn that evidence over to the police and *they* will do the catching. We do not put ourselves in danger. To the contrary, we go out of our way to stay out of harm's way. At Pokrovsky Motors, we gathered a lot of evidence that pointed to what was going to happen and we were exactly right. But when it came time to make that arrest, we were safely on the sidelines. We didn't pull guns and we didn't wield fire extinguishers."

"So, let's talk about smoke." Samantha shifted in her chair. "Alice, you're making fine progress in getting people to talk to you. Keep it up. Keep walking in Cecelia's footsteps and keep your eyes and ears open. And, I like your group's list of poisons, and I could add a couple to it that they don't know about."

"Paula, you need to get out during your break. How hard is it to get into the dispensary? Can someone get drugs without signing for them? Can you get into the patient records system? If so, get me the records of those other people who died of heart attacks. And find out everything you can about this Mandy Ojumbua."

"Jean, keep on digging. You found us Mandy; let's see what Cavendish Woods is going to do about him, and whether there is anyone else management is keeping an eye on."

"Eleanor, you've never signed anything with Liss and Swann, is that right?"

Eleanor agreed that she had not.

"Then they have no financial claims on you for the work they've done. You're within a day or two of being presented with documents to sign and, when you fail to sign them, the fine folks at that firm are going to turn very nasty. They think they have you completely reeled in. We need to see what those trust documents say and what powers they give themselves. They certainly won't let you take them home to 'think about it' and they likely don't want to even give you time to read them over completely. You can use your recorder to read out the salient parts but that might raise suspicions."

"I don't envy you, Eleanor. All I can say is, 'be strong'."

"That is my last name," Eleanor said. "I think I know what I'm doing. Eleanor had not shared her visit to her husband's nursing home or his prognosis.

"And Marilyn," Samantha said. "You also have a tough job. I want you to go see your Aunt Donna and see how she's doing. In fact, I want the entire family's temperature. Your uncle has probably been back to Cavendish Woods to see about a refund. How did that go? You have to be the concerned niece, but you also have to realize that these people may be hiding something."

"And what about my mother?" Marilyn asked. "She also is a suspect."

Samantha shook her head. "You're way too close for that. Talk to her, of course. But talk to her the way a daughter talks to her mother, not the way a policeman talks to a perp. She's going through a very rough period. She doesn't need to think her own daughter suspects her of something."

"And with that, I need to take my leave," Samantha said. "I have an appointment up on the North Shore and traffic can be brutal."

19.

Samantha rang the doorbell of the enormous, gray-shingled house on Ocean Avenue in Marblehead Neck. She straightened her skirt, pulled down her jacket and adjusted the leather portfolio under her arm. This was business and she was in her dark blue business suit; by coincidence, the same one she wore when she testified in court.

The door was opened by an attractive woman in her mid-40s, attired in a pastel cashmere sweater and black slacks.

"Mrs. Pokrovsky?" Samantha said, smiling. "My name is Samantha Ayers. I believe your husband is expecting me." She handed the woman – presumably Al Pokrovsky, Junior's wife – her card.

Samantha had left her coat in the car. If this meeting did not go well, she did not want the awkwardness of attempting to retrieve an item of clothing.

"He's upstairs in his office," Mrs. Pokrovsky said, reading the card. "Let me make certain he's available."

"Available" meant that Al Pokrovsky, Junior had not told his wife that there would be a visitor this evening. In setting up the meeting, Samantha had said only that the meeting was "in both of their best interests" and that it should be just the two of them – no attorneys and no witnesses.

The front door opened into a foyer. Looking left was a spacious living room done in tasteful fabrics and with expensive-looking vases, lamps and professionally framed photographs on every surface. It was a formal room and likely used only on special occasions. In other words, a wasted space, in Samantha's view. To the right was an equally formal dining room set with eight chairs and an enormous hutch displaying fine china. It, too, was dark. The two rooms, plus the two-story marble-floored foyer in which she stood, comprised roughly a thousand square feet. This unused space was larger than her apartment.

Mrs. Pokrovsky came down the stairs, this time with a smile on her own face. "Al asked me to bring you up," she said. As they climbed the stairs, she said, "I'm sorry I didn't introduce myself earlier. I'm Muriel. Al doesn't take a lot of meetings at home."

They went to the third floor, which opened into a spacious loft modeled on a sailing ship captain's cabin, except that most of the captain's cabins Samantha had seen in books were cramped affairs with low ceilings and a porthole or two. This one featured a ten-foot-wide picture window and a coffered ceiling.

The room was filled with nautical elements; a telescope, ship's clock, an anchor and depth charts for various New England shore points. The lone home-like touch was a bookcase filled with family photos and brightly colored toys of the kind an infant might play with.

Al Pokrovsky was waiting for them. Samantha offered her hand and said, "Thank you for seeing me on such short notice."

Pokrovsky accepted her proffered hand but did not respond, instead saying to his wife, "Sweetheart, we'll need a little time."

"This shouldn't take very long," Samantha said, "I just need to go over one or two things." She smiled at both Pokrovsky and Muriel.

As soon as his wife's footsteps could be heard on the stairwell, Pokrovsky closed the door and went to his desk. He was an ordinary looking man, Samantha thought. He was of average height and weight; neither attractive nor unattractive. Just a guy in his late forties who looked as though he could just as easily have been selling cars or repairing them, rather than running a small automotive empire with dealerships in three states.

"You said you had something I would find of interest," Pokrovsky said, sitting back in his captain's chair. He motioned to one of the chairs on the other side of the desk.

"I wanted us to meet privately," Samantha said. "I asked that it be away from interruptions and prying eyes, and I thank you for welcoming me into your home."

"Do you want to get to the point?" Pokrovsky said, annoyance in his voice.

Samantha held the portfolio to her stomach, drumming her fingers lightly on it, making certain that Pokrovsky saw it. "We have crossed paths a few times before," she said. "In those cases, my company paid a claim to you. I don't know if the events of last month are going to change our relationship."

Samantha assumed that Pokrovsky was recording their conversation to share with his attorney and, possibly, his father. She chose her words with care.

"I was troubled by the circumstances of your earlier claims and so, as I believe you are aware, I had your Reading dealership placed under surveillance."

"You mean you had spies who lied their ways into my place of business," Pokrovsky said, anger having replaced annoyance.

Samantha nodded. "As an insurance investigator, I cannot be in multiple places at one time and so I reply on independent operatives to assist me. I also take the time to look through things that people throw away."

She unzipped the portfolio and reached into it, extracting a copy of a receipt. "For example, I came across a sales receipt from Tiffany and Company, dated December 17. It is for an eighteen karat gold Villa Paloma narrow trellis bangle bracelet. Including tax, the price is $6,375."

Pokrovsky looked at the receipt, studied it for a moment and his face – just for a fraction of a second – showed concern. But he recovered just as quickly. He handed back the receipt.

"So?" he said. "I bought my wife a Christmas present. She thought it was very beautiful."

"Two odd things caught my attention," Samantha said, placing the receipt back on the desk between them. "The first is that you paid cash. The second is that you give your address as 515 Revere Beach Boulevard, Apartment 945. We are on Ocean Avenue in

Marblehead Neck."

"They must have made a mistake," Pokrovsky said. "I wasn't paying attention." He made no effort to reach for the receipt.

Samantha gave a small sigh and reached into the portfolio again. "I took the liberty of pulling the lease for that address. The lease is in the name of Dee Simonson, and you are shown as the payment guarantor." She placed two legal-sized sheets of paper on the desk.

"I don't know a Dee Simmons," Pokrovsky said.

"It's Dee Simonson," Samantha replied. "She is a salesperson at Pokrovsky Honda – excuse me – Honda of Beverly. I met her earlier this week when I went shopping for a new car."

Pokrovsky's face turned red.

Samantha patted her portfolio. "I also have a number of clothing receipts from Nordstrom and Neiman Marcus. They're all marked 'size two'. I would guess your wife is a – what? – size eight. She's very attractive. Miss Simonson, on the other hand, was a definite size two…"

"Rummaging through my trash," Pokrovsky said under his breath. Then, looking at Samantha with a cold stare he said, "What the hell do you want?"

"It is very simple," Samantha said, patting the portfolio. "I have here a thoroughly documented history of your relationship with Dee Simonson; the many gifts you've given her, your place in Revere Beach, your trips with her to Mohegan Sun and Atlantis."

"In less than two weeks, there will be a preliminary hearing on your arson charge," Samantha continued. "I note with considerable interest that your lawyers seem to have no interest in deposing me. That tells me that you are attempting to track down the independent operatives who worked on my behalf at your dealership, and that you very likely intend them harm. By not deposing me, you can claim that you never knew of their existence. If they are unable to testify, the state's case gets cast into considerable doubt, and your attorneys would use their 'disappearance' as a means to get the charges against you dismissed."

"What the hell do you want?" Pokrovsky said the words with gritted teeth.

"I expect that in the next seven days your attorneys will depose me. They will ask about my sources of information, and I will be compelled to tell them. The names of my operatives will be on the record which, in turn, says that if anything were to happen to them, suspicion would immediately fall on you."

Samantha rose from her chair. She gathered the papers from the desk and put them into her portfolio. "I offer you a simple trade. You will have me deposed, and you will make no effort to independently seek out my operatives. The hearing and your trial will go forward. If your attorneys are very clever, you will get off."

"But, if any harm comes to any of my operatives, this portfolio will be placed in the hands of your wife. And, if she reacts the way I would react if I were in her place..." Samantha shrugged, "...this will not be a very happy home."

Samantha did not say goodbye, and she did not ask to be shown out. She opened the door to the stairwell and began walking down.

\* \* \* \* \*

Pokrovsky waited until he could no longer hear footsteps. He closed and locked the office door, sat down at his desk and, with shaking hands, punched a number.

"How did it go?" Al Pokrovsky Senior asked. There was no exchange of greetings.

"She had some personal stuff on me," Al Junior said. "She says she'll give it to Muriel if anything happens to what she calls, 'her operatives'. She figured it out. We haven't done a deposition. She figured it out from that."

"What do you mean, she has some 'personal stuff' on you?"

"Me and one of my sales ladies in Beverly."

There was a moment's silence, then thirty seconds of invective. "You stupid son of a bitch," Al Senior said. "How much 'stuff'?"

"Receipts for gifts. Copies of an apartment lease down in Revere Beach. I guess hotel receipts."

"You guess?"

"She showed me some of it. She had one of those leather portfolios. She just kept pulling pieces of paper out of it."

"Where did she say she got it?"

Al Junior squeezed his eyes shut, trying to remember the words. "She said she takes the time to look through things that people throw away. I guess she went through the dumpster."

"You threw away receipts for gifts and hotels?"

"I couldn't exactly bring them home."

"And you never heard of a shredder?"

"How was I supposed to know someone was going to go through the dumpster?" Al Junior was pleading now.

"They didn't go through your dumpster, you dumb son of a bitch. That would take hours every night. They had someone go through the waste basket in your office. You said you saw four old broads plus the insurance lady? I think your friend just helped us out with who the fourth one is. We got the one in accounting, the Registry runner and the one buying the fleet. We couldn't figure out who the last one was. The fourth one was on the cleaning crew."

"But she said she's going to turn everything over to Muriel…"

Al Senior cut his son off. "What else did she say she got?"

"What do you mean, what else?"

"She has the history of you as a cheating husband. What else did she say she had?"

"Nothing. She didn't talk about anything else."

"Then let's put it another way: what else did you throw into that waste basket?"

Al Junior racked his mind. He had never paid any attention to what he threw away. Stuff went into the waste basket, it got collected and went into a dumpster. A garbage truck took it away and probably took it to an incinerator. "I don't think I threw anything else away," he said finally.

"You're a moron," Al Senior said. "If you can put gift receipts and hotel bills from your mistress in the trash, there's no telling what you can throw away."

"I swear," Al Junior said. I just couldn't bring those receipts home."

Al Junior heard his father exhale loudly on the other end of the phone. "Here's what I think. I think your insurance lady just showed us her hand. Not that I don't think she has more stuff, but that her number one goal is to protect those four broads. Now, we know her weakness."

"So?"

Al Senior muttered something unintelligible, then said, "It means we don't have to find four old broads and make them disappear. All we have to do is find one of them. We let your insurance lady listen to one of them scream on the phone, and then *we* tell *her* where to deliver everything she's got."

"Dad, I knew I could count on you."

* * * * *

In the kitchen of the house on Ocean Avenue, Muriel Pokrovsky turned off the baby monitor, the transmitting end of which was nestled in among the colorful toys in the bookcase in her husband's office. The conversation between the insurance investigator and her husband was crystal clear. She could hear only one side of her husband's talk with her father-in-law, but it was sufficient to hint that Al Senior had a plan in mind.

Muriel had suspected that her husband had something going with Dee Simonson. The way they had acted at the dealership Christmas party – forced formality in Muriel's presence followed by Al's inability to take his eyes off of Simonson all evening – left little doubt that this was her husband's latest infatuation. And apparently a very expensive one.

What was unclear was why Al Senior was so anxious to know what else her husband might have thrown into the trash at the dealership. She knew her husband was an idiot. He had been proving it for fifteen years. But for the last seven years, he has presided over the Pokrovsky Auto Group; a smoothly functioning machine that minted the steady income to make this house and their lifestyle possible. Al Junior needed to do nothing more than glad-hand major customers, show up at charity events, and read cue cards for radio and television ads.

Was there a possibility that her husband was doing something that might jeopardize the company? She involuntarily shuddered at the thought. Muriel fingered Samantha Ayers' business card.

She just might need it.

20.

Rudy Davis stared at the twenty-three page invoice and certified check, a look of non-comprehension on his face. He had expected to collect a check for something close to $800,000. The check in his hands, payable to the Estate of Cecelia Davis was for $388,216.

Tiffany Morgan, the red-headed, twenty-something "Senior Finance Manager" had left him alone for ten minutes after handing him a thick envelope containing the invoice and check. In those ten minutes, he had looked at page upon page of twelve-digit codes and truncated descriptions for things like PHY THP S.

Tiffany came back into the room bearing two bottles of water. She proffered one in Rudy's direction. He accepted it but placed it on the table next to the invoice, unopened.

"Do you have any questions?" Tiffany asked.

Rudy blinked. "What is all this?" he asked, picking up the invoice.

"These are your parent's expenses billed against their entrance fee," Tiffany said, seating herself in the chair next to Rudy.

"I was told that the estate would get – and I think I'm quoting it from memory – up to eighty percent less some miscellaneous expenses."

Tiffany gave a disarming smile. "Well, I don't think I would characterize them as 'miscellaneous', but let's give it a try. The 'eighty percent' would have been sixty-two percent under a standard contract, but we made allowance for your parents' advanced age and your father's physical condition. As you can see, your mother's expenses were nominal; I think under ten thousand dollars."

"Most of these are your father's expenses, and most of those are from the time he entered the skilled nursing facility and especially for the final few months of his life," Tiffany explained. "That stay in skilled nursing was not part of your parents' contract."

Rudy's mind, fogged as it was, did some simple arithmetic. "My father's care was four hundred thousand dollars for eighteen months?"

"Your father had state-of-the-art, round-the-clock care in one of the best facilities in the country," Tiffany said. "He was also living separately from your mother. The monthly living expense your mother paid was for the apartment in The Overlook. Your father's room costs accrued separately."

"You charged my father more than twenty thousand dollars a month for his care?" Rudy asked.

"If you look at the invoice, you'll see that he had some of the best specialists in Boston – meaning, the best specialists in the world – consulting on his case. They believed that his stroke was not irreversible and that, with time and intervention, his health could be restored..."

"He was ninety-three," Rudy said, finally comprehending. "You took a terminally ill, ninety-three-year-old man and saw that he had a million dollars to spend. You set out to spend every dollar of it. If you could have kept him alive for another year, you would have succeeded."

Tiffany's face turned red. "That is a horrible thing to say, Mr. Davis. We cared about your father, about his comfort, and his well-being."

"Who authorized these charges?" Rudy asked, genuinely curious but also now getting beyond the shock of seeing the invoice. "Who authorized calling in the world's leading doctors to consult on my father's case? I had his health care proxy, and you never asked me."

"It was all in your admissions contract," Tiffany said.

"It is in the admissions contract that you have the right to spend as much money as is in a patient's account without consulting the family, and without regard for the quality of a patient's life, his age, or the fact that he is already incapacitated?"

"Your father's health care proxy gave us the latitude to make day-to-day decisions about how to care for him. We did what we thought best for your father," Tiffany said. "Money was never part of that equation."

"The hell it wasn't part of the equation," Rudy said. "He came here because his family couldn't provide the care he needed at home. His stroke had been deemed irreversible. You saw a huge pot of money and set out to spend it."

Tiffany rose from the table. "There is no need to stoop to insults or accusations here. Every item of your father's care is documented. You apparently thought his care would be free. I'm very sorry you had to find out…"

"And let me guess," Rudy said, holding out the check. "Cashing this check means I agree to the charges. Is that right?"

Tiffany bit her lip. "There is language regarding limitations to your right to appeal charges on your copy of the check. Perhaps I ought to get my manager…"

"No, Miss Morgan," Rudy said, now also standing. "Perhaps you ought to get your attorney. Because this looks to me like a case of fraud and abuse."

Rudy picked up the invoice, pointedly leaving the check on the table.

"You can't take the invoice without taking the check," Tiffany said. "That's the property of Cavendish Woods."

"Just try to stop me," he said.

21.

Alice found herself getting into the rhythm of the daily *t'ai chi* class. She wasn't certain that "White Crane Spreads Wings" maximized her energy movement and was an expression of a desire for longevity, but neither was she going to question the "master" who led the class. She found it relaxing and, afterwards, she would go with Gwendolyn for a smoothie or a biscotti and tea. The tea, she noted, was invariably served on china.

Her efforts to exactly match Cecelia's schedule were stymied by schedule changes. An intermediate Spanish class was not currently meeting because its members were on a three-week "fluency trip" to Ecuador. Cecelia had planned to be on that trip, Alice knew. It would have been part of her "rediscovery of life" after Harry's death. Another class on wine appreciation had completed its twelve-week run.

Alice also enjoyed the twice-weekly bridge game where she found her skills were improving rapidly with experience against competitive players. On Sunday evening, Celie Sturtevant, the member of the bridge group who had recited a litany of poisons that would mimic a heart attack, had a new one.

"Aconitum or aconite," she said. "I think I first learned about it watching *Dexter* a few seasons back. I thought it was silly because some *femme fatale* had it growing wild in her garden in Miami. Aconitum is a northern perennial that would never survive in Florida. But I did some research, and it turns out that the leaves *are* terribly poisonous. You'd have to brew it into a tea, though. A heavy dose will kill someone immediately but even a lighter one will bring on a heart attack in a few hours. The woman on *Dexter* soaked a pencil in it."

The thought sent Alice's mind racing. Someone could have placed a mild solution in Cecelia's tea or coffee at dinner. Her heart attack would have come several hours later. But it was February.

The ground was frozen. *Only someone with a greenhouse…* Alice was so engrossed in envisioning a poisoning that she misplayed her hand to the dismay of her partner.

"And I was just starting to think you had the makings of a first-rate bridge player," said Marge Constantine, shaking her head sadly.

* * * * *

"We're taking a one-day break from the Pre-Raphaelite Brotherhood because I have something very exciting to share," said Jillian Connolly, who led the Art Appreciation class. An easel covered by a cloth by her side. When Connolly felt she had the full attention of the nine members of the class, she pulled the cover off the easel.

It was an oil painting, recognizable immediately by Alice as the work of Winslow Homer. The other members of the class apparently knew as well, because there was a collective gasp.

"This is a final study, painted at two-thirds size, for 'West Point – Prout's Neck' painted by Winslow Homer in the summer of 1900," Connolly said. "Homer summered in Maine for more than thirty years, and he was sixty-four when he executed this painting. It depicts a time fifteen minutes after sunset, exactly when the sky is at its reddest. In many ways, these preparatory paintings tell us more about the artist's intent than the final work…"

"Where did it come from?" asked a member of the class, astonishment in her voice.

"The painting has a wonderful history," Connolly said. "Because Homer never married, the studies and unsold paintings in his possession passed to his brother upon his death in 1910. No artist other than Vincent Van Gogh had a stronger brother as a supporter than Homer, and Charles Savage Homer inherited a trove of wonderful art. After Charles' death, those works began to be dispersed through gallery sales in New York…" Then Connolly appeared to catch herself in mid-sentence.

"I'm sorry," she said. "I suspect that's not really the question you asked. One of our residents has chosen to share it with us for our spring show." There was a hint of mystery in her voice. "My hope is that the resident will step forward between now and April when our show opens."

For the next ninety minutes, Connolly explained the painting and Homer's brand of realism that was so appealing to American collectors. She veered into Homer's life and his use of women as passive and sometimes sexualized objects in paintings such as *The Life Line*; and linked that observation to feminist theory of "the male gaze" in paintings.

Connolly produced a lithograph of the completed painting and showed where Homer had made subtle changes in composition. She estimated that the painting on display was likely the one painted by Homer just before he started work on the final canvas.

At the end of the session, Alice felt both exhilarated and exhausted. Connolly's passion was infectious. After previous Art Appreciation classes, Alice had gone to the movies. This afternoon, she went to the media center and took a comfortable seat at a computer, where she began reading everything she could find on Homer and his paintings from the coast of Maine. She read about preparatory paintings and their role in the art world.

Inevitably, her search led her to look for the value of Homer's preparatory paintings. She found auction results for two such works painted between 1895 and 1900. One had been sold by Christie's in 1998 for $620,000. Another had been auctioned by Sotheby's with a pre-sale estimate of $500,000 to $700,000. The final price, with buyer's premium, was $1,210,000.

Alice was shocked, but then such surprises were becoming regular occurrences in her life at Cavendish Woods. The walls of Priscilla and Alan Clurman's villa were covered with art. They were wealthy. They had likely been collecting for decades and could easily have purchased the paintings at a small fraction of their current value. All her life, Alice had assumed that when she saw a painting on the wall by a recognizable artist, the painting would be a print or a copy. The lone exception was Cecelia's Fantin-Latour, which she had kept in her bedroom, away from prying eyes and which, sadly, was now known to be a forgery.

But that, in turn, led Alice to wonder if Jillian Connolly had spotted Cecelia's painting as a forgery. Was it good enough to have fooled an expert or had Connolly remained silent because she did not want to injure the pride of an elderly woman who cherished a painting as much for its history as for its value?

Alice closed the browser and felt tired. After such a promising start toward finding Cecelia's killer, Alice felt she was now hearing gossip for the most part. Gwendolyn loved to tell tales of the residents and perceived Alice to be a willing listener. But while there were rivalries among residents, there were no feuds. Alice was reasonably confident that another resident had not taken Cecelia's life.

Alice had asked discreetly about the nurse named Mandy Ojumbua. When Gwendolyn heard the name, a broad smile came to her face. "He's everyone's favorite," she said. "I spent a week in skilled nursing when I was recovering from my surgery. He brought me freshly brewed *real* tea every day. He sneaked in chocolate – good *Belgian* chocolate and said it was 'our little secret'. I never had to push the call button. He seemed to know when my pain medication was running low. The man is a saint."

"Does everyone else have the same opinion?" Cecelia asked.

"As far as I know, yes," Gwendolyn said. "He doesn't just stop to chat. He takes a genuine interest in you. I think he's wasted in skilled nursing, but he told me he wants to stay there because he can do more good there."

Gwendolyn had an additional thought. "You know, he doesn't spend all his time in skilled nursing. I see him in the restaurants or on the Esplanade two or three times a week. He says he likes to check up on his former charges. Would you like me to introduce you?"

Alice said she would, and filed away the information to relay to Samantha.

There were no additional tales to learn about Cecelia's two daughters-in-law. They had come to Cavendish Woods, they had made pleas for Cecelia to provide financial assistance, and they had been turned down. Donna Davis and Clarice Davis were suspects, to be certain, but Alice had no way to propel the investigation forward from inside the nursing home.

She rose unsteadily from the chair in front of the computer and began navigating her way down the shop- and restaurant-lined esplanade to the elevators for The Overlook. In the morning, she would research aconite. For now, what she needed was a nap.

22.

The head of nursing administration dropped the stack of files on Paula's and Leslie's floor station. "I need your help this evening," the woman said. "I have two admins out with the flu." The woman nodded at Leslie. "Leslie, show Paula the ropes."

It was just a few minutes after seven o'clock. Paula had come to work with a plan to excuse herself as early in the evening as possible to investigate the drug dispensary, and then to engage Leslie in a free-ranging discussion of Cavendish Woods' drug control policies. Instead, it appeared that her shift was going to be devoted to data entry.

"It's a breeze," Leslie explained after the head of nursing administration was out of sight. "You enter the resident's name, you pull up their record, and then you enter the codes or notes. The system does the rest. This is, like, two hours' work. We just make it look like it took all night."

"But we don't have access to patient records," Paula said.

Leslie grinned. "Tonight you do." A green Post-it appended to the top folder contained a handwritten note. It consisted of a word – "Zachary" – and a fifteen-digit number.

Leslie pulled off the Post-it. "Here's the password, and here's the security key. Both are changed every day to keep people like me from snooping around the system. But tonight, we have the keys to the kingdom. Let me show you."

She entered the password and number into her computer, and a bright blue screen appeared.

"Let's start with Gladys Kimtanis," Leslie said, opening the first folder. "She went to see a specialist this morning. We enter the code for the doctor." She tapped in a string of numbers from the sheet in front of her. A physician's name appeared – a gerontologist, if Paula's recollection of the Medical Group organization chart was correct. Next was a code representing the type and length of visit.

When the code was entered, a description popped into the field, including a fee - $275.

"These people want $275 for a twenty minute consult?" Paula asked, incredulous at the fee.

"Welcome to the land of rich old codgers," Leslie responded. "Of course, the residents don't see it, and their health insurance carrier will bargain it down. But the higher figure you start with, the higher amount you'll get in the end. And the difference between the insurance payment and the specialist's charge just gets deducted from their admission fee. The real fun part is that some of these guys can do five twenty-minute consults in an hour. The Cavendish Medical Group has a peculiar set of clocks."

For ninety minutes, the two entered codes into resident records; a task that required accuracy and, more important, an understanding of the logic of medical treatments. At 8:30, Leslie left to take a break.

"Take your time," Paula said, and hoped she would.

Paula held her breath and went to the "Resident Name" tab. She typed in "Cecelia Davis".

This time, the screen filled with a timeline.

Paula exhaled.

\* \* \* \* \*

When her shift ended twelve hours later, Paula had searched and printed out fifty pages of records on Cecelia Davis and the six residents that had died of heart attacks in the preceding twelve months. The two hours when Leslie took her sleep break were the most productive, but even the five-minute bathroom breaks were put to good use. For the first time, Paula felt that she was contributing to the solution of the mystery.

The file on Cecelia Davis confirmed everything her granddaughter, Marilyn, has told the group. There were no heart issues. Her health was excellent for her age. Cecelia Davis had every reason to believe that she would live to the century mark or longer.

Her death certificate and Dr. Downey's notes were part of the file. The head of the Cavendish Medical Group's examination had been cursory at best. No fluids had been drawn. Downey had noted skin and muscle tone, lips and fingernail color. Everything was consistent with death by a "coronary event" and so that is what he concluded. There was a notation that Rudy had been notified and a hearse called to take Cecelia's body to an area funeral home.

Now, spread out across the dining room table in her home, she began looking for patterns. One resident was ruled out immediately. He was in his late eighties and had developed, over two years, acute coronary disease that had been treated with drugs and surgery. While the cause of death was labeled "heart failure", the more accurate description would have been "a chronic and irreversible heart disease".

Four of the others were residents that had died in the skilled nursing facility. Two had been incapacitated by strokes, two by dementia. One of the four had suffered a heart attack two years earlier, but the other three had no markers apart from high blood pressure or elevated cholesterol levels.

The deaths were roughly two months apart, the most recent one a month earlier. No autopsy had been done on the bodies and no blood samples had been drawn on the first two. The lone commonality was that the four had prognoses that indicated no recovery was likely.

Were these deaths related to Cavendish Woods' sudden interest in Mandy Ojumbua? Paula wondered. The fact that the most recent two deaths had been followed by blood and fluid draws with full toxicology analyses indicated that someone's suspicions had been aroused. She set those four records apart. It was an interesting question, but not one that had bearing on her investigation right now.

Instead, Paula spread out the seven pages of records on Margaret McClellan. She had died the previous October of a heart attack, in her cottage. Like Cecelia, McClellan had failed to respond to her evening "wellness" call and had been found when a staff member went to check on her.

McClellan had been in good health for someone in her eighties. She had a quarterly physical exam two weeks before her death, and her physician's overall assessment had been positive. Paula focused on test factors affecting her heart. There was no indication of blocked arteries or abnormal heart rate; the note on her electrocardiogram indicated it was normal.

This woman had suffered a fatal heart attack, and it had gone uninvestigated.

Two deaths – Margaret McClellan and Cecelia Davis – hardly made a pattern. It was two deaths by heart attack, six months apart, in a community of six hundred elderly people.

But it *felt* like a pattern. If McClellan lived in a villa, she was one of Cavendish Woods' wealthier residents. She apparently lived alone – otherwise a spouse would have summoned assistance as soon as the heart attack occurred. *Had* she been married?

The medical records told only one part of McClellan's life. It would be up to Alice to find any other intersecting points in the lives of Margaret McClellan and Cecelia Davis.

It was now ten o'clock and Paula was exhausted. Outside, the sun shone weakly through clouds that emitted occasional flurries. She changed into a nightgown and climbed into bed.

*I'm finally onto something*, Paula thought, and then fell into a deep sleep.

23.

Marilyn Davis stared intently at the menu in front of her, wondering what furies were being suppressed across the table where her Aunt Donna glared at her own menu, her napkin already crushed into a ball and tableware continually moved from one location to another.

Marilyn had thought a lunch at a "neutral site" would be the best way to broach the subjects she wanted to discuss. It was clear that Donna Davis had arrived in an agitated state and that anything said was fraught with the possibility for misinterpretation.

It was better, perhaps, to allow her aunt to vent whatever was on her mind.

"That nursing home is run by thieves," was the first statement uttered by Donna over their salads. "They are crooks who ought to be in jail."

Marilyn did nothing more than offer her aunt a sympathetic look.

"Every day that she and Harry were there, that place just kept piling on secret charges," Donna seethed. "Oh, they'd send a bill every month; but that just covered Cecelia's apartment and some 'incidentals' like fifteen dollars for a cup of coffee and some biscuits. Nobody ever handed you a bill for anything. You didn't sign for anything. You never got a receipt. They just smiled and put it into some computer."

Marilyn murmured that it was terrible.

"And what they did to Harry just sickens me," Donna said, bitterness in her voice. "He had a stroke. He wasn't going to recover. That's why they went into the nursing home in the first place. Then they moved Harry into some special care building and brought in every specialist in the country to 'consult', all the time keeping the bill a secret. Rudy had their health care proxy, but they didn't ask his permission."

"Did Grandmother know any of this was going on?" Marilyn asked.

Donna gave her niece a sullen stare. "Well, if she did know, she wasn't telling anyone in the family. You trotted out there to see her all the time, didn't you?"

"We had lunch every week."

Angrily, Donna said, "Did she tell you she had changed her will? Did she say that she was giving everything to 'charity'? Did she tell you about that estate planning outfit that put together some phony 'competency' test so she could turn everything over to them to manage?"

The last of Donna's tirade was loud enough to attract attention from diners at nearly tables.

"We never talked about anything like that," Marilyn said, softly. "I know you and Uncle Rudy went out to see her, too."

"She was a spiteful old woman," Donna said. "Harry was the only thing that kept her in check all those years. When he died, she just went to town, getting even with all of us. It wouldn't surprise me if she had it all worked out ahead of time. Rudy said she went to see that firm within two weeks of burying her husband. He was barely in the ground and she was out getting even."

"But what did you talk about when you went to see her?" Marilyn asked.

Donna glared at her. "You don't understand, child. Cecelia hated me. I was never good enough for Rudy. He should have married someone who kept her mouth closed and knitted booties. She couldn't abide anyone who disagreed with her and, as soon as she could, she got back at us all."

"And that damned painting. Rudy wants to hang onto it for sentimental reasons. 'It meant so much to them,' he says. Well, I want to throw it into the fireplace. You know it's worthless?"

Marilyn nodded. "We all heard."

"I'd strike a match to that thing, but Rudy would never forgive me. I can't even bring myself to look at it. It reminds me of her and the way she treated me all those years."

*Was this a woman who could have killed her mother-in-law?* Marilyn thought. *Was this anger always there, or did it come to the surface after she learned that there was almost no money in her estate?*

They left the restaurant thirty minutes later. Donna's tirade never stopped, only ebbed for a few minutes at a time. The emotions were still raw; this was anger that had been bottled up for a very long time.

On the one hand, Marilyn thought as she drove home, the luncheon had answered none of the questions she had expected to ask her aunt. Each question, however gently phrased, had resulted in a fresh stream of invective directed at Cecelia. But the luncheon had also been instructive: her aunt's dislike for her mother-in-law bordered on hatred.

If Donna thought Cecelia's death was the only way to release an intergenerational transfer of wealth that would ease her family's financial problems, might she had gone to Cavendish Woods and killed Cecelia?

Marilyn decided she would try again in a few days, perhaps using a different tact. For now, she felt emotionally drained.

\* \* \* \* \*

While his wife lunched with his niece, Rudy Davis carefully looked through his house for clues that might implicate Donna in the death of his mother.

The thought that his wife might have somehow caused the heart attack that had killed his mother had been growing in Rudy's mind ever since the night of the call from Cavendish Woods. Her reaction had been baffling: She had listened to his side of the conversation, then pretended not to have known what the call was about. Upon being told that Cecelia was dead, she then began sobbing mournfully. The two women disliked one another. It had to have been an act.

The newest piece of the puzzle had come a few days earlier. Donna had gone out on the late afternoon of Cecelia's death, ostensibly to go to her book group. She had returned three hours later, announced that she was tired and had no desire for dinner, and retired to their bedroom.

Two members of the book group had now confirmed that Donna had called to say she couldn't attend because she wasn't feeling well.

When Rudy confronted Donna with the two statements about the book group, she had glared at him. "I don't ask you where you go every time you leave the house," she had said.

"But I hardly go anywhere," he had protested.

"Maybe that's the problem," she had responded, a snigger in her voice.

Today was the first time he had been alone in the house since that confrontation. Rudy set to work as soon as he heard the garage door go down.

He knew only that his mother had died of a heart attack. Six years of medical school and forty years of practice had given him a good working knowledge of the things that could cause cardiac arrest. Using latex gloves from the boxes he had brought home from his dental practice, he probed through the medicine cabinet looking for things that did not belong. When he finished there, he went through his wife's cosmetics and the contents of her bedside table.

Each bottle and tube was examined for its ingredients listing, each prescription for its toxicity. There was a two-year-old bottle of a generic equivalent of Ambien. Three pills remained from what would have once been twelve. Five, ten-milligram pills, pulverized and dissolved in a warm liquid, might well have depressed an elderly woman's heart rate to the point that it stopped beating.

When had Donna last taken these pills? He could not remember her ever taking them and talking about a need for them. According to the bottle, the prescription had been filled at their local Walgreens almost three years earlier. Had she planned the murder years in advance?

He continued looking through her dresser drawers, gently

pushing aside clothing. But, as he did, he wondered why, if Donna had set out to kill his mother, she would have kept evidence around. She could just as easily have tossed the prescription bottle into the recycling bin the next day.

There was also, he realized, his own stash of medical supplies. In their basement was a cabinet with dozens of vials of benzocaine and xylocaine together with disposable syringes. The sales people who came through his office had made it clear that even low doses administered to the elderly could be extremely dangerous; even fatal. What if Donna had taken a vial of benzocaine and injected it into his mother?

Shaking, Rudy stripped off his gloves. What did the police shows talk about? Means, motive and opportunity. Donna had the motive and, for the past two days, he knew she had the opportunity. Here, in their own house, were the means.

It was barely noon, but he went to the liquor cabinet and poured out a large bourbon. He sat down in the living room to wrestle with the idea that his wife might be a murderer.

24.

Al Pokrovsky, Senior, was getting angry.

For ten minutes he had been listening to excuses. They now knew the name of the old lady in accounting was Alice Beauchamp. They knew that her address of record with the Department of Motor Vehicles was a dump of a public housing project for senior citizens next to the town of Hardington's sewage treatment plant. They knew that, three months earlier, she had moved to a much nicer "over 55" community called Olde Village Square.

And, there, she had disappeared.

She had not been around long enough for her new neighbors to get to know her, and many of them were in warmer climates for the winter. Her neighbors in her old apartment in Hardington Gardens vaguely knew she had a son somewhere out west and a daughter in either Maine or New Hampshire.

What little mail she received was being held at the post office, something usually connected with being on vacation. Her car was in the garage of her condominium. No one had gone into or out of her unit. The condominium manager in the sixteen-unit development did not live on site and said it was not his responsibility to know where the owners were vacationing.

The only intriguing aspect of Alice Beauchamp's existence was that, according to public filings, the deed for her unit at Old Village Square was held in the name of something called the 'GCG Trust' with a Boston post office box address, and GCG Trust was not registered with the state office of corporations.

"We've just got to wait for her to show up," said Mike McDonough.

"And if she shows up on May 15 with the rest of the snowbirds, where does that leave us?" Pokrovsky asked. "You keep looking. 'Beauchamp' is not a common name. Her son has to know where she is."

McDonough made a note to start looking for men named 'Beauchamp' who lived 'out west'.

"Tell me about the skinny broad," Pokrovsky said impatiently.

McDonough opened his notebook. "Six different sales guys talked to her at one time or another. The driver's license was a good phony with a non-existent address. She told one that her husband's company was in software service and was located in Wilmington. She told another guy that she and her husband are looking at property in Beverly. The lady salesperson who took her on a test drive got to swapping stories, and she said she has a grown daughter down in Washington D.C. working at the State Department."

"When are you going to tell me something interesting?" Pokrovsky said through gritted teeth.

McDonough flipped through pages of the notebook. "They also talked about breast cancer."

"Breast cancer," Pokrovsky repeated.

"The skinny lady said she had an operation last summer and that they had caught it in time."

Pokrovsky started to say something dismissive, then checked himself. "People don't lie about that kind of thing." He thought for a few moments. "Everyone says the skinny lady was the real deal – she had good taste in clothes and spoke like she understood business."

He shifted in his seat. "How many women in that age group – say, a couple of years either side of fifty – got breast cancer operations between June and August last year? Try the best hospitals and clinics; not the little suburban ones. This lady would have wanted the best care, and she could have afforded it."

"Isn't there some kind of confidentiality on that sort of stuff?" McDonough asked.

Pokrovsky waved his hand. "Figure it out. What about the other two?"

McDonough pulled a grainy photo from the notebook. "This is the Registry runner. The RMV came through for us. It isn't great, but we can show it around. The question is, where?"

Pokrovsky stared at McDonough. "I pay you to answer questions like that, not to ask them. And the fourth one?"

McDonough shook his head. "You were right. She was working for Suffolk Janitorial. A guy there owed your friend, Miss Ayers, a big favor. He never met the woman. She just showed up every night with the crew that cleaned at Reading. She got paid with a debit card, just like the rest of the crew, so there were no names and no records. I talked to two people on the crew. She didn't speak Portuguese, and their English isn't all that good. They said she worked hard. They had no idea she was a plant."

"Damn," Pokrovsky said. He drummed his fingers for the better part of a minute. "The lawyers tell me I've got less than a week. If they haven't deposed Ayers by then, she's going to be certain we're trying to squeeze her. She already pushed back on Junior with some stuff she found tying him to some woman in sales up in Beverly. I could care less about that. What I need to know is if she has something bigger that could come back to bite the business. Which leaves the question of what kind of stuff was my idiot son tossing into his trash can?"

McDonough shook his head. "You want me to find out?"

Pokrovsky exhaled sharply. "You find me Alice Beauchamp or the skinny broad. Or either of the other two. Then we'll find out what else 'my Miss Ayers' might have on us. I already lost one dealership because of her. I'm not going to lose any more."

25.

Paula Winters held up two cashmere sweaters in the large, well-lighted walk-in closet. The yellow one highlighted her blond hair but made her face look pale. The pink one complemented her face but looked like she was trying to look too young.

She sighed and started over.

She had promised Martin that her job would not interfere with their relationship. She had called Martin almost every evening from Cavendish Woods, taking her cell phone to an alcove thirty feet from the nurses' station and out of earshot of Leslie. But the conversations were constrained by the reality of her mission. She had so much she wanted to tell him – especially about the halting progress in finding Cecelia's killer. He could offer so much advice and guidance.

But she couldn't confide those things because, if she did, it would inevitably lead him to Samantha Ayers and, from Samantha, to the Brookfield Fair heist. So, all she could say was that she was discovering that she had probably moved past nursing and that she would leave in thirty days or less.

"Why wait the thirty days?" Martin would ask.

"Because I made a promise to myself." The answer sounded dubious at best. It also sounded evasive.

So, instead, she coaxed out of him the stories of his day at the Brookfield Police Department. For all his charms, Martin was not a natural-born storyteller, at least on the telephone. Someone had broken into the science lab at Brookfield Middle School the previous weekend, and he had quickly narrowed down the suspects to four teenage boys, all of whom had parents with lawyers on speed dial.

He had tried reasoning with the parents: if their sons were responsible, they should acknowledge what they had done and accept whatever punishment was coming their way. The parents, though, could not see past some hypothetical Ivy League college admissions form that asked for disclosure about past criminal mischief. So, instead, Martin doggedly pursued physical evidence and interviews with classmates, all of which pointed to the boys, but as of yet without conclusive proof.

All of this came out, though, as dry as the weekly police blotter report in the local newspaper. "I spoke with two more of Tyler's friends who at first denied any knowledge…"

Worse, when the call was over, Paula would come back to Leslie's barrage of questions. As of the past weekend, Leslie was now "between boyfriends", which thankfully spared Paula what she feared would otherwise be graphic descriptions of "hook ups" and "friends with benefits". It wasn't that Paula was a prude. She just wasn't a voyeur.

Leslie, however, was fascinated by the idea of a woman on the "other side of fifty" having a romantic relationship because she was certain that her own parents – both in the same age range as Paula – hadn't (as she put it) "crossed the center line of the king-sized bed" in their Needham home in years.

"What did he say?" "What did you talk about?" "Where are you going tomorrow night?" Variations of those questions would be the first three sentences out of Leslie's mouth when Paula came back after twenty minutes.

Tonight, because of the threat of snow, Martin had insisted they meet for dinner in Hardington, which meant going to Zenith, which was fortunate because she was supposed to be at the restaurant in fifteen minutes and she was still choosing clothes.

Was this the night that she invited him back to her house?

The question had been on her mind after every dinner, film, museum exhibition and play. The question had only intensified because for those four nights a week when she was at Cavendish Woods, their communication was so abbreviated. She wanted Martin to truly understand how she felt, and not lead him to believe that their relationship was deteriorating into some kind of "phone pal" thing.

Paula felt like she was back in high school.

Still undecided about sweaters, she carried both into the bathroom. She stood in front of the full-length mirror and stared at her reflection. Slowly, tentatively, she reached behind her back and unhooked her bra.

She took a step closer to the mirror. Standing, the long, pink scar underneath her breast was visible only if she lifted the breast. Otherwise, she looked as she had looked for years before, if a little thinner. This was the benefit of having money. Her surgery had been planned with reconstruction as an integral part of the recuperative process.

*Is it just vanity?* she wondered. *Other than me, does anyone care?*

She had told herself that the reconstruction was part of beating the cancer. If the cancer was to be fully vanquished, it must appear afterward as though there was never a battle. Even if no other person other than her doctors ever again saw her breasts, this was her validation that she had won.

Someday soon – if not tonight then in the next few weeks – she would invite Martin for dinner, and they would both know that this was *the* night. This was the pleasure of being an adult: there was no adolescent groping or sly hands in the wrong places. Their evenings together ended in kisses and embraces. Martin would enfold her in his arms, and she would feel his warmth and revel in the pleasure of being held.

And she had made it clear that the relationship would include sex. She had asked him to circle the fifteenth of April on his calendar and to make no plans for the week than followed. That date was seven weeks away and, whether their vacation meant someplace tropical or urban, it would certainly not include separate rooms.

She held up the sweaters one last time. The yellow one, she decided.

26.

When Alice first brought up the name of Margaret McClellan, the first responses she always heard was, "Poor Peg…"

Margaret "Peg" Dowd McClellan had lost a daughter and a husband within three months of one another. That she died just a month after burying her daughter seemed to complete the reversal of what had otherwise been a charmed life.

The Dowds were New Money Boston Irish, and Peg had been the beautiful daughter that was the apple of the eye of her father (in true Boston Irish fashion, a bootlegger turned celebrity restaurateur). She was educated at St. Mary's College, the all-women "companion" school to Notre Dame, and she had married William Xavier McClellan, Notre Dame '55, one month after her own graduation.

The couple settled in Boston where Bill put his law degree to work on behalf of the Diocese of Boston. His practice, coupled with a keen eye for real estate, made the family sufficiently and securely well off that, when a judgeship on the Suffolk Superior Court was offered, Bill was able to jump at the opportunity to become Judge McClellan.

They raised two girls in their gracious Chestnut Hill home. Rosemary would follow in her father's legal footsteps, Lucy earned multiple degrees in Computer Science and rose through the ranks of Hewlett-Packard to become one of its senior executives.

Then, seven years earlier, Peg fell and broke her hip. Six weeks later, daughter Rosemary called to say that a pap smear had showed ominous signs. And Bill's behavior on the bench became erratic. He attributed it to concern for his wife and daughter, but reporters and the courthouse staff saw the incipient signs of memory loss.

Within a year, the McClellans had sold their home. Moving to Florida or Arizona was not an option: they wanted to be near Rosemary, who now had a confirmed diagnosis of ovarian cancer. While Aricept had helped stabilize her husband, Peg also worried that Bill's care would suffer at the hands of Sun Belt medicine. They became one of the inaugural residents when Cavendish Woods opened.

The McClellans set the tone for the new community. Their presence and their continued entertaining in their villa helped entice other couples of means to accept that a nursing home – under the guise of a "continuing care retirement community" – was an acceptable next step when in-home care was no longer feasible. Peg's hip eventually left her using a cane, and Bill's dementia gradually worsened to the point that he no longer recognized even long-time friends.

Then, in one horrific four-month period the previous year, the McClellan family imploded. Bill's dementia was found to be masking a brain tumor that might have been caught at an operable stage had he been able to communicate his disorientation. When the diagnosis was finally made, the tumor was as large as a baseball. He died two weeks later. Six weeks after his death, Rosemary's ovarian cancer went from remission to extreme malignancy. She was dead within weeks at fifty-one.

Peg McClellan fell into a deep depression following her daughter's funeral. She stayed in her villa, declining invitations from friends. Then, one evening, three months after her husband's death and four weeks after burying her daughter, she suffered a heart attack. She failed to respond to a "wellness call" and, as was policy, an aide went to her villa where she was found, in bed, dead at least three hours.

Alice heard this story, amplified in some areas and truncated in others, from everyone with whom she spoke. Most ended their telling of the tale with, "What she really died of was a broken heart."

A few carried the tale into the weeks after Peg's death. The younger daughter – Lucy, the one who lived in California and jetted around the world on company business but who couldn't be bothered to come see her father and sister until they were on their deathbed – showed up the day after Peg's death and began clearing her family's belongings out of Cavendish Woods.

"She got into shouting matches with the people in the front office," one person confided. "She questioned every item on the care invoice and called in an attorney."

Another person said Lucy, "showed photos of the interior of Bill and Peg's villa with every piece of art and pottery circled, and demanded to know the whereabouts of every item she claimed was missing. She raised an awful stink. She was a real bitch."

Several residents said Lucy cornered them and asked pointed questions about staff members. "She was relentless," one person said.

Alice decided that Lucy McClellan was a thoroughly unpleasant woman, but likely someone to whom Samantha needed to speak. She put her notes into an email and sent them off to both Samantha and Paula. Paula was an afterthought, but Alice had great respect for her intuitive grasp of why some people behaved the way they did.

\* \* \* \* \*

It was after *t'ai chi* class when Gwendolyn tugged at Alice's sweatshirt and said, "There he is!"

The tall, dark-skinned man sat at a restaurant table with three women, none of whom Alice recognized. Alice could hear their laughter from thirty feet away. The man was dressed in the light blue uniform worn by Cavendish Woods' nursing staff.

Gwendolyn tapped the man on the shoulder. He turned and grinned broadly. "Miss Gwendolyn!" he said. He stood up and wrapped his arms around her. "And how is that right leg of yours? Does it still give you problems?"

He spoke with an accent that Alice thought of as 'Colonial English'. Not a Caribbean lilt, but a melodic cadence that conveyed warmth.

"Mandy, I want to introduce you to a friend of mine, a new resident." Gwendolyn gestured at Alice. "Alice Beauchamp, this is Mandy Ojumbua."

He bowed. "Mandeville Tompkins Ojumbua at your service,

Miss Alice Beauchamp. Please join us."

The three women looked at one another. One of them said to Ojumbua, "Actually, we're going to the cinema. They're showing *The Maltese Falcon.*"

"Then please join me," Ojumbua said. "Though I must return to work in ten minutes."

Alice and Gwendolyn took the seats vacated by the three women, who each gave Ojumbua a hug as they left.

"Beauchamp," Ojumbua said, rolling out the name slowly. He pressed a finger to his chin. "You are descended from the ninth through fifteenth Earls of Warwick who built Warwick Castle? I have seen that grand building, which still stands on the River Avon."

"My late husband never mentioned it," Alice said.

"Ah," Ojumbua said. "Then you must go there and investigate the family tree. Perhaps you are the Countess of Warwick and do not even know it. There is a very strong resemblance between your visage and that of the last Countess, whose portrait hangs in the castle. Things became somewhat unsettled during the English Civil War. Such a query could be highly profitable."

Ojumbua turned his attention to Gwendolyn. "And you have been avoiding me..."

And so they spoke for ten minutes. Ojumbua possessed charm and wit and a prodigious memory. He inquired after Gwendolyn's grandchildren by name and remembered that her daughter's husband had diabetes. He demonstrated a hand massage technique that he said he had learned at a training course; one designed to relieve rheumatism.

When he looked at his watch and saw it was nearly one o'clock, he looked genuinely disappointed. "This has been a pleasure. One old friend and one new friend. This is why I love being here."

With that, he rose and kissed Alice's hand. "Miss Alice Beauchamp, whom I suspect is secretly the dowager countess of Warwick. I take my leave, your ladyship."

Gwendolyn beamed as he left. "You asked if I knew who

Mandy Ojumbua was. Well, that's who he is."

"And he's always like that?" Alice asked.

"Every time," Gwendolyn replied. "He is the nicest man I have ever met."

That evening, Alice wrote a long report to Samantha, detailing the encounter. She did not say so in the report but, as she wrote, she could not help thinking to herself, *there is no way this man could be a murderer.*

\* \* \* \* \*

Even though she had been there just a little over two weeks, Alice fell into a routine: breakfast and morning *t'ai chi* class followed by a long conversation over tea with Gwendolyn and, sometimes, other members of the exercise group.

The Art Appreciation class met four times a week, and the time in that group re-awakened Alice's love of art and art history. Jillian Connelly brought paintings to life, delving into the backgrounds, histories and politics of both the artists and those who modeled for the paintings. By the end of each session, Alice wanted to rush to the computer center and read everything she could find on the painting – and read ahead so that she would have the grounding necessary to dissect the next work of art.

She learned that Peg McClellan, too, had been part of the art appreciation class. Peg had been a kind of "star student", able to match wits with Connolly and to offer alternate points of view that kept the class in rapt attention. Gwendolyn told Alice that, far from being annoyed by having a prodigy who talked back in her class, Connolly encouraged the class to be more like Peg and that, when Peg's husband and daughter died, she stopped coming to class.

"It was never the same afterward," Gwendolyn said. "We all tried reaching out. We even went to Peg's villa as a group. She was just too overcome by her loss."

The bridge group was also a constant in Alice's new life. She read books on contract bridge strategy from Cavendish Woods' library and downloaded articles from experts on bidding. Her play improved markedly from session to session to the point that Celie Sturtevant said, "I believe we have a ringer in our midst." Everyone now wanted Alice to be their partner.

But it seemed there was nothing more to learn about Cecelia. Alice spent an evening hearing about Peg McClellan from the bridge group. Peg was not a card player and so the group's knowledge of and friendship with her was based on other interactions. She was certainly well-liked, but no one with whom Alice spoke could be truly said to have been close friends with either of the McClellans.

Alice put these thoughts, too, into a late-night one call to Samantha. "I don't know what else I can do," Alice said. "I'm not hearing anything new, and I feel like I'm wasting Paula's money."

"You're inside," Samantha said. "The people there accept you. When something breaks, you'll be the one who knows it first."

"That's what happened at Pokrovsky Motors," Samantha continued. "You figured out the processing fee scam and thought you were done. Two weeks later, you saw the transfer paperwork coming in for the cars Pokrovsky was going to torch. You told us what to look for."

The words soothed Alice, who slept more comfortably that evening than she had in several days. She resolved that, starting the next morning, she would befriend yet another group of residents and learn what they knew about Cecelia and, now, Peg.

\* \* \* \* \*

Samantha, though, was more worried than ever after saying "sleep well" to Alice. She still had nothing she could take to the police. She had suspicions but nothing else. And, without "meat", both the state police and Town of Cavendish police would dismiss her or, worse, make a few cursory calls to the management of Cavendish Woods that would inevitably tip off the person who had murdered Cecelia Davis and Margaret McClellan.

And it *was* murder, Samantha had concluded. The two deaths overlapped too neatly. The worst possible case was that the two deaths were the product of someone with a deranged mind; "mental defect" in the parlance of the law. The person chose victims at random and killed when the pleasure of the previous kill wore off. That person would be difficult, if not impossible, to catch.

*We need more information*, Samantha concluded. The question was, where could they get it?

And another thought crowded into Samantha's mind: everyone's safety. It had been three days since her meeting with Al Pokrovsky. It had produced, the following morning, a call from lawyer Gerald Turow inquiring about Samantha's availability during the coming week. She had said that her calendar would be open for a deposition on the day and time of Pokrovsky's convenience.

But instead of setting a date, Turow had said only that he would be back in touch. That was two days ago, and no date had been set. It had been a bluff, and Pokrovsky clearly had something else in mind.

Her impression of Al Pokrovsky, Junior was that of a man who was weak. He had blustered until she placed the first sales receipt on the table. Then, his eyes widened and dilated. He had been caught by surprise; he had no recourse. When she left the house, she felt that she had put things back on a track she could control.

But these two days said things were not as they should be. Which made Samantha wonder if Al Pokrovsky, Junior, was really the person she should be worried about. In the legal documents she had reviewed, Al Junior was the sole owner of the Pokrovsky Auto Group; his father had cashed out of the business and no longer held voting stock. He was listed as a "consultant" to the corporation with an undisclosed monthly retainer. That was not unusual in privately held businesses being passed down from one generation to another.

What if Al Senior, had put himself back in the picture? What if he was the person who was making the decisions?

She had read everything she could find on the elder Pokrovsky. There was a carefully cultivated image of the man who sponsored the charity golf tournament, who gave generously to good causes, and who now enjoyed the good life in Florida and on Cape Cod.

More diligent research showed that, underneath that layer of benevolence, was another Al Pokrovsky. It was a man who had been linked to bribery of zoning boards (though never proven), lawsuits charging illegal sales practices (each dropped inexplicably), and reprimands for unethical treatment of employees (each accompanied by a denial of wrongdoing and a promise not to do so in the future). There was also, courtesy of Al Junior's waste basket with its tantalizing but incomplete evidence of Al Senior's dealing in counterfeit auto parts.

If Al Pokrovsky, Senior, was planning his son's defense strategy, Samantha was playing for far higher stakes than she thought when she said that if any harm came to Jean, Paula, Alice or Eleanor, that she would turn the evidence of Al Junior's infidelity over to his wife.

Were they vulnerable? Samantha's instructions had been given with a sense of urgency: *never* park where a camera could capture an image of your license plate, *never* give even cursory details about your life or where you lived, and don't intimate to *anyone* why you were really at Pokrovsky Motors.

Had everyone followed those instructions? The women were bright, but this was their first time being "undercover", and they might not understand the risks they were taking – even as Samantha only now understood the true nature of the risks she had placed these women in.

Who was the most vulnerable? Probably not Jean. She had worked with the cleaning crew. and no one should have ever known her name, much less why she was there. As a Registry runner, Eleanor was at the dealership only sporadically and should have attracted little attention. It was Paula and Alice who were most visible. They would be the ones that Pokrovsky Senior would go after if he learned their identities and home addresses.

Alice needed to stay at Cavendish Woods. She was far safer there than at home. Paula was also safer working, but getting her out of town would be better. Samantha needed to think of a purpose that would seem reasonable without being frightening.

An idea came to her.

The death of Peg McClellan was the best clue to the death of Cecelia Davis and the daughter, Lucy, was the lone first-hand link to information about her mother. Under any other circumstance, Samantha would have tracked down Lucy McClellan at work and arranged a time for a phone interview. What if, instead, the interview *had* to be done in person? And what if Paula *had* to be part of the interview team? It would be a day out, a day back, and a day in California. It would be expensive, but it was certainly somewhere that Pokrovsky would never think to look.

\* \* \* \* \*

It took just a few minutes on Google and LinkedIn to find Lucy McClellan at Hewlett-Packard in Cupertino. It took two hours to get her on the phone. McClellan was at or near the top – Samantha could not tell based on her title – of Hewlett-Packard's cloud computing activity within its Software Division. She was at a sufficiently high level that messages were left with an administrative assistant rather than on voice mail.

When Samantha finally convinced the administrative assistant to connect her to McClellan, the conversation was, to say the least, awkward.

"My mother didn't carry life insurance," McClellan said.

"This isn't about life insurance," Samantha said. "It's about an investigation into the circumstances of your mother's death."

"My mother died of a heart attack. She was in her eighties. End of story."

"Another woman at Cavendish Woods died under almost identical circumstances earlier his month…"

"But you're not with the police."

"If we find the link, I'll turn the information over to the police."

"The name of the other woman who died?"

"Cecelia Davis."

Samantha heard the tapping of computer keys in the background. "You're the Samantha Ayers quoted in stories about a robbery at the Brookfield Fair." McClellan said.

"We carried the fair's insurance."

"Who is the chairman of the board of Mass Casualty?" McClellan asked.

Samantha had to think for a moment. "Charlie. Charles Penzler." She had met him perhaps twice in three years.

"And you're also quoted in articles about an arrest for arson at Pokrovsky Motors."

"We carried their policy as well."

"But you don't carry Cavendish Woods' policy?"

"This is a purely private investigation on behalf of the family of the woman who died recently."

"And we can't do this over the phone because…."

"There are some discussions best done in person," Samantha said.

There were several moments of silence except for the tapping of keys. Finally, McClellan said, "Tomorrow evening. Seven o'clock, at my home. If this is anything other than what you say it is, the meeting will be over very quickly, and you will have come a long way for nothing."

"I'll be traveling with Paula Winters, who was a close friend of the other woman who died."

"Fine," McClellan said. "I can throw out two people as easily as one."

27.

"We're going *where?*"

Paula was fairly certain she had heard Samantha correctly, but what she said made no sense.

"I need you to be ready to go with me to San Francisco tomorrow afternoon. We may have to stay overnight."

"Why me?"

"Because I've never been to California, and I bet you've been there a dozen times, and because I need a second set of eyes and ears, and I trust you."

Samantha recapped the conversation with Lucy McClellan. "McClellan is up there," Samantha said. "Fancy office, fancy title. She made it clear that we have about two minutes to make our case and, if we don't, she's going to throw us out. I need you for support."

"It's also our last, best hope to find the link between Cecelia and Margaret McClellan," Samantha added. "I've been going over what we've got and it's very thin. If I took this to the state police today, they'd laugh me out of the barracks. I feel like we need to do this."

"But why tomorrow?" Paula pleaded.

"Because that's the time she gave us," Samantha said. "Tomorrow night at seven."

Conflicting thoughts crowded Paula's mind. She had made plans with Martin. They were going out for ribs and then to a movie. She was going to have to cancel, she had no logical excuse, and the truth was out of the question.

"And there's one other thing," Samantha said, hearing the void on the other end of the line and needing to fill it.

"What's that?" Paula said, doubt creeping into her voice.

"You're the only person who won't laugh at me," Samantha said. "I've never been on an airplane."

"Never?"

"Both sides of my family come from Worcester. My brothers and sisters live in Worcester. When we went on vacation, we drove to Canobie Lake or Six Flags. I've never had to fly for business."

"Well, I guess that changes tomorrow," Paula said. "I'll take care of the tickets and I'll email you the details."

* * * * *

Samantha closed her eyes and said a silent prayer. She had to reach deep into her own psyche to find a plausible reason to get Paula out of Boston, but she had told the truth. Paula *was* the most polished of the four ladies and would make the best impression. It was entirely true that she had never been to California or, indeed, on a plane. But she had no intrinsic fear of flying, and she imagined that she could navigate the twenty miles from the San Francisco airport to Palo Alto without incident.

Getting Paula out of possible harm's way was the goal, and she had accomplished that goal, or at least part of it. Now, she needed to work on developing the rest of a plan.

* * * * *

Paula buried her head in her hands. *Why does this have to be so hard?*

And she knew the answer: *Because, if I told Martin the absolute truth, he would know that I had made a fool of him. And you can't love someone who not only made a fool of you, but who ought to be in jail.*

Martin had confessed one evening over dinner – it was their third date – that he had at one point suspected she, Jean, Eleanor and Alice had been responsible for or at least played a part in the Brookfield Fair robbery. It was only the convenient car crash in front of the state police headquarters in Framingham that provided a neat solution that allowed Paula to laugh off Martin's suspicion.

Just as it was only wanting Martin – loving Martin – that made it hard. He was the lone link to that event. Take him out of the equation, and it was just a secret among four friends.

But there was a sense of remorse at work. She had talked four friends into breaking the law, and they had gotten away with it.

Remorse required some act of contrition, and contrition meant doing good deeds.

Going undercover at Pokrovsky Motors had been such a good deed. They had played their parts well and, as a result, a man who had repeatedly cheated an insurance company had been caught. Going undercover at Cavendish Woods was another good deed, perhaps an even better one. If they found Cecelia's killer, it would be both justice done and some karmic repayment for a robbery that, with hindsight, had likely been conceived in Paula's depression and fear of her own death.

But performing both good deeds had meant lying to Martin. The trips to the Pokrovsky dealership had been easy: she was at a gym; she was at physical therapy; she was at a doctor's appointment.

But going to work at Cavendish Woods required a different kind of lie: that she was considering a return to nursing or at least uncertain about the arc of her life. She sensed that Martin felt *he* was the cause of the sudden interest in resurrecting her career. He had either pushed her too quickly into being her "boyfriend" (what a horribly unsuitable term!) or she felt some need to demonstrate that she was not merely some alimony drone (which in some sense, she was, though her "alimony" was a multi-million-dollar lump sum payment).

She could not admit that she was going to California with Samantha Ayers, even though the reason was both noble (find a link to Cecelia's killer) and true. She could not because the truth always led back to the Brookfield Fair.

Paula felt the sense of doom. As she laid her head on the desk in the bedroom she had converted into an office, she bumped the photographs of her son and daughter, tipping them over. She turned them upright.

*Perry.* Her twenty-three-year-old son was in Tacoma, Washington; still "finding" himself but making his own living. He had come east to his sister's home near Washington, D.C. for Thanksgiving, and Paula had talked for weeks thereafter about Perry and Julie. It was perfectly plausible that Perry was in San Francisco and needed to see his mother. It was important enough that Paula was prepared to fly across the country to aid her son.

*He had been in an accident while visiting friends and job hunting in the Bay Area. It was a car crash on a freeway and he was in a hospital. He said he was OK but you never knew about these things. He might be in pain or need something. That he had called her to say he was in a hospital meant something was wrong.*

It was another lie. But at least it postponed that day of reckoning.

\* \* \* \* \*

"Martin? It's Paula. I know this sounds crazy, but I have to go to San Francisco tomorrow. My son, Perry, has been in an accident…"

28.

Eleanor was greeted warmly by the receptionist at Liss and Swann. It was, Eleanor thought, a fairly certain sign that the word had gone out that she was about to be converted from a prospect into a customer.

Steve Turner bounded through the glass doors seconds after being called by the receptionist. He smiled broadly as he held out his hand. "I hope we didn't keep you waiting," he said.

They were back in one of the small meeting rooms. Arranged on the table were two pens and an inch-thick stack of papers with yellow "sign here" tabs on a dozen of the pages. There was no coffee or water. This was a meeting that was intended for speed.

"We've prepared all the documents, Eleanor," Turner said. "Everything is in apple-pie order and ready for your signature."

Eleanor smiled, nodded and took a seat.

Turner picked up the top document, and turned it to the first signature page. "You need to sign your full name here," he said, pointing to a space.

Eleanor picked up one of the pens and held it, poised just above the page. "What exactly is this?" she asked.

Turner looked at her, and then to her hand with the pen, ready to sign. "This is your irrevocable trust," he said. "We went through all this before."

"No," Eleanor said. "We didn't." She put the pen down and picked up the second document. "And what is this?"

"It's an irrevocable pre-paid burial policy," Turner said. "Eleanor, we've been through…"

Eleanor picked up the third document. "And this?"

"A Medicaid qualifying annuity. Why don't we…"

She picked up the next document in the pile and looked at its title. "At least I know what this is. It's my will."

Turner smiled. "And it is, word for word, the same will that you gave us. All of the beneficiaries are the same. All it does is name Liss and Swann as executors."

She picked up a fourth, very thick document. "And what, pray tell, is this?"

"It's a reverse mortgage on your home," he said.

Eleanor held up another document; this one of just three pages. "What's this little one?"

Controlling his exasperation, Turner said, "It's a service contract."

Eleanor saw that the next document was a duplicate copy of the irrevocable trust. She went back to the service contract.

"Tell me why I need a service contract?"

Turner blinked rapidly. "If you're in a nursing home, you need someone to pay your bills and look out after your interests. If you just give money to your children for that purpose, the IRS counts it as a qualifying asset and they'll come after it. But, if it's a written contract and spells out the duties, it doesn't count."

Eleanor flipped through the pages. "But I'm not in a nursing home, and I don't have children."

"There may come a time when you are, Eleanor," Turner said. "It's good to have this kind of document in place for that eventuality. And, with your assets in the trust, paying those bills will be more complicated."

"And who will be providing these services?" Eleanor asked.

"I will," Turner said. "Well, Liss and Swann will."

"I can pay my own bills perfectly well," Eleanor replied. "We don't need this."

"That's not right, Eleanor," Turner said. "Once these other documents are in place, you have no assets. You have no money with which to pay bills. That's the whole purpose of what we've done. On paper, you and your husband have no money. Once you sign these, you don't have to pay that nursing home any more. Your assets are out of their reach and Medicaid starts paying. Of course, we know different. We know your assets are safe."

"And how much will I be paying you to pay my bills?'

"It's a very modest sum, Eleanor," Turner said, soothingly. "Especially for the certainty and peace of mind."

Eleanor began looking through the three-page document for a dollar figure. At first she didn't see one. Then, in a footnote at the end of the document, she read, *Payment for the initial term will be sixty thousand dollars per annum. Payments will be adjusted annually for changes in the consumer price index and may be further adjusted at the discretion of the service provider if additional duties are required.*

"You want sixty thousand dollars a year to pay my bills," Eleanor said. "I *live* on less than that."

"These are accountants and lawyers, Eleanor," Turner said. "They're professionals and they're very careful. They often find ways to save their clients substantial sums."

"But I'm agreeing to pay you more *than* a dollar for every dollar you're paying for my property taxes and groceries right now," Eleanor said. "Does that sound reasonable to you?"

"It's all part of the peace of mind, Eleanor," Turner said. "And for our help in keeping the nursing home from seizing your assets."

Eleanor picked up the reverse mortgage document. "And you decided I needed a mortgage."

"It's for liquidity, Eleanor. We discussed this…"

"No, we didn't, *Steve*." Eleanor thumped the word, "Steve" as she spoke. "In fact, I'm quite certain that the subject of a reverse mortgage never came up in any of our conversations. It seems like the purpose of the reverse mortgage is to pay your service contract. Except that I won't own my home. I'm turning it over the trust."

"Your assets go into the trust," Turner said. "That's right."

"Who shopped around for this reverse mortgage, *Steve?*" She again emphasized Turner's name. "What's the annual percentage rate on it? Did Liss and Swann get a finder's fee?" Eleanor now picked up the annuity agreement. "Who is the underwriter for this, *Steve?* Does that underwriter pay finders' fees? If so, how much?"

Turner straightened his jacket. "Eleanor, this meeting is

supposed to be taking place in a spirit of trust. We are one of the top-rated firms in the country. Our reputation is impeccable."

"Fine," Eleanor said. "Then just let me take these documents home. I'll read them and have my personal attorney review them. He'll make the calls to the annuity and mortgage underwriter to see if Liss and Swann receives any compensation for throwing business their way. He'll tell me if the service contract is as fair and reasonable as you say it is. If everything is fine, we can set up a signing date for next week."

Turner opened his mouth as though to speak, then caught himself. He thought for a moment, then said, "This is our work product," he said. "It's proprietary to Liss and Swann and not subject to modification by a third party."

"I can't show this to anyone?" Eleanor asked, incredulous.

"Not until it's signed," Turner said.

"Well, then," Eleanor said, "give me a few hours with it. I'll read it and then decide if I'm going to sign or if I want to make changes."

"You can't make changes," Turner said quickly. "It has already been through legal review here. We've already made all of the adjustments. We can't make any more. It's cast in concrete."

""But I can *read* them," Eleanor said. "You can give me a few hours and I can at least read them."

"If I'm in the room," Turner said. "I have to be in the room. We can read them together and you can ask me questions."

"Why can't I be alone with documents you want me to sign?"

Turner pulled at his collar. "You could photograph them with your cell phone. You could email them. You could just get up and walk out with them."

"You don't trust me," Eleanor said.

"I do trust you, Eleanor," Turner said. "And I hope you trust me."

"Let's see," Eleanor said. "You've read these documents, right?"
Turner nodded. "I went through them several times."

"Is there a termination fee?" she asked.

"What you mean, a 'termination fee'?" Turner responded.

"Let's say I sign these papers today and I take them to my lawyer and he says, 'Eleanor, this is not a good deal for you.' And I come back here and say I want to call this off. Do I have to pay anything? If you want me to trust you, you can tell me that."

Turner looked at Eleanor for perhaps thirty seconds, saying nothing. Then, he said, speaking slowly, "There is a discontinuance clause. If you choose to work with someone else or cancel our agreement then, yes, there is a cost to compensate us for the work we've put into this."

"And how much is it?"

Turner was silent again. Then he said, "You're not going to sign these papers, are you?"

Eleanor said, "I'm not going to sign them if you won't tell me what it will cost me if I change my mind or if my lawyer tells me I'm doing the wrong thing."

"Seventy-five thousand," Turner said. "The breakup cost is seventy-five thousand dollars."

"And I would pay that even if I came back the next day?"

"Yes."

It was Eleanor's turn to be silent. Turner wasn't going to leave her alone with the papers and so she wasn't going to be able to photograph them with her cell phone as she had planned. She had the recording of the conversation in her purse. It might help Samantha, but it wasn't admissible in any court in Massachusetts.

"Mr. Turner," she said when she had thought through her answer, "I learned this week that my husband is going to die very soon. I have asked that he be placed in hospice care. No feeding tubes and no heroic measures. Phil lived a good life, I love him dearly and I will cherish his memory to the end of time. My circumstances have changed. When I first met you, I thought my husband might live for many years, if the condition he is in can be called 'living'. Instead, he is going to die with dignity much sooner. I have not only come to terms with that reality, I am satisfied that it is the best choice for him."

Eleanor continued, "So no, Mr. Turner, I won't be signing the papers. I won't be needing your services."

The look of anguish – probably over lost commissions and fees – on Turner's face was palpable. "Then why did you come this morning? Why didn't you stop as soon as you knew about your husband?"

Eleanor noted there were no words about Phil's impending death; no "I'm so sorry for you". It was strictly business.

"I wanted to see what you had in mind for me."

Another, more frightened look crossed Turner's face. "You're not with the *Globe*, are you? Or some government agency?"

Eleanor smiled. "Wouldn't that be poetic justice? Is that why you won't let anyone take home the paperwork to study? Because you're afraid you'll see it across the front page of a newspaper or have to justify your charges in front of a congressional committee? I think I'm going to leave the answer to that question to your imagination."

Eleanor rose from the table and collected her purse. She did not say goodbye or offer her hand. She left the room and walked through the glass doors to the waiting area where one of the smiling receptionists said cheerfully, "My, that didn't take long! Congratulations!"

Eleanor did not acknowledge the receptionist. She walked out through Liss and Swann's solid, oak doors and, a few seconds later, into the damp cold of a February morning in New England.

She got into her car and started the engine, waiting for the heater to kick in. *It is done*, she thought. *These people are thieves, but I don't think they're murderers. Their goal is to get your name on contracts. Once you've done that, they don't care if you live one year or fifty. They collect either way.*

After a few seconds, she put the car in gear and headed for home.

29.

Marilyn Davis heard and felt the tension.

Her Aunt Donna slammed drawers and kicked shut the lower cabinet door that disguised the kitchen wastebasket. She gave the coffee maker a *thwock* with her hand in an attempt to make it drip faster.

Marilyn had invited herself over on the pretext of having something important to tell her aunt. They had as yet barely exchanged 'hellos'.

"I think I've come at a bad time," Marilyn said.

"Every time is a bad time lately," Donna said, bitterness in her voice.

"Can I help?" Marilyn asked.

Donna gave the coffee maker another slap. "Help *how*? Do you have any idea what's going on around here?"

Marilyn shook her head. She wished she could leave.

"Rudy thinks I killed his mother." Apparently dissatisfied with the wastebasket door, she kicked it again.

Marilyn could not suppress the shock on her face. Her uncle, too, suspected Donna.

"Why does he think that?" Marilyn asked, keeping her voice neutral.

"Because he's an idiot!" Marilyn yelled. "Because he blames himself and because I'm the convenient outlet for everything he's brought on himself."

"But what's his evidence?" Marilyn asked. "He must have something…"

Donna jerked the coffee pot out, a thin stream of liquid still falling on the heating element, boiling and spitting as it hit the plate. She poured two mugs and offered one to Marilyn.

"You don't need evidence when you're an idiot," Donna said. "All you need is your own reflection in the mirror." She tasted her coffee, grimaced, and began spooning sugar into it.

"Please," Marilyn said. "Tell me what happened."

Donna stared at her niece for several long seconds. The rage on her face subsided. She took another sip of the coffee; this time it apparently passed muster because she nodded imperceptibly. "Someone told Rudy that I went to see Cecelia a number of times…"

"It wasn't me," Marilyn said quickly.

"I know that," Donna said. "As a matter of fact, the person who told him was your father. He told Rudy because he learned that your mother also went out to that damned gold-plated nursing home several times. He also told Rudy why I went there, that I wasn't invited when I went, and that Cecelia told both your mother and me, in her most ladylike way, to go to hell."

Donna took another, longer drink of the coffee. "But Rudy also caught me in a lie. The night Cecelia died, I said I had been at a book club. When he found out that wasn't true, he jumped to the conclusion that I must have gone to the nursing home and killed her. He found an old bottle of Ambien I hadn't thrown away, and then he started rooting around his old dental supplies. He apparently figured that I either forced pills down her throat or shot her full of Novocain."

"When I came home from our lunch the other day, he confronted me with this 'evidence' and said I needed to start working on my 'alibi' before the police figured it out."

"But what made him think you killed Grandmother?"

Donna put down her coffee cup. Her gaze went to the floor. "Because I did one other really stupid thing. When the call came from the nursing home that night, I could tell from what Rudy was saying to the person who called that Cecelia had died. But I wanted Rudy to tell me, and so I pretended I hadn't heard anything. And then, to hide what I was really feeling, I went into these histrionics of grief. Rudy, being Rudy, jumped to a conclusion."

"If you weren't at the book group, where were you?" Marilyn

asked.

Donna pushed her coffee cup to one side of the kitchen counter, closed her eyes, and started to laugh. "That's the part that hurts the most. I was at a weight loss counseling group. It was our third meeting, I was with eight women and a counselor, and I was telling everyone that the reason I couldn't lose weight was because my mother-in-law was tearing apart my family. And, after spilling my innermost secrets to this group of total strangers, I come home and, an hour later, learned that Cecelia had died."

"So you told this to Uncle Rudy…" Marilyn started to say.

"He didn't believe me." Donna began to cry, first in little sobs and then in great, heaving bawls. "My own husband didn't believe me. He would rather think that I had gone to that nursing home and killed his mother."

Marilyn went to the other side of the kitchen counter and wrapped her arms around her aunt. For the better part of five minutes she stood, consoling her. But as she did, and as she whispered that no one could or should have suspected a daughter-in-law of such a heinous crime, Marilyn was fully aware that, until this moment, she too had suspected this woman.

"We're going to wait for Uncle Rudy to come home," Marilyn said, soothingly. "We're going to talk to him together. And I'm not going to leave until I'm certain he accepts the truth."

"Thank you," Donna whispered.

"Where is Rudy now?" Marilyn asked when Donna's sobbing subsided.

"He's at the library," Donna said. "Doing computer research that he says he can't do at home."

"On what?"

"Diminished capacity as a legal defense," Donna said, and then she began crying again.

30.

Jean continued to mine the trove of data coming out of the purchasing manager's office. By now it was well established that Mandy Ojumbua, every resident's favorite employee, was the subject of a discreet but hurried and thorough investigation by the management of Cavendish Woods.

Ostensibly, Ojumbua was not supposed to know about the investigation. He was still on the job but being monitored at all times by his supervisor, and he had no access to drugs except when another nurse was present.

His resume was being thoroughly vetted: each previous employer contacted and asked, bluntly, if they harbored any suspicions about Ojumbua's work. In a world of pervasive lawsuits, responses came back in carefully couched, lawyer-vetted responses. *Mr. Ojumbua left Highland Ridge Life Care LLC after eight months employment. His departure was of his own choosing. Please refer any subsequent queries on this subject to the law firm of Witley & Bailey at...*

Reading between the lines, Jean concluded, everyone suspected and everyone had been too frightened to take action. The first hospital or nursing home to call in law enforcement officials would have to deal with the questions, *How many patients/residents died after you began to suspect...* and *Why weren't you more vigilant earlier?* Conversely, if a staff member left of his or her own volition and was subsequently discovered to have been involved in a crime, then all the previous employers could pronounce themselves shocked that a one-time employee could have behaved in such a manner.

It was like re-gifting an unwanted present. Except that the unwanted present had been murdering innocent people.

There was no indication that Cavendish Woods had, as of yet, notified either the local or state police or had any intention of doing so. But it *was* clear that the legal consequences had been discussed. All emails on the subject of Mandy Ojumbua now included a paragraph-long warning that the email was protected by confidentiality agreements, was the property of Cavendish Woods and was subject to attorney/client privilege. None of these admonitions, of course, stopped the purchasing manager from printing out the emails and then throwing them in the trash.

Jean found several worrisome nuggets in the emails. The first was that Ojumbua's five-day-per-week shift was from 7:00 a.m. to 4:00 p.m. and, while his work was in Cavendish Woods' skilled nursing unit, he frequently stayed considerably later and was regularly seen in other buildings. One employee had been assigned to create a time-and-location map for Ojumbua's pre- and post-work wanderings around the Cavendish Woods complex.

A second document being compiled listed the name of every Cavendish Woods resident that had died in the previous two years with all known facts about whether and when Ojumbua could have come into contact with that individual.

Cecelia Davis' name appeared on that list with the notation that Ojumbua regularly chatted with independent living residents in the hours after his shift ended. It was known that Cecelia had gone down to dinner at 6:00 p.m. and then retired back to her room where she was not found until four hours later.

Given that the ground floor restaurants were one of the locations where Ojumbua encountered residents, it was conceivable that Ojumbua's and Cecelia's paths could have crossed on the day of her death as he had completed his regular shift two hours earlier.

The final piece of information contained in the emails was an evolving theory that Ojumbua may not have set out to deliberately kill anyone. Rather, it appeared that he was attempting to advance his career and standing among the staff as someone who saved lives by reacting quickly.

Both residents for whom a full blood workup had been done showed elevated levels of potassium chloride, a chemical that was normally present in the body and which was given to patients intravenously under certain conditions. An excess of potassium chloride would cause the heart to become unstable, then stop. If there was no intervention, the person died. If there was quick intervention, a life was saved.

In at least five instances dating back six months, Ojumbua had resuscitated a resident in the skilled nursing unit who was in heart failure. Three of those interventions had resulted in letters of commendation going into his employment file.

Could Ojumbua have been practicing on Cecelia? Or on Margaret McClellan?

Jean put the latest emails into her "keeper" envelope. As usual, no one paid any attention to what she was doing.

31.

Samantha spent her morning working on three fronts. She *did* have a job, and Mass Casualty demanded that she handle the cases that were sent her way. She conducted telephone interviews and combed case files. She drew charts and wrote memos. She made a conscientious effort to do everything well while cramming two days' work into a few hours.

The second front was getting ready for her two o'clock flight to San Francisco and her interview with Lucy McClellan. She reviewed notes and rehearsed her pitch. She would have one chance to get an audience. If she did not, it would be her own fault.

Worse, it would mean, barring some jolt from the heavens, that their investigation into the death of Cecelia Davis had reached a dead end.

She did not know if she would be able to work on the plane. And, as the morning progressed, the apprehension inside of her grew. She was truly nervous about this flight.

And it was all so *stupid*, she thought. For the past five years she had the means to fly somewhere on vacation. She could have gone to Aruba or the Bahamas and gotten some winter warmth. She could have flown out to Chicago or down to Washington D.C., two cities she wanted to visit. But instead she squirreled money into bank accounts and 401(k) retirement funds. She spent little on herself and nothing on entertainment.

She just hoped she didn't throw up in front of Paula.

Her third front was the most delicate. It involved a stop in downtown Boston on her way to the airport, and she hoped she had allowed enough time. She would meet people she did not know and hope they would hear her out. There, too, she needed a sure-fire pitch.

After packing her small overnight case and putting on her best testifying-in-court suit, she looked at herself in the mirror.

*Girl, you're playing in the big leagues now.*

32.

"We found her," Mike McDonough said, grinning.

Al Pokrovsky, Senior, swiveled in his chair to face McDonough. "Which one?"

"The skinny one," McDonough said. "Her real name is Paula Winters."

Pokrovsky nodded and smiled. "Nice work. And just how did you do that?"

McDonough's grin widened and he tapped the side of his head with his finger. He had pleased his boss. "We thought about it. The bookkeeper lives in Hardington. We figured that would be a good place to start looking for the others. We had plenty of her photos from security cameras inside the dealership. So, we picked out the most flattering one, printed it up and put it in a frame. I took it around to places that aren't in the business of being suspicious of people. I got lucky at the town library."

"I just showed the photo in the frame, and this girl at the desk said, 'Oh, that's Mrs. Winters. She's one of our trustees.' I go look on the wall and, sure enough, there's Paula Winters, library trustee, smiling back at me."

"But I wasn't satisfied. I had *Boston* magazine's list of the top cancer specialists in the city. I had this girl start calling to say that her mother, Paula Winters, 'is going to need to change her appointment.' I got a hit on the fourth call. The receptionist for Dr. Melissa Peterman was happy to change Ms. Winters' appointment to a morning one, even though it isn't for another month."

Pokrovsky smiled and nodded. "Nice work. What's the next step?"

"You give the word, we grab her."

"She lives alone?"

"Divorced, no kids at home," McDonough said. "She won't be missed for a while."

"And take her where?"

"We figure an empty house, maybe a warehouse," McDonough said. "I know a couple of places where we won't attract attention."

"Are you worried about her seeing your faces?"

"That depends on the end game."

Pokrovsky nodded. "And that depends on how quickly and thoroughly this Ayers woman responds. My idiot son thinks that all she has is some receipts that prove he has a mistress. For Ayers to have figured out what night he was going to burn those cars, she had to have a lot more than that. She had people watching the dealership, she had people inside the dealership. One of them was in accounting and another of them was going through Junior's trash every night."

McDonough cocked his head. "But doesn't all that stuff come out in discovery, anyway?"

Pokrovsky laughed. "You sound like my worthless lawyer. I don't *want* this to go to trial. I want this whole, sorry mess to end here. *I want my good name back.* And my biggest fear is that Junior was doing something else even more stupid. The dealerships pay him more than half a million a year, yet he felt compelled to torch cars to collect an insurance settlement. Why?"

Pokrovsky rose from his chair and walked to the window overlooking the water. "Well, I'm not going to let him bring me down. I was a fool to turn the business over to him but I thought that at forty-one, he had finally settled down. And I needed someone I could trust."

Pokrovsky turned to McDonough. "Do it tonight. Call me when you have her, and I'll make the call to Ayers."

McDonough gave a short salute and left wordlessly.

Two minutes later, Pokrovsky called his son's home in Marblehead. As the phone rang, he looked at his watch and then out the window: it was just after five o'clock. Sunset was technically half an hour away but, under a slate-gray sky it was already dusk. Al Junior's wife answered.

"Muriel, I need to speak to Al," he said.

"He isn't home yet," Muriel said. "I don't really know when to expect him."

Pokrovsky exhaled deeply. "I'm sure you can find him. Don't settle for a phone message. Talk to him and make him come home. You and he are going to drive into Boston tonight. You're going to have dinner somewhere very nice and, after dinner, you're going to check into a hotel together and, tomorrow morning, you'll have breakfast together. This is all my treat. Please tell me you'll do this for me."

"Of course, Al," Muriel said.

"You're a good girl," Pokrovsky said. "Take the kids with you. Get a suite. It's my gift to you."

"Thank you, Al," she said.

\* \* \* \* \*

The phone seemed to have gone into some kind of silent vibrate mode in her hand, and Muriel realized that her hand was shaking. In fact, both hands were shaking.

*What in the hell is going on?* she thought.

Muriel sat at the little desk in the kitchen for several minutes, trying to piece together clues. She knew all too well that underneath the smiling veneer, her father-in-law was a crook and a monster. For some reason, Al Senior wanted his son to be visibly and publicly somewhere else tonight.

It all had to come back to the attempted arson which meant it had to do with the young African-American woman who had come to her house a week earlier. Al Senior was capable of anything, she knew.

Muriel opened the desk drawer and looked among the scissors, tape and screwdrivers. She found Samantha Ayers' business card and, as she had done that earlier evening, fingered it; turning it over and over in her hand.

She picked up the phone and dialed the first number on the business card. An automated switchboard intercept told her that

Mass Casualty's offices were closed for the day but that she could use the search-by-name function to leave a message.

Muriel hung up and dialed the second number. It went to voice mail. She paused, wondering if leaving a message was the right thing. If something happened to Samantha Ayers and a message warning Ayers that something bad was about to happen was found on her phone, it could mean that she, Muriel, was an accessory to whatever it was that happened.

She hung up a second time.

There was an email address but that made whatever message she wrote even easier to find should something happen.

Muriel began shaking again. When she felt her composure return, she put the business card in her purse. She would find a way to keep trying until she got through to Ayers without leaving a message.

With that, she began the arduous task of tracking down her husband.

33.

Lucy McClellan's home in Palo Alto's Crescent Park neighborhood did not seem especially rich to Samantha. Less than twenty feet separated it from its neighbor on either side, and the front yard was barely large enough to contain a small bib of grass behind the wooden fence. A few minutes before she departed for the airport, she had idly tapped the address into Zillow. The "make me move" price was five million dollars, and nearby homes were listed for that amount or more.

*Only in California*, Samantha thought.

Paula, too, took in the property, but her eyes were drawn to the full canopy of trees – oaks by their appearance – bright green lawn and pots of flowers on every available surface. Seven hours earlier, she had left leaden skies and temperatures in the low twenties. Here, it was spring in February.

Samantha rang the doorbell. They squeezed one another's hands. *This is it*, Paula thought.

The porch light came on, and the front door was opened by a woman in her mid-40s, wearing jeans and a red, faded Stanford sweatshirt. Lucy McClellan had one of those no-nonsense hair styles that looked effortless. Paula, though, could see an expert's hand at work in the cut, dark blonde color and highlights.

"You must not have had any trouble getting here," Lucy said. Then, opening the door fully she said, "Please come in."

Lucy led them to a study that was likely once a bedroom. The walls contained diplomas and photos, the desk surfaces framed photos. The photos, Samantha noted, looked to be vacation shots with friends. She saw nothing that said family.

"I don't know how long I can give you," Lucy said, indicating two chairs. "You've come cross-country, so I know this is important to you. For me, it's something I've tried – so far without success – to put behind me."

Samantha introduced herself. "I'm the one who spoke with you on the phone." Indicating Paula, Samantha said, "Paula Winters has been working with me and has a personal interest in your mother's death…"

"You knew my mother?" Lucy asked, looking at Paula.

Paula shook her head. "We never met. I had a friend at Cavendish Woods who was good friends with your mother. She died earlier this month, also of a heart attack."

Looking back at Samantha, Lucy said, "And you think there's a link."

"Two women, both in good health and neither with a history of heart disease, suffered heart attacks under nearly identical circumstances," Samantha said. "Both lost their husbands a few months earlier. I'm looking for that link."

"And that's worth two round-trips tickets to San Francisco?" Lucy asked.

"If we find the link, it's worth ten round-trip tickets."

"You said you work for Mass Casualty," Lucy said. "They don't write life insurance. They'd be more likely to have a policy on the nursing home."

Samantha quickly shook her head. "This is strictly extracurricular for me. And, no, Mass Casualty doesn't have any nursing home clients." Samantha indicated Paula. "I owe this lady and a few of her friends a debt of gratitude. They think a woman named Cecelia Davis died under…"

"A debt of gratitude for what?" Lucy interjected.

"For one thing," Samantha said, "this woman saved my life. She beat off a man who was trying to kill me."

Lucy looked at Paula and re-appraised the thin, fifty-ish blonde woman traveling with the tall, twenty-something African-American.

"I'd like to talk about your family," Samantha said. "We can start with your father and sister. I understand they passed away within a few weeks of one another."

Lucy saw Samantha taking in the photos on the wall and desk.

"No," Lucy said. "You won't find any warm, fuzzy family snapshots in here. I do have one of my mother and sister in my bedroom. I'm pretty sure that I've never had a photo of my father."

Paula heard the words and immediately thought, *child abuse.*

Lucy saw the look and smiled. "No, it's not what you're thinking. In some ways, it's worse. Are either of you Catholic?"

Paula and Samantha both shook their heads.

"Then let me give you the unexpurgated story. My father got out of law school and went to work for the Diocese of Boston. The Diocese probably had two lawyers when my father got there. By the time he left, they had at least half a dozen on staff and three times that number on retainer."

"My father got to the Diocese in the glory days of the late fifties. Rich little old ladies died off and left everything to the Church. One of my father's jobs was to sift through their estates looking for the good stuff – things the Diocese could sell to raise money to keep expanding the empire. His reward – with the Archbishop's blessing – was to be able to buy certain items for basically nothing. We bought the house I grew up in for less than ten thousand dollars. Even in 1960, a house that size in Chestnut Hill was worth thirty or forty thousand."

"We owned fine art and oriental rugs. We owned alleyways in Beacon Hill and tiny buildings in the financial district. We owned vacant lots in Newton and Brookline and undeveloped land along Route 128. Why did he get it so cheap? Because there was so much of it coming in, and my father was very good at converting the rest to cash on behalf of the Diocese. He was their golden boy."

"But my father had a second role. He was technically a lawyer, but he came to be more like a *consigliore.* And, when Bernard Law became Archbishop of Boston, my father's career kicked into overdrive."

"For years, my father had been buying off families – the cheaper the better. He could get a signed, legal document absolving the Diocese of Boston of all wrongdoing for five hundred bucks. The documents, of course, never mentioned Father Jones or what he had been doing to little Billy, but it was legally binding all the same."

"Law and my father became best buddies. My father was the keeper of the secrets. Law set out to find every priest who was abusing kids, and my father was the guy who kept it quiet. I remember sitting around the dinner table, and he would ask my sister and me what we had done that day, and we would wax enthusiastic about tennis or geometry. And, when my mother would ask him about *his* day, he would just shrug and say, 'same old same old'."

"He got his appointment to the bench about four years before it all blew up into the open," Lucy said. "Law – excuse me, 'Cardinal Law' – pressed all the right buttons, and William McClellan became Superior Court Judge McClellan, who now got to use his powers as an impartial arbiter of the law to coerce families into settling rather than bringing lawsuits."

"I was in college when I figured out what was going on. When the *Globe* broke their series in 2002, I called my father and asked how much he had known and what he had done about it. The bastard just lied and said he had 'tried to make it less painful for the families'. I don't think I ever spoke to him after that. I certainly wasn't going home for family get-togethers, and it ought to explain why I wasn't at my father's funeral."

Lucy paused, collecting her thoughts, then continued. "On the other hand, I grieved for my sister. Rosemary was four years my senior, and I looked up to her when I was young. But once I understood my father's role in the Diocese, I expected her to be as outraged as I was. Instead, Rosemary talked about 'God's will'. She followed my father into the law, though she stayed clear of anything having to do with priest abuse."

"But my father's role was a shadow that hung over the family; the elephant in the room. I couldn't *not* talk about it, and no one else in the family could or *would* talk about it. And so I became the family's un-member. And, of course, two divorces and no children didn't exactly endear me to my mother."

"When my sister's cancer began to spread, I made several trips back to Boston to be with her and with my mother. It wasn't quite a reconciliation, and it wasn't quite not one. My mother and I had a couple of heart-to-heart talks. She couldn't forgive me for not coming to my father's funeral, but she said she understood my principles even if she didn't agree with them."

Lucy shifted in her chair. "Anyway, while I was with my mother, I took photographs of her. I wasn't trying to document the villa she was in. It's just that the things in the villa were in the background. I expected her to live a long time – she was eighty-three and, apart from her hip and some osteoporosis, she was in good health. After my sister died, I came back here and got on with my life."

Samantha spoke. "Did you talk with your mother in those last few months?"

Lucy nodded. "Twice, maybe three times a week. Not for very long. It was clear she was depressed and, short of my moving in with her, nothing was going to speed up the grieving process. I let her know I was there for her. Other than that, it was just the two of us talking."

"When was the last time you spoke with her?" Samantha asked.

Lucy did not need to think about the answer. "Two days before she died. Nothing had really changed. She didn't want to go out, and she didn't want to see her friends. She apologized that she had been very curt with some of them when they descended on her to 'cheer her up'. It was a conversation that lasted about five minutes. I said I'd call again in a few days. Two days later, the nursing home called me to say she had been found in her villa a few hours after she died."

"So you flew back to Boston," Samantha said.

Lucy nodded. "Rosemary's husband, Jeff, had his hands full with three kids. And, I was the executor of the estate as some kind of afterthought. I thought it would take a day or two." She shuddered. "It was a nightmare."

Samantha gave her an encouraging look.

"When I got to Cavendish Woods, I went to her villa and things were... not in order, and certainly not the way they had been a few months earlier. Then I noticed that a beautiful Lalique vase was gone. I had been let in by someone on the office staff, and I demanded to speak with the general manager. It took two hours to round him up and, by that time, I was comparing what was in the villa to the photos I had taken on my last visit. It looked like at least a dozen valuable objects were gone."

"Do you think someone on the staff stole them?" Samantha asked.

Lucy's face had a pained look. "The general manager said my mother must have given those things away in the weeks after my father's death. As it turns out, he was right. My mother gave them to my nieces after my sister's funeral. All the pieces were there. I think I was more distraught than I was willing to admit to myself."

"What happened to your mother's body?" Paula asked.

"By the time I got there, she had already been taken to a funeral home in Cavendish. I made the funeral arrangements; she was buried three days later. I think everyone at Cavendish Woods was there."

"There was no autopsy; nothing by the Medical Examiner?" Paula asked.

Lucy shook her head. "I had no reason to ask. The head of the medical staff signed the death certificate and called the funeral home. If there were any tests or exams, I never heard about them."

"She was embalmed?"

Lucy nodded. "Does that preclude any kind of post-mortem testing?"

Samantha shrugged. "It makes it harder."

"You believe my mother's death was not just grief taking its toll?"

Samantha answered carefully, "We came here looking for any kind of correlation. So far, we don't have any. You mother and Cecelia Davis died under similar circumstances; they were friends, they were both widows of means, but that describes basically everyone at Cavendish Woods."

"Let me try one thread we're following," Paula said. "Did your mother and father have an estate advisor? In particular, did they have any dealing with a firm called Liss and Swann?"

"Brown Brother Harriman for financial," Lucy replied. "Ropes and Gray for estate."

"*Dammit,*" Samantha said under her breath.

"Were things stolen from your friend's room?" Lucy asked.

"No," Paula said. "As far as anyone knows, her belongings were intact."

Samantha had an idea. "What did you do with your mother's belongings?"

Lucy leaned back. "Rosemary left two daughters and a son. The son is still at home – he's in high school. One daughter is in school at B.C. She took off the semester after Rosemary died, and I don't know if she is back at school now or not. The oldest has been out of college for a year or two. She's down in Austin, Texas, doing whatever it is that kids with degrees in French Literature do for a living. Probably working at Starbucks."

"Anyway, I made up an inventory of everything in the villa and everything I knew to be in storage. I had everything shipped to Rosemary's house, and the kids can claim what they want or need. There were a couple of items that I knew my mother wanted donated to the MFA – some ancient Greek coins and a Roman vase that had been in storage. Thank God those weren't left around the villa because I'm sure they would have disappeared. I'm still not sure what to do with the Canaletto."

"I'm sorry," Paula said. "The Canaletto?"

"It was one of my father's 'estate find' pieces from the late 1950s. The Diocese let him buy it for about a hundred dollars. It was the one piece of art that didn't go to the MFA when my parents moved to Cavendish Woods, although it was promised to MFA in their will. It was a beautiful scene of the Piazza San Marco and the

Basilica. I had the painting delivered to MFA. They sent it back about three weeks later with a very kind note saying that, unfortunately the painting was a copy."

Samantha and Paula looked at one another. Paula's mouth was open. Samantha could not breathe.

Lucy saw the reaction. "What did I say?" she asked.

"Lucy," Paula said, "Tell me everything you know about that painting. This could be important."

"Canaletto," Lucy said. "Eighteenth century Italian painter..."

"No," Samantha said, recovering. "Did it have a provenance? Did your parents ever have it authenticated?"

"You think this is that 'correlation' you were looking for?"

"Please," Samantha said. "Provenance. Authentication."

"OK," Lucy said. "The painting came from the estate of a family in Cambridge. I think their name was Callahan, or at least that was the last surviving member. It came into our house before I was born, and always hung in the library over a fireplace. If there is a provenance, it would be with my father's papers, which I have in a safe deposit box at Bank of America here in Palo Alto. I ought to have sent them to the MFA along with the painting, but the papers were back here, and I was doing all the sorting in Boston."

"Authentication?" Lucy continued. "My father had the painting appraised several times for insurance purposes over the years, and I would think that someone would have spotted it as a copy..." Lucy paused, remembering something. "When they last made out their wills, they stipulated what items were going to the MFA, and MFA sent someone out to look at the artwork and antiquities."

"I know that because my sister wrote me about it – I pretty much wasn't talking to my parents by then – and she said they were very thorough and provided appraisals for estate valuation purposes. The Canaletto was worth close to a million dollars."

Then Lucy stopped. "I'll tell you more, but only if you tell me why you need to know."

Samantha said, "Cecelia Davis had a Henri Fantin-Latour

painting, *White Roses*, in her room. Her son went to an auction house and was told it was a very good copy."

"Mother of mercy," Lucy said. "What happened next?"

"This all just happened a few weeks ago," Samantha said. "Cecelia and her husband bought the painting from a gallery in the south of France in the 1950s. It had gallery stamps and a history, but the auction house said the gallery stamp was hand-painted. The family was devastated."

"So someone could have copied and swapped both paintings?" Lucy asked.

"The curator at the art gallery…" Samantha said.

"Jillian Connolly," Paula said. "She would have known about both paintings. She had Cecelia's Fantin-Latour for a show."

"How do you copy a painting?" Lucy asked.

"What did you do with the Canaletto?" Samantha asked.

"It's in a closet," Lucy said. "I think this might be the right time to take a close look at it." She paused, then added, "I'm going to order in some dinner. What do you guys like?"

* * * * *

Ten minutes later, they began unwrapping the box sent by the Museum of Fine Arts. Lucy had read only the accompanying letter with the polite let-down that the painting was a forgery. She had thrown the box into a closet until she could decide how to offer a worthless painting to her sister's children.

Now, they cut through the layers of cardboard and bubble wrap to get to the painting, from which they took the last pieces of plastic and paper.

It was a beautiful painting of Venice in its eighteenth century glory, the Piazza San Marco was golden and, beyond it, St. Mark's Basilica. The painting *looked* to be more than two hundred years old.

"My mother loved it because it incorporated Canaletto's *imaginaria*," Lucy said, holding the painting at arm's length. "He painted canvasses for the rich English tourists on their Grand Tour. He would get bored and start re-arranging Venice just to amuse himself. This painting puts the *campanile* on the wrong side of the piazza."

"It doesn't look like a copy," Samantha said, taking the painting from Lucy. "The surface is cracked and the varnish is discolored."

Lucy went back to her desk, tapped on her computer and found an entry. "Apparently, with the right tools, you can make a week-old painting look like it has a couple of centuries on it. I've got at least a dozen web pages with step-by-step instructions. Sugar-solution underlays, rabbit-skin glue and dark-brown caseins, amber shellacs, bake it in an oven at a hundred and forty degrees for a week…. it's all here."

"But you have to start with the painting," Paula said. "Someone has to copy that painting perfectly…" Paula looked at her watch. "I'm going to call Jean," she said to Samantha. "She can see if anything is in Jillian Connolly's office."

"Who is Jean?" Lucy asked.

"She is undercover at Cavendish Woods doing the most thankless task in the world – working with the overnight cleaning crew, going through trash cans, looking for clues," Samantha said.

"Talk about jobs you can't pay people enough to do," Lucy said.

"Oh, no," Samantha replied. "She's not getting paid for this. She's doing this because she wants to find out who killed Cecelia."

Lucy looked at the two of them and blinked. "Who are you people?"

"We call ourselves the Garden Club Gang," Paula said. "It's a long story."

"Who has the Fantin-Latour?" Samantha asked Paula.

"Probably Rudy," Paula said. "Unless his wife burned it."

Samantha, too, looked at her watch. "It's eleven o'clock on the east coast. You call Jean, and I'll call Marilyn. She has to get that painting from Rudy before he uses it for kindling."

"Marilyn is part of this Garden Club Gang?" Lucy asked.

"Marilyn is Cecelia's granddaughter. She was the only person who thought Cecelia's death was suspicious," Paula said. "She approached us."

"And this Jillian Connolly is…" Lucy let the question hang in the air.

"The curator of the little 'art gallery' at Cavendish Woods," Paula responded. "If these paintings are the common link, then Jillian Connolly is either the murderer or else she is complicit. Alice says she's very good at art history…"

"Alice?"

"Another member of the gang. She's undercover as a resident. I'm undercover as a nurse. Eleanor is undercover looking at Liss and Swann, the 'save your assets from the nursing home' outfit."

"I hate those commercials," Lucy said to Paula. "And this is a business? 'The Garden Club Gang' is an enterprise, and you…" She indicated Samantha. "…are their advisor?"

"No," Paula said. "The four ladies are members of an actual garden club. We got together last summer to…. do something. In the process, we got to know Samantha…"

"Where you saved her life," Lucy said. "I remember that part."

"But we owed Samantha something, too. And so in December and January we helped her uncover an insurance fraud at a car dealership. A dealer about to torch his own cars…"

A look of awe came over Lucy's face. "In Boston. The guy who was filmed as he was about to light those cars on fire. I thought that sounded familiar. He peed his pants. That was you?"

"That was us," Samantha said.

"The YouTube video of that has gotten, like, thirty million hits," Lucy said.

"We weren't after hits," Samantha said. "My company had paid out half a million in claims to that guy. If he had gotten away with it, we would have paid almost two million more."

The doorbell rang. Lucy excused herself to answer it.

"We need to get back to Boston tonight," Samantha said to Paula when Lucy was out of the room. "Tomorrow could be 'the day' when we wrap this up."

Samantha's phone rang. She looked at the caller ID. "Marilyn," she said. A brief conversation ensued.

"Marilyn is going over to her uncle's house at the crack of dawn and getting *White Roses*. Assuming Donna hasn't incinerated it. She'll keep it safe until we can get it to an expert."

Lucy came back with two tote bags of food. "The great thing about Palo Alto is that you can get anything delivered. Who's up for Italian?"

"We're going back to Boston tonight," Samantha said. "If we're right, we can have this in the hands of the police this time tomorrow."

"Are you on United or Jet Blue?"

"United," Samantha said.

"I have about three million miles on United and an elite status so high they want to name a terminal after me," Lucy said. "One of the perks is being able to do nice things for other people. When you get to SFO, somebody will be waiting for you."

"You don't have to do that," Samantha said.

"When you walked in here an hour ago," Lucy said, unpacking food, "I was going to give you five minutes and, if you were trying to sell me something, I was going to have you out the door before you sat down. An hour ago, I believe my mother died of grief brought on by the loss of her husband and daughter. Instead, now I know something awfully damned important about someone I cared for dearly. Call this a small 'thank you'. If you're right, there will be a much larger one coming."

34.

"Anything you can find," Samantha said, emphasizing *anything.* Take as long as you need and make copies of anything that looks even remotely suspicious. In fact, take a camera and photograph everything."

"You understand it's not part of my normal cleaning schedule," Jean said. "Someone might get suspicious." Samantha's phone call had caught her as she was getting ready to leave for Cavendish Woods.

"Jean, I think we have our person," Samantha said. "Two very expensive paintings that just happen to turn out to be copies after they've passed through Jillian Connolly's hands, and then two women dead of heart attacks. If she didn't do it, she knows who did."

Two minutes later, Samantha closed her phone, a satisfied look on her face. "She'll do a good job," Samantha said to Paula. "She's just nervous.

They were sitting in the United Club at San Francisco International Airport. Paula sipped a scotch, Samantha drained the last of her Diet Coke. Upon leaving the rental car center, they had called a number provided by Lucy McClellan, and a young woman with a sign bearing Samantha's name had met them at the AirTrain station. Less than ten minutes later, they were in the lounge, a pair of boarding passes for first class seats in their hands. "That woman has pull," was all Samantha could say.

She looked across at Paula, who had a confused look on her face."What's the matter?" Samantha asked.

"I called my home phone to see if I had any messages," Paula said. "Listen to this one." She held out her phone so that Samantha could hear.

*"Hi, Paula. This is Melissa Peterman. Jo told me your daughter called and asked to change your March 13th appointment to ten-thirty. She's done that,*

*but I just wanted to give you a call to see how you're doing otherwise. Give me a call when you get a minute."*

"Who is Melissa Peterman?" Samantha asked.

"My oncologist. What I can't figure out is why on earth my daughter would call to change an appointment. She doesn't even know my oncologist's name…"

"Call your daughter," Samantha said. "I know you'll probably wake her up, but please call her."

The look on Samantha's face was one Paula had seen only once – late one evening in an SUV in the parking lot of a building that housed a long-closed fortune teller. She looked at her watch: it was after midnight on the east coast.

She found her daughter's number and tapped her phone. Fifteen seconds later, she heard her daughter's sleepy voice.

"Mom?"

"Julie, I have an important question; then you can go back to sleep. Did you call my oncologist – her name is Dr. Peterman – and change the time of my appointment for next month?"

"No, that's crazy," her daughter said.

"That's all I needed to know," Paula said. "I'm sorry to have awakened you."

"But what's this all about?"

"A prank, I guess. I'll call you tomorrow. Good night." With that, she tapped her phone and put it down.

"Do you want to tell me, or make me guess?" Paula said.

"Dear God," Samantha said. "What have I gotten you ladies into?"

"You can tell me now, or I can badger you for six hours on the plane," Paula said. "I can take it."

"Al Pokrovsky," Samantha said. "We're less than two weeks away from the preliminary hearing, and I've never been deposed by Pokrovsky's attorneys. If and when they depose me, they'll ask for all of your names, and I'll be required to give them. That cuts two ways: it means they can talk about unfair investigative tactics in court, but it also means that the four of you are safe: even Whitey Bulger would think twice about going after someone whose name was unknown until it came out in a deposition."

"Last week, I went to Al Junior's house and gave him an ultimatum: either depose me or else I'd turn over the stuff we got on his stepping out on his wife. I showed him a couple of receipts to get his attention, and he looked like he had caved. But, apart from one call asking for available dates, I haven't heard a thing. That made me realize I've been worried about the wrong person: it isn't Al Junior who is calling the shots. It's his father, Smilin' Al himself."

"I think Al Senior has been looking for the four of you ever since I was stupid enough to let you go to the sting. Al Junior saw all of us. He went crying to daddy. And Al Senior is a mean enough son of a bitch that he'll come after you if he can figure out who you are."

"But how could he have found me?" Paula asked. "I parked my car a block away, and I stayed in character."

"Did you ever talk to anyone about your cancer?" Samantha asked.

Paula thought for several moments. At first, she thought 'no'. Then, she remembered a conversation with one of the sales staff, a woman who also had a grown son and daughter. She had let slip that Julie was working at the State Department. And, when the woman said her own recent mammogram had raised a warning flag, Paula had urged the woman not to hesitate about seeing a specialist... and, for emphasis, had said she had breast cancer surgery over the summer.

"Oh, Lord," Paula said. "I did say something. Once. To a salesperson to urge her to see an oncologist."

"That's all it took," Samantha said. "They certainly had photos of you. They showed them around until they got a name. And, once they had a name, they checked out the rest of the information they had to verify that it was you. It's exactly what I would do."

"Does this mean they know all of us?" Paula asked.

"I don't think they need everyone," Samantha replied. "I made a mistake, too. I told Al Junior that if anything happened to *any* of you, he was going to be toast. That's as good as a sworn statement that I'll give him everything I've got to keep the four of you safe."

Samantha continued, "So, they're going to grab you and anyone else they've identified. And then, they're going to call me. The problem is, they're going to go to your house, and you're not going to be there, because you're in California. And that's where you're going to stay until this gets resolved."

"No," Paula said. "I'm not going to hide anywhere. If you're in trouble or the rest of us are in trouble, I'm going to be there to help. End of discussion."

Samantha stared at Paula for several seconds. She saw an adamant, determined expression on Paula's face and decided that trying to talk her into staying would not be useful.

"Then the first thing we do is alert everyone else," Samantha said. "I'll get in touch with Jean and have her tell Alice – which ought to be nothing more than making certain she keeps her door locked tonight. I'm going to tell Jean to check into a motel when she leaves work. I'm leaving you the delicate task of calling Eleanor and getting her out of her house."

An overhead loudspeaker informed them that Flight 1728 was ready for boarding and that first class ticket holders were welcome to board at any time.

"We make our calls, we get some sleep, and tomorrow we pull together a plan," Samantha said. "Tomorrow is going to be one very busy day."

35.

Jean put away her phone and looked around warily. *"Don't go home,"* Samantha had said. *"Don't even go there for a change of clothes. Stop somewhere and buy what you need for a day or two. I'll let you know if anyone is watching your house. We'll talk tomorrow and I'll explain everything."*

In the background, Jean thought she could hear announcements and bells, like what you would hear on an airplane. Was Samantha leaving town? But, if so, how could she tell Jean if someone was watching her house?

No, Samantha must be flying home. She had found something that led her to believe that Jillian Connolly either murdered Cecelia or was somehow complicit. The urgency in her voice in both conversations was real. This was not a suggestion: it was a command.

Jean had never been inside the small art gallery, and its access was controlled by a keypad. The crew chief, the only person with whom Jean worked who spoke English, readily opened the facility but said she would need to stay with Jean.

The gallery itself held no interest. The paintings and sculptures were just that: well-displayed art objects. Jean had been asked to go through Connolly's office and work room. That room, somewhat surprisingly, also had a keypad entry. Jean turned on the lights in the workroom.

At the center of the room was a painting on an art stand. It was a seascape with rocks in the foreground, a large wave crashing over the rocks, and a red line of a sunset bisecting the painting. All around the room were photographs of parts of the painting including four that captured the part of the canvas that folded over the frame. A large photo showed the painting's obverse with detailed shots of what appeared to be ink stamps and imperfections in the canvas.

Someone, Jean concluded, was intent upon copying this painting. She took out her camera and began photographing everything in the room that could conceivably be of interest to Samantha. When she had completed that job, she turned to Connolly's office desk and photographed it thoroughly, paying careful attention to papers on the desk and around the computer on that desk.

She pulled at the desk drawer. It was locked. The wastebasket held only tissues.

In less than fifteen minutes, Jean was through. She mumbled a thank you to the crew chief and could only imagine what was going through the woman's mind. Jean had taken nothing from the office and showed no interest in the presumably valuable art in the gallery. Just a hundred photographs.

Before going back to her regular schedule, Jean needed to alert Alice. Going to the room on the fourth floor of The Overlook, and managing not to be seen by the two nurses on the floor, Jean tapped lightly at Alice's door.

When there was no response, she tapped harder and was rewarded with sounds from inside the room and light underneath the door. After two minutes, the door opened a crack. Jean held a finger to her lips and motioned that she needed to come in.

"Samantha said you were to stay in your room tonight and lock your door. Don't let anyone in," Jean said. "I'm supposed to go to a motel and not even stop for a change of clothes."

"Don't be ridiculous," Alice said. "You can stay here. I have plenty of room."

The idea was appealing. Jean, always frugal by nature, did not relish the idea of paying the Holiday Inn in Cavendish more than a hundred dollars a night for a room.

"I have to finish my rounds, so I may be a few hours," Jean said.

Alice went to her purse and found her key ring. She held out the one to the suite they were in. "I'll have made up the sofa. Don't wake me."

\* \* \* \* \*

Paula's call to Eleanor awakened her from a troubled sleep.

"I usually yell at people who call at this hour of the morning, but I was not fond of the dream I was having," Eleanor said. "You're really in California?"

Paula said she was and explained the discovery that Jillian Connolly had likely switched two paintings for forgeries.

"Sounds like a motive to me," Eleanor said. "I really feel like I was out of the cast on this one – chasing Liss and Swann. I was kind of hoping that I would finally get to be the one to finger the bad guys."

"I thought I had done everything right at Pokrovsky Motors," Paula said. "I thought I never let my guard down. It was just one time – one conversation when someone on their sales staff said her latest mammogram showed some abnormalities. She wasn't going to do anything about it because she wasn't certain if her insurance was going to cover the cost. It set me off. I talked about my own history. Pokrovsky tracked me down from that one, five-minute conversation."

"We'll figure out something," Eleanor said. "Samantha is pretty smart that way. Do you think she'd mind if, instead of a motel, I went to Phil's nursing home instead? We're getting down to the end game and, while he has no idea who I am and is mostly unconscious, I feel like every visit may be my last one…"

"I think she would understand," Paula said. "I certainly understand. They'll let you in even though it's…." Paula looked at her watch. "After one in the morning?"

"By now, I know everyone there and the executive director is an old friend," Eleanor said. "They'll take me in. Call me when you get back to Boston."

The call ended, and Paula turned to Samantha. "Eleanor is leaving now. She'll be at her husband's nursing home."

Samantha frowned, then thought through the idea. "It's not ideal," she said. "But I understand."

36.

"She wasn't there," McDonough said. "She never came home. I did the stakeout myself."

It was not what Al Senior wanted to hear, either in person or, as now, over the telephone. "Does this mean she knows you're onto her?"

"We've been too careful for that," McDonough said. "I don't think so. I could go into the house and look for clues, but I think she just wasn't home last night."

The answer was not satisfying to Pokrovsky. "She could also be on vacation. We may not see her for two weeks."

"No," McDonough said. "There's a newspaper in the driveway. Just one. Not a pile. If she was on vacation, there would either be a pile or none. I'm certain we just picked the one night she wasn't home."

"How many guys can you get that you can trust?" Al Senior asked.

"Two or three," McDonough replied. "I want to keep this as tight as I can."

"You get one of them to sit on the house and another to sit on that Beauchamp woman's townhouse," Al Senior said. "And you go full court press to find one of the others. If two of them live in that town, maybe they all do. We've got to finish this thing."

"You're the boss," McDonough said.

\* \* \* \* \*

Pokrovsky put down the phone and stared out across Green Pond and the white sky. Even on the normally placid narrow inlet, there was a light chop pushing water against his dock. It was going to snow for sure, which would further complicate things.

His first job was to keep his idiot son out of sight. Hopefully, Muriel was doing her job, but his instructions had gone no further than breakfast this morning. When this came down, Al Junior had to have impartial witnesses that he was somewhere else, and preferably with his family.

He had been up much of the night waiting for the call from McDonough. During that time, he rehearsed what he would say when he called Samantha Ayers. He wanted the tone of menace to be just right: utter certainty of what would happen to her friend if she did *not* comply exactly with his wishes, but with just enough magnanimity that she should expect that her friend would be freed when she *did* comply.

He had, of course, come to the conclusion that none of the five should live to give depositions, much less to testify. It was a matter of honor. For nearly four decades, his name and reputation had never been questioned. He had *respect*. Charities and organizations sought him out for his endorsement; people brought him quality investment opportunities.

Then, in a heartbeat, that reputation had been demolished. And not just sullied in New England. Every news network had aired the footage, every news anchor spoke his family's name with a sneering laugh. The video of his flesh and blood wetting his pants was all over the internet.

At the epicenter of the entire event was this woman – Samantha Ayers – who had *set out* to entrap his son. For a few miserable dollars of insurance payments, she had *deliberately* ruined the name he spent his life building. The four women were willing accomplices. They had taken money without thinking what incalculable harm they were causing. They must all pay the ultimate price.

Toward two in the morning, when it became clear that McDonough was not going to call, Pokrovsky turned his attention to the means of extracting the names and whereabouts of the remaining women. It was good that he had come up to Falmouth alone. Some things were best done quickly and efficiently. Others, like what he had in mind, were better savored when time and distractions were not a factor.

In one way, the day's delay was a gift. Anticipation allowed him to savor what was coming.

37.

They were still at Logan Airport when Samantha heard the ringtone for an "unidentified caller" and glanced at the number. It seemed vaguely familiar. Her first instinct was to let it go to voicemail, but then saw five missed calls from the number in the preceding twelve hours. She tapped the key to answer the call.

"This is Muriel Pokrovsky," the voice on the other end of the call said. "We met very briefly when you came to visit my husband last week."

Warily, Samantha asked, "How can I help you?"

"I think you and some people you work with are in danger," Muriel said.

"I thank you for the warning, Mrs. Pokrovsky, but why are you telling me this now?" Samantha asked.

"Because my father-in-law is about to try something. I overheard the conversation between you and my husband. I know you were trying to scare him into leaving you and your people alone by showing him receipts for things he bought for... that woman. After you left, he called my father-in-law. I could only hear my husband's side of the conversation, but it was clear that my father-in-law wants to kidnap the women you work with and use their abduction to force you to turn over everything else you have on him or my husband."

Muriel continued. "Last night, my father-in-law called me and told me to take everyone into Boston, go out for dinner, and check into a hotel. The only other time he ever did that, one of his business partners was found shot to death in Providence the next day. I tried to call you as soon as I got off the phone with my father-in-law, but you didn't answer, and I couldn't leave this kind of message. I've tried several times since, but you weren't answering your phone."

"I was on an airplane most of that time," Samantha said.

"Well, my father-in-law just called again. He's ordered us to stay here another day."

"Where is your husband?" Samantha asked.

"He's showering. I'm out in the hallway," Muriel said. "Ms. Ayers, I'm well aware of my husband's shortcomings. I already knew about Dee Simonson, and before her there was another woman. I also know my husband has a gambling addiction. But he's not a monster. It's my father-in-law who is the monster, and my husband's problem is that he has lived his entire life in a monster's shadow."

"Are you asking me to just turn over anything I have to your husband and father-in-law?"

"I can't tell you what to do, except to warn you that my father-in-law is going to do something. He has a man who works for him…"

"What's the man's name?" Samantha asked.

"Mike McDonough," Muriel said.

"Describe him," Samantha said.

"He's big – two hundred and fifty pounds, six-four. Maybe fifty years old with thinning black hair. He may have been a football player at some point. He has that kind of a build. He also has a couple of younger goons that he hangs around with. They've been to the house once or twice. I told my husband that any time they were coming over, I didn't want me or the kids to be in the house with them. They scare me."

"You know this could turn out badly for your husband, Mrs. Pokrovsky," Samantha said.

"I know that," Muriel said. "Right after the…. incident… up in Reading, my husband got several calls. A private equity firm offered to buy the whole chain. My husband asked what the top offer might be. When he heard it, he told the person who called that the offer was 'insulting'."

Muriel continued. "My husband doesn't know I listen in on what goes on in his office and, if he knew, he'd never forgive me.

But the next day, I asked if he would ever consider selling the business. He shook his head and said, 'Dad would never let me'. He sounded so mournful. He isn't a bad man, Ms. Ayers. He's in over his head."

Samantha had an idea. "Your father-in-law – Al Senior – he's up here or down in Florida right now? "

"He came up after he saw the news," Muriel said. "He has a house down in Falmouth. He was here at our house about a week later, screaming."

"He's married, I know," Samantha said. "His wife came up with him, I assume."

Muriel snorted. "You couldn't pry Roxanne out of Naples with a crowbar before Memorial Day. It's high season down there."

"So, if I give him the stuff I've got, and I take it down to him, I'll be safe – no house full of goons."

"You're never safe with him," Muriel said. "But he lives alone if he comes up in the winter. Just some day help, and he eats out."

"Mrs. Pokrovsky, I consider myself and my people warned," Samantha said. "I will make certain they stay out of sight. And you keep your husband occupied. If you hear something else, call me. If I can't pick up, it's OK to leave a message."

Samantha ended the call, her mind racing. Paula had heard one side of the conversation and seemed eager to learn what Muriel Pokrovsky had told her. Samantha provided an abbreviated version, then said, "We need to find someplace to plan our next move."

"There's a hotel on the airport property," Paula said.

"Then let's get a room," Samantha replied. She looked at her phone. "If it's eight o'clock on the east coast, it's five in the morning in California. How early do you think we can call Lucy McClellan on a Saturday morning?"

Her question was interrupted by the ringing of her phone. Samantha looked at the caller ID: it was Lucy McClellan.

"I guess I answered that question," Samantha said.

"I think I've found the Canaletto," Lucy said, dispensing with 'hello' or 'how was your flight?'. "I spent an hour on the phone with the person on the Art Crime Team at the FBI field office in San Francisco after you left, and I had a web image search done using the copy I have here. There's a gallery in New York, Hao Ming, that specializes in fine art sales to China. The painting was on their website for about three days in December."

"Can it be recovered?" Samantha asked. Her mind was filled with other, unasked questions such as *how do you get an FBI agent on the phone at eight o'clock on a Friday evening* and '*what do you mean you had a web image search done?*. What kind of resources does this woman have at her disposal?

"That's what the FBI and I will be talking about this morning," Lucy said. "What I need from you is a high-res jpeg of that Fantin-Latour painting. Given when my mother died and when the painting showed up on the website, we're right in the middle of the sweet spot when the painting might be at that gallery – assuming it went through the same channel."

"I can't thank you enough," Lucy added.

"I can tell you exactly how you can thank me," Samantha said. "You have a lot of people with a lot of resources. I need two things done today, and I bet you can do it." Samantha described what she needed.

"It won't be easy, but it won't be impossible," Lucy said. "I'll be in touch. In the meantime, please stay away from the Cavendish Woods gallery lady. I don't want to spook her in any way."

As that call ended, Samantha heard the call waiting tone on her phone. It was Jean.

"There's a beautiful painting in the gallery workroom," Jean said. "It looks as though someone is about to make a copy of it."

*Which will mean another dead body*, Samantha thought. "Send me all the photos," is what Samantha said. "And don't go back into that studio. We don't want to tip off Jillian Connolly in any way."

38.

Jillian Connolly tapped in the alarm code to enter The Cavendish Collection. It was two minutes after eight and, as was her routine, she checked the "last access" tab on the touch screen and saw that the cleaning crew had been in at one o'clock that morning and had reset the alarms at one-thirty. She glanced around the gallery and saw that, as usual, the crew had done only a cursory dusting. Connolly sighed and made a mental note that she would need to do a proper cleaning herself later this morning before the gallery opened at noon.

She then tapped the alarm code to enter her workroom at the back of the gallery and, also as was her routine, she checked the entry log to make certain that no one had been in her workroom since she left yesterday at five o'clock.

She froze in her steps when she saw that there was an entry immediately after the main gallery had been accessed, and that the codes had been reset fifteen minutes later. She went back and re-checked the exit log for the main gallery. The time stamp was fifteen minutes later than the exit from the workroom.

Someone with knowledge of the access codes had been in her private studio.

She went back to the workroom and examined everything in it carefully. Nothing was out of place; nothing appeared even to have been touched. There was a negligible chance that the cleaning crew had come in just to look around.

But not for fifteen minutes. You did not spend fifteen minutes to just look around.

She now looked at the contents of her studio from the perspective of someone trying to gain information. The possibilities were terrifying.

There was, of course, the final study for *West Point – Prout's Neck* on the easel. By itself, it meant nothing. But all around it, covering every work surface, were her annotated photographs and notes. Particularly damning were the details of the painting's obverse – the gallery mark, the ancient gouge in the canvas backing, and the pencil note made sometime in the preceding century.

These were the things that only the painting's owner would ever have seen, and it was possible that the owner had never taken any note of them. But they were the necessary details that needed to be copied exactly in the event that the owner was observant.

The most damning evidence was the draft artwork for the sales receipt conveying the painting from a New York gallery to Mr. William Hunter of Boston. Connolly had made multiple notes on the artwork; thoughts to herself on typefaces and word choices.

The painting's owner was a haughty woman in her late seventies who told Connolly she had inherited the painting upon her parents' death thirty years earlier. Connolly's own research showed that the painting passed from Winslow Homer's estate to that of his brother and, in June 1938, to the Macbeth Gallery in New York. It was one of three Homers – the other two were watercolors – purchased by the current owner's parents.

It was one of the cleanest provenances Connolly had ever seen. A digitized copy of Winslow Homer's will was freely available through Bowdoin College as were inventories of Charles Savage Homer's paintings from 1911 and 1919 showing "unsigned late study for sunset at West Point" as being in the brother's possession. The Archives of American Art had thoughtfully posted online a copy of the works conveyed to the Macbeth Gallery by Charles Savage Homer's estate.

Only the sales receipt to a buyer other than the woman's parents (the fictitious William Hunter) needed to be produced – not that a buyer in China would give a damn about such things. Still, Connolly prided herself on her thoroughness and attention to detail.

She went back over the workroom surfaces. There were sticky notes surrounding her computer screen and one of them was a reminder to call her contact at the Hao Ming Gallery.

*Careless*, she thought. Gradually, though, her mind turned to who would have done this and why. She wrote down a list of names, but only the one at the top of the page made any sense. She circled it, and then circled it again.

*Alice Beauchamp.* She had entered Cavendish Woods just two weeks earlier and had been in Connolly's class the very next day. A casual conversation with a friend on the admissions staff provided the information that Beauchamp was here on a thirty-day "get acquainted" stay, and a quick look at her apartment had shown she had brought no artwork with her.

At the time, Connolly had dismissed Beauchamp as a nuisance; the kind of idiot savant that interrupted the flow of her lectures with off-topic questions or to volunteer information gleaned from a cursory reading of a Wikipedia entry.

Now, it was clear that this was an act. Beauchamp had immediately gravitated to Gwendolyn Durham, a notorious gossip and close friend of Cecelia Davis. Beauchamp apparently fancied herself some kind of Jane Marple, out to investigate the death of her friend.

The question was how Beauchamp had befriended the cleaning staff and convinced them to allow her into the gallery when they cleaned. There should be video footage; she knew the security staff well.

\* \* \* \* \*

Connolly scrolled back the video feed a third time. It didn't make sense.

Two women approached the gallery door together. They both had cleaning carts. They both sported the same, dark blue uniform worn by workers of the company that provided janitorial services to Cavendish Woods. They both had security badges dangling from lanyards around their necks. Neither one was Alice Beauchamp.

The taller of the two punched in the codes and pushed in her cart. The shorter woman followed, leaving her cart in the esplanade.

What followed was less distinct because the security camera

recording the event was thirty feet away with The Cavendish Collection's plate glass windows intervening. Through the glass, though, Connolly could make out the taller woman apparently entering the codes for her workroom. The shorter woman went inside the workroom and turned on the lights; the taller woman did some desultory dusting and wiping in the gallery.

The lights in the workroom were turned off after fifteen minutes, and the shorter woman spoke with the taller woman for a few seconds. Then, the shorter woman left the gallery, retrieved her cart, and began pushing it toward the meeting room complex.

Connolly called over her friend on the security staff. "Can you identify these two women?"

The man shook his head. "They're outside contractors." He tapped the screen, indicating the taller one. "She's been here for a couple of years. I think she's the crew chief. I've never seen the other one, but she has the right badge. You'll have to talk to the night crew to find out when she started."

"How do I find out who she is?" Connolly asked.

The security staff member cocked his head. "Did she take something from the gallery? Do you want me to call the police?"

"No," Connolly said quickly. "It's just that she…" She paused, not wanting to plant ideas in anyone's mind that might later prove inconvenient. "…she looks familiar. I think I know her from somewhere."

"Well," the security staff member said, "start with the night shift." Assuming the discussion was at an end, the staffer tapped keys to return to a real-time view.

Connolly returned to her workroom, deeply disturbed by what she had seen. Someone had talked – or bribed – their way onto the cleaning detail. Last night, that person had been let into the gallery and then gone directly to this room.

The object was not theft. The person had not even looked at the items in the gallery (which, in any event, were on pressure pads and would cause alarms to sound if they were moved). The object was *discovery*.

The "cleaning lady" had discovered that the Homer was in the process of being copied. The question was whether the person was acting in concert with Beauchamp. Connolly realized that she could have potentially answered that question by asking to follow the woman on other security cameras, but her lame excuse of thinking she knew the person precluded such a request.

On a Saturday morning, only a skeleton office staff would be on duty. It was possible Connolly could casually request the name of the contract cleaning service and a phone number for its crew chief. She could then call the crew chief on the pretext of reminding her that only certain cleaning products should be used in the gallery, and then work in an "oh, by the way…" and ask if someone had been in her workroom.

It would be a delicate negotiation, but the knowledge that someone had seen her preparatory work for copying the Homer was potentially devastating.

She locked her workroom and gallery and began walking down the esplanade toward the administrative office. She was deeply in thought, rehearsing the plausible reason she would give for needing the crew chief's contact information, and it was only by chance that she glanced into the coffee shop.

There, in a corner but clearly visible, was Alice Beauchamp. And sitting across the table from her was the cleaning lady.

The two were engrossed in a conspiratorial conversation that required both of them to lean across the table. Connolly was certain she had not been seen, and she immediately turned away from the tableau. She retreated a few steps and stood, admiring the poster for the next film at the Cavendish Cinema.

She had her answer. The cleaning lady – whoever she was – had broken into her workroom at the behest of Beauchamp. Unless, of course, the cleaning lady, who appeared to be a decade younger than Beauchamp, was the true sleuth and Beauchamp was her agent.

But now Connolly knew there were two. It took no special leap of faith to conclude that the two women had deduced that Connolly had also reproduced Cecelia Davis' Fantin-Latour. *How* they knew was an interesting question but not one that was germane to finding a solution to the immediate problem.

Connolly's mind went to work on the problem and its solution. The first requirement was to clear her workroom of incriminating evidence.

The second step would be to pay a visit to her neighbor's greenhouse.

39.

Samantha drove past Paula's house at a leisurely twenty miles an hour. With the passenger seat partially reclined, Paula could just see out the windshield.

In a neighborhood in which no one parked on the street and even cars in driveways were unusual sights, the black Jeep stood out. It had a thin coating of snow except for the hood over the running engine. It was not parked in front of Paula's house. Rather, it was two houses down and across the street. The driver's window was cracked open two inches, and the occupant of the car had wiped a six-inch-wide circle in the window through which to peer.

"That's two out of four," Samantha said. "You and Alice. Except that they can wait outside Alice's condo from now until the cows come home, and it isn't going to do them any good."

"Does that mean you have a plan?" Paula asked, raising the seat upright.

"It means now I can *make* a plan," Samantha replied.

\* \* \* \* \*

Jane Cronin tapped at the door where Eleanor was curled up in a large upholstered chair in her husband's room.

"I heard you came here last night," Jane said. "Would you like to come down and join us for breakfast?"

Eleanor looked over at her husband's still form. "I look a mess," she said.

"It's Saturday morning, and we make allowances for that," Jane said. "I'll meet you down in the cafeteria in ten minutes."

Ten minutes later, Eleanor was explaining Paula's middle-of-the-night call to find somewhere to stay. Over breakfast, she found herself telling Jane the story of her undercover work at Pokrovsky Motors, though not her earlier adventures at the Brookfield Fair.

"And it wasn't even any fun being a Registry runner," Eleanor concluded. "The pay was lousy, and the folks at the RMV are really some alien pod people. They have no sense of humor."

Jane listened with fascination. "And this thing with pretending to sign up with the 'asset protection through instant poverty' – that's all part of determining if a member of your garden club was murdered."

Eleanor nodded. "I guess, when you put it that way, it sounds like I lead a fascinating life. Don't be fooled."

"Two elderly women have died because someone wanted their paintings," Jane said, as much to herself as to Eleanor.

"That about sums it up," Eleanor said. "I'm hiding until the coast is clear."

"You can stay here as long as you need to," Jane said, "and we can find you a better accommodation than that chair."

Eleanor shook her head. "I don't know how many more nights I'm going to be able to hear the sound of Phil's breathing. The chair is fine. Being in the same room is important."

"Then how about a cot?" Jane asked. "I can have one put in Phil's room today. What I don't understand is why you aren't with your friends right now. They may well need an extra set of hands."

Eleanor considered the question. "Apart from the fact that I don't know where they are, you're absolutely right. I just followed orders." In her mind, though, she thought back to an evening in August when she helped "bury" a very bad man who had been sent to kill Alice and who, given the opportunity, would have killed any one of them.

"Then why are you sitting here?" The question snapped Eleanor out of her reverie.

"You're right," Eleanor said. "If Smilin' Al is looking for us, we ought to be ahead of him, not reacting."

"Tell you what," Jane said. "I'll put a cot in Phil's room. If you can't go home, you come back here tonight. This will be your safe house."

Eleanor finished a plate of eggs and a blueberry muffin and gave Jane a long hug of thanks. Back in her husband's room, she made herself as presentable as she could under the circumstances. She leaned over Phil's bed and kissed his cheek.

"It won't be long, my love," she whispered.

40.

Mike McDonough could not help but smile as he put down the phone. He had figured it might take a hundred calls. It took only eleven. Tennille Beauchamp of Cherry Creek, Colorado – a woman whose antipathy toward her mother-in-law smoldered in every sentence – was only too glad to provide the information that Alice Beauchamp of Hardington, Massachusetts, had taken up temporary residence at a nursing home in nearby Cavendish.

She also said she hoped that every floorboard in that townhouse condo she was so smugly proud of was being warped by the water from the toilet that had been overflowing for two days.

"When you next speak with her, tell her she really should have given the management office an emergency phone number and let us know she was going to have been gone so long," McDonough said. "We could have checked her unit every day."

"If I don't talk to her for the rest of her life, that's fine by me," Ms. Beauchamp said. "You tell her."

*Families*, McDonough thought.

So, he finally had the second woman. Two of his men were babysitting houses, although one could now be pulled off and put on photo duty, showing the flattering shot of the Registry runner around shops in town. The fourth one – who worked as part of the cleaning crew – was turning into a dead end. Yes, the company responsible for the Reading dealership had taken on a fifth cleaning crew member at the request of the Mass Casualty investigator, but the woman had been functionally invisible among the Portuguese-speaking full-timers. She said nothing but also asked nothing and pulled her weight. All anyone could say was that she was short – not more than five feet tall.

Pulling Alice Beauchamp out of a nursing home shouldn't be too hard. The old people were usually in wheelchairs and some were confined to beds. But the Beauchamp woman had worked in the accounting department, and she certainly wasn't in a wheelchair. So, this must be one of those assisted-living kinds of places. There would be attendants or nurses, but there were always side doors.

His plan was to reconnoiter the nursing home to determine how many men he needed and whether it could accomplished without attracting attention.

\* \* \* \* \*

An hour later, McDonough drove through the entrance of Cavendish Woods. He noted the statue of Athena, the globe, and the carefully trimmed, though snow-covered, shrubs. He passed the villas. *This is your high-class nursing home*, he thought.

Finally, he came to a large building labeled "The Lodge" and marked with a sign that said "Reception". He parked, walked in, and found a circular desk staffed by a cheerful young woman. Apparently, no one in this place wore a nurse's uniform.

"I'm looking for my aunt," McDonough said. "Where would I find Alice Beauchamp?"

The young woman tapped a computer screen. "Room 417," she said.

"Is that one of those little buildings I passed?" McDonough asked.

The young woman smiled. "Those are The Cottages," she said. "Your aunt is in The Overlook." She pointed to a corridor lined with restaurants and shops. "Go down The Esplanade to the elevators on the right."

McDonough did so, but did not go up the elevator. Instead, he retraced his steps to one stairwell, then went past the elevator to find a second set of stairs. A short corridor by one of the sets of stairs led to a door that went onto a long outdoor plaza. There were no steps down from the plaza to the ground, some twenty feet below.

By law, though, he knew there had to be exits that led directly outdoors. He went back outside, keeping his face away from the reception desk.

What the nursing home called "The Overlook" was a long,

multi-angular five-story building. There were three fire doors, each marked, "ALARM WILL SOUND." In a place like this, the alarms would certainly work.

McDonough went back inside and again faced the young receptionist. "I was wondering if it's OK to take my aunt out to lunch," he asked.

"Of course you can, but we have five restaurants," the receptionist responded. "What kind of food are you looking for?"

"Swedish," McDonough said.

"That's tough," the receptionist said. "But then I don't know of any Swedish restaurants around here, either."

"I'll ask her when I see her," McDonough said. "Room 417?"

"Room 417," the receptionist affirmed.

As he suspected, the elevator opened onto a nurses' station. Oddly, it was tucked into an alcove as to make it unobtrusive. He also noted that the corridor turned just thirty feet down either direction. The nurses could see very little. The most satisfying thing he discovered, though, was that there were no security cameras. He had spotted at least a dozen on the ground floor.

The nurses did not challenge him; only made mental note that he was there. He saw a sign indicating Rooms 401 to 420 were to the right. He nodded to the nurses and turned right.

McDonough paused by 417 but made no effort to try the door. Instead, he went down the stairwell that was thirty feet past the room. As he suspected, the stairwell's principal exit was to the first floor corridor. The stairs went down one more floor to a basement level where one door was locked and a second was marked as an alarmed fire door. Turning around to go upstairs, he also saw a security camera pointed at the two doors.

As he exited the stairwell door into The Esplanade, he found two men waiting for him. They wore security guard uniforms. McDonough sized them up: they were not your standard "mall cops". They were athletic looking and had intelligent faces.

"You appear to have had a problem finding Mrs. Beauchamp,"

one of them said.

"She wasn't home," McDonough said. "I like taking the stairs."

"We've been observing you for the past fifteen minutes," the other security guard said. "You appear to be taking quite an interest in our stairwells and the placement of our security cameras."

"It's a hobby," McDonough said.

"We've posted your photo at the reception desk and in the security office," the first guard said. "The next time you enter the building, we will notify the Cavendish Police. May we escort you out of the building?"

McDonough said nothing. He turned toward the lobby and began walking.

*Not quite as easy as I first imagined*, McDonough thought as he walked. *Cavendish Woods isn't a high-class nursing home. It's a high-class prison with one way in and one way out.*

41.

The call from Lucy McClellan came at one o'clock. Samantha saw the caller ID and answered immediately.

"The building you're looking for is in the Myles Standish Industrial Park in Norton," Lucy said. "The sign out front says 'Wellfleet Candle Company' and it's on John Quincy Adams Road."

"How did you find it so fast?" Samantha asked.

"Big data," Lucy replied. "It's fascinating what you can find when you know what you're looking for."

"Do I want to know if this is legal?"

"Go ask the NSA," Lucy said. "It's all a gray area. Companies collect data on everyone who uses a computer every day. Google and Yahoo scan your email for key words. They're looking for things they can sell you. Facebook does the same with everything you post. We lay our lives bare. The one thing I can say with complete honesty is that at no point did I use my employer's data set; that would be unethical. This all came from third parties and, if you looked long enough, you could have found this on your own. Of course, it helps speed up the process when you know people in the industry."

"What do you mean, 'this all'?" Samantha said.

"You're going to need more than an address," Lucy replied. "That building has two levels of security. But security is only as good as the humans who set it up, and the geniuses who monitor the building put the codes on a server, probably so their own people wouldn't have to flip through sheets of paper. God, I love stupid people. I'm texting you the codes now."

Samantha's phone buzzed. She looked at the screen and saw a listing of alarm codes and even instructions on the sequence in which they were to be used.

"What about the invitations?" Samantha asked.

"I have the names and the email addresses," Lucy said. "They all go out at seven tomorrow morning your time. The invitation will say the party starts at nine."

"Do you think anyone will show up early?"

"If I got that message, I'd drive like a bat out of hell to get there as soon as possible," Lucy said. "If I remember my Boston geography correctly, you've got one guy in Cohasset and another in Duxbury. They could be there half an hour after they get the message."

"What else do I need to know?" Samantha asked.

"I have the full paper trail on the building lease," Lucy said. "It's convoluted, but it's all there. I'll email that to you when we get off the phone. I'll be out of pocket for a few hours working on Jillian Connolly. The FBI out here has a different view of working on Saturdays than the high tech industry. I'm trying to make someone's career, and they're asking why it can't hold until Monday. Go figure."

"But I'm supposed to stay away from her," Samantha confirmed.

"Just pretend she doesn't exist until I say otherwise," Lucy replied. "Besides, your plate seems pretty full already."

"Very full," Samantha agreed.

The call ended, and Samantha shook her head. She had twenty hours to pull off the biggest operation of her life. Four people's lives were at stake – five including her own.

It was time to get started.

"Paula, are you willing to be kidnapped?"

\* \* \* \* \*

It took an hour to assemble everyone at Jean's home. A drive by her house showed no cars on the street, and the one that had been near Alice's condo had disappeared, which Samantha took as an ominous sign.

Samantha first told the four women about Paula's and her flight to San Francisco and the revelation that Jillian Connelly was either the person who murdered Cecelia Davis or was at least complicit in the crime.

"As much as I want to, we don't do anything about Connolly until after we deal with Al Pokrovsky, Senior," she said. "He is a danger to us all, so listen carefully."

"We're going to make a lot of guesses," Samantha continued. "If any of them are wrong, we could be in a world of trouble. Muriel Pokrovsky told me there may be three or four of them, and we can't deal with that many. The one we know about is out in front of Paula's house. He's the one we can take by surprise. Paula goes up her driveway. That will make the guy in the car out on the street call his boss – this McDonough character. McDonough will call the other bad guy or guys and tell them to come to Paula's house. But as soon as the guy in front of the house calls McDonough, we disable him..."

Eleanor looked at the diagram Samantha had sketched. "Where are we hiding? That's five acres of lawns and bare trees with an inch of snow on top of everything. Tell me where we're hiding. And then, while we're "disabling" this guy, tell me why he isn't hitting re-dial and telling McDonough it's a trap."

Samantha started to speak, but then looked at her own diagram.

"It's no good," she said in a low voice. "You're right. This would work on a city street or even some densely packed suburb. But in Paula's part of town we'd be completely exposed."

Samantha ripped up the sheet, defeat showing on her face.

Alice asked, "Is your goal to use one of us as kidnap bait to get Smilin' Al to call you and demand you bring him everything you have on him? And then to spring some kind of trap on him, instead?"

"That's oversimplifying things, but yes," Samantha replied. "I wanted him to think that he had won, then pull the rug out from underneath him."

"Then, why are we going through this kidnapping charade?" Alice asked. "You call him directly..."

"Tell him 'you win'," Jean interjected. "Cut out the middle man."

Eleanor added. "He's on the Cape. His people are up here, at least an hour away. Instead of waiting for one of them to grab one of us, we grab him…"

"And then we…" Paula started to say.

Samantha held up a hand. "Wait a minute. One at a time." Samantha pointed at Eleanor. "You go first…"

\* \* \* \* \*

An hour later, a plan was in place and tools – if a large, black plastic trash bag and two rolls of packaging tape could be called tools – had been assembled.

"Are we ready?" Samantha asked.

Jean raised her hand and said in a low voice, "I have one more thing we ought to talk about…"

Everyone's eyes were on her.

Jean pulled two sheets of paper from a manila envelope. "After I went through Connolly's office last night, I did my regular rounds." She indicated the sheets of paper. "This was in the purchasing manager's wastepaper basket. I think it's important. I'm sorry I don't have copies for everyone." She handed it to Samantha.

Samantha quickly read the sheets and murmured, "How could they…" She looked up at the group. "What Jean has found is an interoffice memo. It has a lengthy legal notice both at the top and the bottom, which I won't bother to read, saying that it is intended only for the recipients. The meat of the memo is that Mandy Ojumbua will be fired Monday morning. He is an 'at will' employee so no reason needs to be given. He will be offered a month's severance and escorted from the premises."

"So. they're not going to do anything," Paula said, her voice shaking. "They're just going to kick the problem down the road; turn a murderer loose. Mandy Ojumbua disappears for a month or so, then reappears at another hospital or nursing home…"

"This isn't our fight," Samantha said. "We know Ojumbua had nothing to do with Cecelia's death. We are up to our collective necks in things to do right now. On Monday, I promise I'll…"

"I'm not up to my neck," Paula said. "You've got the folder

with all the other memos. Give me a few hours, and tell me where to meet you."

"Paula…" Samantha started to say.

"I can't let this go," Paula said. "You know and I know what's going to happen if we don't do anything."

The two women looked at one another for a long moment. Then Samantha nodded. "Martin Hoffman is very smart. He knows people, and those people know other people." She went to one of three boxes and took a thick file folder from the top of one of them. She added the most recent memo to the folder and handed it to Paula.

"Call me when you're done," Samantha said. "I'll let you know where to meet up with us."

Eleanor cleared her throat. "It won't take four of us to deal with Smilin' Al. In fact, four of us would probably get in one another's way. I can join you for the second part of the operation, but I have a sense that Phil is very near the end. With your permission, I want to spend the rest of the day with him."

"You don't need anyone's permission," Samantha said. "I'll call you when we're ready for you."

42.

Paula sat in the parked car outside the entrance to Martin Hoffman's Framingham apartment. Driving here, she realized how tired she was from the events of the past few days. Twenty-four hours earlier she had been on a westbound flight to San Francisco where the uncertainty of what might or might not happen when she met Lucy McClellan weighed on her. A first-class sleeper seat on the return flight had been responsible for perhaps two hours sleep, but adrenaline-fueled elation kept her mind racing through much of the night.

Now, she was committed. She clutched the file folder and got out of the car.

\* \* \* \* \*

Martin hugged her. "You look very tired," he said.

"I *am* very tired," Paula replied.

"Your son is going to be OK? You were only out there a few hours."

"He was afraid," Paula lied. "Perry has still not gotten over the divorce. There's a part of him that thinks he was responsible…" She stopped herself. "He needed to see me. He needed to know that I would come. I got there and found a room full of his friends." She shrugged. "There was no reason to stay."

"You said you have something very important to show me…" Martin started to say.

"I don't know who to turn to," Paula said. "I'm making something your business. I have no right to do that."

"Why don't you let me decide?" Martin asked.

Paula nodded. She sat down on the sofa in Martin's living room. He sat next to her, and she took his hand.

"Two and a half weeks ago," she began, "I took a job as a night nurse. You asked me why, and I said something about needing to 'give something back' because the people who provided my care had been so good to me. That was partly true, and you were kind enough not to press me on details."

"I had another reason," Paula continued. "You know that I went to a wake for an old friend from the garden club – Cecelia Davis. When I was at that wake, her granddaughter approached me and said that she suspected Cecelia's death hadn't been of natural causes."

"Why did she approach you?" Martin asked.

"I'm not sure. I never asked," Paula replied. "Maybe she asked a lot of people. But I said I'd help. And so I applied for the nursing position. And because the overnight shift at a nursing home is such a do-nothing job, it gave me ample time to poke around. One of the things I did was to look through wastebaskets…"

"You looked through the trash because you thought you might find clues to a patient's death?" Martin asked.

"I was looking in a lot of places, including at patient files on the computer system. I was also talking to residents and to other nurses," Paula snapped back. "I'm not a detective. I just started looking. And I found something."

"You found your friend's killer?"

Paula shook her head. "I found something worse. I found a nurse named Mandy Ojumbua. He works in what is called the 'skilled nursing' facility, meaning he takes care of patients who are either in for short rehabilitation stints or who are permanently confined to a bed. I saw that six patients had, like Cecelia, died of heart attacks over the previous year. Four of them were in the skilled nursing facility. Three of them had no apparent history of coronary disease."

"And then I found these." Paula opened the folder and spread out the memos. "Cavendish Woods' administrative staff also thought something didn't seem right. They drew blood samples from the last two residents who died and found elevated potassium chloride levels. They also found multiple incidents in which Mandy Ojumbua had 'saved' patients who went into cardiac arrest."

She pulled out several pages from the folder. "Cavendish Woods contacted the nurse's previous employers. The responses came back like letters from lawyers. Apparently they all had suspicions, and they all did nothing. They let Ojumbua go, and they hoped he'd stop. Then, they built legal barriers around themselves. Cavendish Woods tightened up access to drugs and made certain Ojumbua had no access without someone else present."

"I thought all of this was in preparation for calling in the police to have him arrested," Paula continued. "Instead, I found this one last memo." She handed it to Martin, who read it carefully.

"They're more afraid of lawsuits than they are of turning a killer loose on the next hospital," Martin said.

Paula nodded. "Exactly. And, on Monday morning, he will walk out of the nursing home, and he'll disappear for a few weeks or a few months. Until he applies for a new job in a new city."

Marin looked again at the memo. "Who is Christine Jortberg? These memos all seem to be addressed to her."

"She's the purchasing and supplies manager at Cavendish Woods," Paula said. "I've never even met her. She's one of those people who prints out everything instead of reading it on a computer screen. After she reads it, she throws it away."

"By the way," Martin asked. "Were you at Cavendish Woods today?"

"No," Paula said. "They're not expecting me until Monday evening. Why do you ask?"

"Just wondering," Martin replied. "I thought you might know if Ojumbua is on duty today or tomorrow."

"I know the answer to that one," Paula said. "He is working Sunday from eight to five."

Martin read through several of the memos, including ones from other hospitals and nursing homes. "I see why you came to me," he said.

"I can't let this happen again," Paula said. "And, I know if I walk into the Cavendish Police Department…"

"They'll sit on it and discuss it for three days, and then mail it off to the state police," Martin said, nodding. "Giving Mandy Ojumbua time to disappear." He flipped through the pages again. "This is a Barracks H issue. They've got a couple of intelligent homicide people there."

"Do you have to use my name?" Paula asked.

Martin paused to consider his answer, and to reflect on why Paula would not want credit for such a thing. "If this came in over a tip line, it would have to be taken seriously; it just wouldn't happen as quickly. The only name that consistently appears on these memos is Christine Jortberg. When I take it to Barracks H, I just say the source is anonymous. If they jump to the conclusion that Ms. Jortberg is the whistle-blower, so be it. But I have to ask: why not let them know it's you?"

"Because I have no desire to have a TV news crew camped out in my driveway," Paula said. "This isn't about me or about who deserves credit. What I don't want is to learn on Monday that Cavendish Woods' management succeeded in burying its problem. If Ojumbua was caught at his next job, the people here could just say they were shocked that such a thing had happened. Now, they're going to have to deal with liability."

"Then I guess it's their tough luck," Martin said. "Film at eleven."

"You're going now?" Paula asked.

"I know the guy who is on duty weekends," Martin said. "And this will take some time to explain."

"Do you mind if I stay here for a few hours?" Paula asked. "I am bone-weary tired, and I don't want to drive out in this mess just yet."

The request caught Martin by surprise, and he was uncertain if there was some deeper meaning. "I'll likely be at least two hours," he said. "Maybe three. We can get some dinner when I get back if you like."

She kissed him. "Thank you. I'll probably be gone, but the offer is wonderful."

When Martin left, Paula set her phone to make maximum noise in two hours. She found a blanket and lay down on the sofa. In minutes, she was sound asleep.

\* \* \* \* \*

As Martin cleared the snow off the windshield of his car, he tried to piece together why Paula was telling him only part of the truth. While her story had a surface plausibility, it did not stand up to closer inspection. If she were working as a nurse, how could she have spent hours going through wastebaskets, and what did she expect to find in wastebaskets if she was investigating the death a month earlier of a nursing home resident? How did she have hours to talk to residents and other staff members?

The lone certainty that there was more to what she was saying was the final memo. It had been sent to Christine Jortberg at 4:37 p.m. on Friday. At that moment in time, Paula was in an airplane en route to the west coast. Paula could only have possession of the document if she were at Cavendish Woods this morning, or if someone else found it last night and gave it to her today. If someone else was helping her, why would she lie about it?

The sudden trip to San Francisco was its own mystery. He had no doubt but that she had taken the trip. But why had she stayed just a few hours if she did not need to be back at work for two days? Had she even, in fact, gone out to see her son or was there another purpose to the trip?

He knew this much. Complete trust – the kind that allowed you to tell another person the absolute truth even if it would cause pain – was something that was built over years. It could not be demanded in a relationship that had existed for only a few months.

He knew all too well that they both came with what people nowadays called "baggage". Part of his was the inability to let go of the memory of a wife now dead nearly five years. Hers must inevitably include the deception of a cheating husband and, perhaps, her bout with cancer.

He put the thoughts out of his mind and concentrated on the slush-covered roadway. He loved this woman. Fortunately, the Framingham barracks were just four miles away down a major road. This was turning into one of those rain-snow-sleet mixtures that were just plain nasty.

43.

Carefully wearing latex gloves, Jillian Connolly cut two dozen leaves of the blue-flowering *aconitum* in the greenhouse of her next-door neighbors. The neighbors, away in South Carolina from Thanksgiving until the end of April, did not care what Connolly grew in the greenhouse; only that the cherished houseplants and tender orchids were watered and fertilized according to the schedule on the building's door, and that any temperature alarms were promptly attended to.

Connolly, in turn, had potted the plant, commonly called monkshood for the distinctive shape of its flowers that grew in her own small yard. In September, she had placed it in an inconspicuous corner of the greenhouse where it would not be noticed when the neighbors made one of their periodic two- or three-day trips back home to meddle in the lives of their adult children.

Back in her own kitchen and still wearing gloves, Connolly cut the leaves into tiny pieces, which she then placed into a saucepan together with a pint of water. She placed the saucepan on her range, set the flame to "low" and a timer for fifteen minutes.

She remembered the first time – three years earlier – she had offered a cup of her "herbal tea". The recipient was Mary Ann Klempa, who had brought a yellowed, but brilliantly executed Constable landscape with her to Cavendish Woods. It had, she said offhandedly, been in her family for generations. Klempa knew nothing about art and did not care to learn. She had sought out Connolly only because the painting seemed "dirty", and she had read somewhere that a conventional kitchen cleaner could damage oil paints.

Connolly had spent a month removing shellac, dirt and soot from the canvas. When Klempa saw the result she was astonished. The old woman offered Connolly fifty dollars for her efforts and announced she was going to put the painting up for auction. She did so the next day, consigning it to Skinner in Boston, where it sold a few months later for more than a hundred thousand dollars.

Connolly had been so taken aback by the proffered fifty dollar bill that she could not respond. Inside her, though, a fury grew into a malignant hatred of a cheapskate woman. The fury begat a need for revenge which ended in a thermos of herbal tea laden with aconite.

Klempa had nodded approvingly of the tea, but said it would be better with just a hint of sweetening. In two hours, Klempa was dead of cardiac arrest.

It was revenge, but not a satisfying one. Klempa's children had the proceeds of the sale of the Constable. Connolly had only a fifty dollar bill taped to her refrigerator as a reminder that humanity was essentially rotten to the core.

She developed a plan and set out to execute it. Where she had previously stayed aloof from the residents, Connolly began an assiduous cultivation of them. Her classes grew from three or four attendees to a dozen or more, and she made a point of welcoming new residents individually. With each month her knowledge of the art holdings of Cavendish Woods residents increased. Many had disbursed paintings to children and grandchildren before downsizing to an apartment or villa, but a sizeable number kept superb pieces in their residences.

Connolly identified some of these as reproductions or outright forgeries. The owners of those works were struck from Connolly's list. Her goal was one painting per year. She would befriend its owner, talk the individual into displaying the work as part of a show, and then make a copy that would pass all but a museum's scrutiny.

Nine months after her brush with Mary Ann Klempa, Connolly heard of a small Matisse in the possession of Ruby and Donald Broderick. It was from the 1940s and hardly a major work. Moreover, it was not in the Matisse *catalogue raisonné*, yet it was undeniably by that artist.

In two months, Connolly had acquired a canvas of the proper

size and vintage and assembled paints appropriate to the era. In another month, while the original painting hung as part of a group display, Connolly had executed a brilliant copy. One night, the new painting – aged to appear identical to the original – was slipped into the existing frame and the Matisse went home in Connolly's Volvo.

She had already identified and visited a New York gallery that specialized in sales of Western art to Chinese collectors. On her day off, she drove to New York and asked if the gallery would be interested in representing the painting. They would, of course, provided the painting's chain of ownership – its provenance – was impeccable. Connolly opened her portfolio and produced five documents attesting to the painting's passage through galleries to its present owners, the squabbling children of the late Marion Kimball of Essex, Massachusetts.

The owner of the Hao Ming Gallery studied the painting for two hours, and Connolly paid careful attention to how the gallery owner authenticated the work. Just as important as the painting were the gallery stamps and minor detritus that had attached itself to the back side of the painting through the years.

The painting was accepted; the gallery's commission would be twenty percent. It was possible, Connolly was told, that the owner knew of a collector with a keen interest in Matisse's work from that era.

The commission was far steeper than would have been paid to an auction house, but a swift sale was promised, and Connolly had made clear that the heirs of Marion Kimball prized liquidity and, if possible, cash.

The sale went through in three weeks. Three days later, Connolly and Ruby Broderick enjoyed a cup of tea in the Broderick's villa. That evening, Mrs. Broderick went into cardiac arrest. Donald Broderick, devoted to his wife of more than half a century, died a month later. The Matisse, which still hung as part of the gallery show, was collected by the Broderick's daughters. They had, they said, no intention of selling their parents' wonderful painting. It would go to the Museum of Fine Arts.

Less than a month later, Connolly heard through other Cavendish Woods residents than the painting had been turned down for auction by Christies, which called it a "very good" copy.

Connolly, in turn, collected $385,000 in cash from the gallery, with an invitation to bring more works. Apart from taking five months to deposit the money in a dozen accounts, Connolly had found her system, and set her sights higher.

A year later, Connolly sold a Paul Signac pointillist work and collected $627,000. Colleen Stanton, a widow in her mid-nineties who had already endured open-heart surgery, suffered cardiac arrest two days after Connolly brought home a Louis Vuitton suitcase filled with hundred dollar bills.

Her next target was Margaret 'Peg' McClellan, a wealthy Boston woman who owned a fabulous Canaletto. McClellan took great pride that the bulk of the works that she and her husband had purchased through estate sales were already in the possession of the Museum of Fine Arts. Though it, too, was promised to the museum, the Canaletto was the one piece they held back, a reminder of their palatial Chestnut Hill home.

The Canaletto was her hardest forgery. Third-rate Italian paintings of that era were scarce commodities, and Connolly had substituted a mid-nineteenth-century canvas; something that would not fool an expert for a moment. When the MFA's art experts received the painting, they were going to be in for a major surprise.

McClellan's husband and daughter died while Connolly worked on the painting. It did not, however, stop Connolly from handing the original over to the Hao Ming Gallery or from collecting her first million-dollar payoff. When she returned the copy, Connolly found the woman in a profound state of depression. Giving her the cup of tea seemed almost like a mercy killing.

Connolly had not expected to find another quality painting so quickly. Cecelia Davis had sat through her art history seminars for two years without ever once mentioning that she had a beautiful

Fantin-Latour in her bedroom. When Davis first made reference to the painting, it was in connection with her husband's failing health and how he cherished waking up to see *White Roses* every morning.

Connolly had to slip into Davis's apartment to see the painting and, when she did, she was stunned by its quality. She immediately knew she had her second, million-dollar score.

The death of Cecelia Davis's husband sent the woman into the same kind of depression that Connolly had seen in Peg McClellan but, surprisingly, Davis snapped out of her condition. She became active in more groups and made it known that she was seriously considering leaving Cavendish Woods to live more independently.

Connolly could not bear to lose the painting. She talked Davis into allowing her to clean the Fantin-Latour in exchange for displaying it for a few days in the gallery. Connolly worked four days virtually non-stop and, in the end, produced a copy indistinguishable from the original.

With the original in New York and prospective buyers being shown the painting, Connolly decided that it was time for Davis to take tea. The two met in one of the Cavendish Woods restaurants for dinner. Davis thanked Connolly profusely for cleaning the painting and offered a check for five thousand dollars. Connolly declined, humbly saying that working so close to a top-of-his-form Fantin-Latour was reward enough.

Davis drank the tea that Connolly touted as her own chamomile recipe. Three hours later, Cecelia Davis suffered a heart attack while watching television.

It all seemed so easy; so straightforward. Less than three weeks after she turned *White Roses* over to the gallery, a new Cavendish Woods resident, Elissa Franco, aged 82, sought Connolly out to look at the art in her villa. Connolly's eye had immediately gone to the Winslow Homer study. She knew the finished work was one of the Clark Art Institute's most prized paintings, a cachet that would add several hundred thousand dollars to the painting's value.

Copying and selling the Homer would have been the capstone of her career. A third million-dollar payday would have given her enough money to quit. She could travel and paint. She could buy into an established gallery or open one of her own.

Connolly reminded herself she could also have done those things after the sale of *White Roses*. She pushed the thought out of her mind.

Now, there was Alice Beauchamp to deal with, as well as a short woman posing as a member of the cleaning staff. For the first time, someone appeared to have both taken an interest in the frail, forgotten owners of these beautiful paintings and deduced Connolly's role in their deaths.

Perhaps it was just the two of them. Perhaps there were others. It was no matter. Connolly would track them down and silence them.

Connolly looked at her phone and noted the time: just after four o'clock. She checked her messages and mail. Oddly, there were none from the gallery. Yes, it was Saturday, but Connolly had established herself as a valuable conduit for master works, and there was a $200,000 commission in the offing.

The silence was worrisome. Looking through paperwork in her tiny home office, Connolly found a slip of paper with the gallery owner's home phone number. It was a breach of the art world's formal etiquette, but this unexpected delay was worthy of an exception. She tapped in the number; the phone was answered.

"Mr. Li, this is Jillian Connolly calling. Can you tell me…"

"I do not think we should be speaking right now," Li said.

Connolly was dumbfounded. "Is there a problem with…"

"I do not think we should be speaking right now," Li repeated. "Goodbye."

With that, the phone went dead.

Connolly stared at her phone, unable to parse the meaning of the conversation. Li's voice, warm and resonant when he first answered, turned to a careful monotone as soon as she identified herself.

Something was wrong. Horribly wrong.

If Li would not speak to Connolly over the phone, he could not refuse to speak to her in person. A quick check of a weather map showed that the snow ended just south of Providence and that it was only cloudy south to New York.

The same slip of paper also provided Li's home address in Greenwich. Connolly checked the time: she could be there in a little over three hours.

Her plan had been to go to Cavendish Woods this evening. Meeting with Li was more urgent. It made no real difference if Alice Beauchamp died tonight or tomorrow morning. In five minutes, Connolly was in her Volvo and on the road.

44.

At seven o'clock, Martin Hoffman finally felt he had achieved what he came to the state police barracks to accomplish. Detective Frank Shugman "got it". The cocked head, impassive mouth and furrowed brow that had characterized the first hour of their meeting had changed to a series of quick nods as Martin completed the explanation of the sheets of paper he had brought. Most telling of all, Shugman's foot began tapping. This was a man who smelled a high-profile arrest and some lead-the-six-o'clock-news-career-advancing exposure.

"We can't wait until Monday," Shugman said, echoing what Martin had said ninety minutes earlier. "At nine o'clock Monday morning, Ojumbua will be gone, and Cavendish Woods will be cleansing its files."

"I think you're exactly right," Martin said. "Monday morning, the evidence will be evaporating before our eyes."

"If we're going to go in tomorrow morning, I need a judge tonight," Shugman said, looking at his watch. The subtle shift was in the use of the first person. Shugman had signed on. His finger ran down the papers. He tapped on one page.

"Judge Grimes has a mother in a nursing home," Shugman said. "She has groused about 'high-handed management' any number of times. I think she would sign off on this in a heartbeat..."

"You'll need to catch her at home," Martin offered.

"She'll take my call," Shugman replied. "I think she even owes me a favor."

Martin did not want to know what kind of favor a judge could owe a state police homicide detective.

"Two or three computer guys," Shugman said as he wrote. "Figure three or four uniforms to make the arrest and seal the exits if Ojumbua tries to run. And the media relations guy. We need something to feed the stations." Shugman's pen was moving furiously across a pad of paper.

Shugman paused. "You know, I can't ask you to be there."

Martin nodded. "I know. This is a state bust. I'm not even Cavendish."

"I feel bad about that," Shugman said. "You've handed this to me on a platter."

"The bad guys are going down, Frank. That's what counts."

\* \* \* \* \*

Martin arrived home at a few minutes after eight. Paula was not there; a note thanked him profusely for the use of his couch for a much-needed rest. Her note also, somewhat cryptically, said that she would be "out of pocket" for the rest of the evening. He considered calling her. She would certainly be interested in the outcome of his discussion with Shugman. But he also respected her wish for privacy. This was the time to show sensitivity by giving her the space she needed.

Instead, he opened a Sam Adams and found the Celtics game on NESN.

45.

The telephone in Al Pokrovsky, Senior's Falmouth home rang promptly at ten o'clock. The caller ID gave a '774' area code – a cell phone somewhere in the Boston area. He considered letting the call go to the answering machine but, curious, picked up the phone.

"This is Samantha Ayers. We've never met, but I think you know who I am."

"What do you want?" Pokrovsky said.

"I want to put an end to all this," Samantha said, adding a strong tone of weariness to her voice. "I've got four women hiding out in motels, afraid for their lives."

"And what does that have to do with me?"

"It's your people that are looking for them."

There was a pause on the line. "How do you know that?" Pokrovsky said.

"Because I'm smart," Samantha replied. "And because I'm stupid."

"I'm listening."

"I'm the person who got your son busted," Samantha said. "I told the state police where to be and when. If it hadn't been for me, your son would have been nearly two million dollars richer because my insurance company would have paid his claim. I had four women working undercover for me. I was stupid because I invited them to see the arrest. I know that your son saw them and saw me. And he recognized them – or some of them."

"That's got nothing to do with me," Pokrovsky said.

"Yes, it does, and that's where I'm smart," Samantha said. "Your attorney has deposed everyone in this case except me, and there's a preliminary hearing in ten days. There's only one reason why you haven't had me deposed: because you want those women dead and deposing me would put their names on the record."

"That's my son's problem, not mine."

"That's what I thought at first, Mr. Pokrovsky. I went to see your son, and I tried to blackmail him. I showed him some of the documentation I have on an affair he's having and said if he *didn't* depose me, I'd give those receipts and leases to his wife. Obviously, I have a lot more, but I just wanted to show him enough to get any ideas out of his head. When I left his office, he was scared. But I made a mistake: I told him that if anything happened to my operatives, I would make certain he paid."

Samantha continued. "My guess is that he relayed that conversation to you, and you realized I had shown him my weak spot. That was me at my stupidest. I didn't count on you. Well, I'm telling you now: you win."

"I win what?"

"I have everything that your son threw away into the trash," Samantha said. "I have complete documentation on how he's been underreporting sales and siphoning off funds from the business – things that the IRS would use to shut down the business and put him in jail. I have all the documentation on his moving the cars he was going to torch. I have that complete paper trail. Without it, the state's case falls apart. I also have his own notes on ways he's screwing his employees – withholding commissions, not paying overtime. The kind of things our Attorney General would use as a steppingstone to the governorship."

"And you're going to turn those things over to me?" There was a note of sarcasm in Pokrovsky's voice.

"You get every scrap of paper," Samantha said. "I have all the originals, right here in my hand. You call off your wolf pack. You agree to leave my operatives alone. You get everything, including my assurances that there are no copies and that I will not cooperate with investigators."

"Doesn't the state police have all of this already?" Pokrovsky asked.

"I laid it out for them," Samantha said. "I told them what was going to happen and how your son was going to do it. I told them where to be. But they don't have the documents or even copies of them. They looked at what I showed them but figured they could get the material later."

"And how do I know you'll keep your word?" Pokrovsky asked. "And how do I know you aren't recording this for the police right now?"

"You know I'll keep my word because I've seen that you can track down at least two of my operatives despite their very best efforts to leave no trail. I assume you'll find the other two. And, of course, I know you can easily get to me if it comes to that."

"And, as to a recording," Samantha added, "there isn't one. Nor am I wearing a wire. This is two people agreeing to a business transaction in which one has the upper hand. You get back the reputation of your business. My operatives get to go back to their lives. You won."

Pokrovsky paused. "Tell me again what 'crimes' you think you have evidence of?"

"Your dealerships – excuse me, your son's dealerships – tack a $299 charge onto every sale for 'paperwork'," Samantha said. "One hundred of that disappears into an incentive account. It never makes it onto the books, and your son is the sole signatory on that account. It's under-reported revenue and open-and-shut tax fraud on both the state and federal levels. That's the big one."

Samantha continued. "Your son also has a habit of adding things to window stickers that aren't actually on the cars. I have three dozen examples just from the Reading dealership where he changed engine sizes, added clear coating or undercoating, made standard tires premium tires; that sort of thing. He jacked up the price of the cars by about eight hundred dollars apiece. There's both state and federal law on the subject and once it's know he was doing it at one dealership, they'll start looking at every car sold by a Pokrovsky dealer for the past ten years."

"The eighteen cars that were to be torched supposedly had all kinds of aftermarket goodies on them and, of course, Mass Casualty would have paid full list. I have your son's instructions to fabricate invoices for that aftermarket equipment, about three hundred thousand in all. Do you want to hear the rest?"

"Absolutely," Pokrovsky said.

"Your son routinely declined to pay overtime to hourly employees by a whole book full of subterfuges, and he reneged on commissions by assessing penalties against your sales people or claiming the commission for himself. Anyone who complained was fired. He made lots of notes on things to say about those employees. That's the one the AG will have a field day with, and it will keep your son's photo on the evening news for two of three months while she dribbles out the details."

"That's everything?" Pokrovsky asked.

"That's everything unless you want me to go through these boxes and look for more stuff," Samantha replied. "I can be creative, but it seems like enough to me."

"If I agree to this," Pokrovsky said, "how do we make the handoff?"

"That's easy," Samantha said. "I'm in a car right outside your gate. We can do this right now. I would have hopped the fence and rung your doorbell, but I would have probably set off alarms."

"You're damned right you would have," Pokrovsky said, allowing anger to edge into his voice. He peered out the window but saw nothing. "I need to think this over. Call me back in five minutes." With that, he hung up.

*Jesus Christ*, he thought, his heart racing.

Two things stood out in the conversation. First, Junior was even more stupid that he thought. Illegally pocketing a hundred dollars from every sale was a catastrophe waiting to happen. Now he knew what had been feeding Junior's gambling habit for the past several years.

The additions to the window sticker, though, were something Junior had learned from him, except that *he* had never been dumb enough to throw paperwork in the trash. The Ayers woman was right: whoever investigated this was going to go back ten years – comparing cars on the road with what was claimed on the sticker – and when they found it was going on ten years ago, they'd go back to every car ever sold under the Pokrovsky name.

Cheating sales staff was something new. You needed those people on your side. It was the ultimate sign that his son was a moron.

But the other thing that stood out was what the Ayers woman *hadn't* said. Not a word about parts. Nothing about Norton. He had kept Junior out of that business. And it was a good thing because Junior would doubtlessly have screwed it up as well.

Pokrovsky picked up his cell phone. Mike McDonough answered on the first ring.

"The Ayers woman is down here on the Cape," Pokrovsky said. "In fact, she's right outside the house. She says she had all her papers on us – all originals – and she's willing to turn it over to me because she knows you and your people are sitting on what she calls 'her operatives'. She says they're scared and hiding out. If I call you off, she says everything goes away because she never turned anything over to the state police."

"And you believe her?" McDonough asked.

"I heard the fear," Pokrovsky said. "That was real. And, if she's willing to turn over the originals, it throws a wrench into the state's case. She also told me about some really stupid stuff Junior has learned how to do."

"I'd say take the papers," McDonough said. "We can always do something later. Give them a few days to come out of hiding. One of them is holed up in this high-class nursing home that's so secure it's like a prison."

"How fast can you get down here?" Pokrovsky asked.

"Call it an hour and a half. It's snowing," McDonough said.

"I'll hold her until you get here – by force if she gets antsy. Then you and I go through the papers," Pokrovsky said. "We'll have a nice fire in the fireplace while we decide what to do with her."

"Sounds like a plan," McDonough said.  "I'm on my way."

A few moments later, the house phone rang.

"I'm unlocking that gate, Miss Ayers," Pokrovsky said.  "I'm also putting on a pot of coffee.  You and I have a lot to discuss."

46.

Jillian Connolly pressed down on the accelerator, pushing her Volvo past 75 miles an hour. The Connecticut Turnpike was dry and traffic was sparse. She was angry. No. She was *beyond* angry. She was livid with rage.

She was also more than a little frightened.

Winston Li had met her at the door of his Cos Cob home.

"I fear my telephones are tapped," he said. "You have placed me in an awkward position. We should talk outside."

There was no "hello". There was not even an expression of surprise at seeing her.

They talked in her car, with the engine on and the heater running. His tone was as emotionless as the features on his face. Connolly, usually good at reading people's emotions, was taken aback by the new tone of the man who was her main source of income.

"I have spent several hours on the telephone with the FBI," Li said. "They want to know who purchased the Canaletto and how I came into possession of the painting." He paused and added, "They also made the same requests of the Fantin-Latour."

"What did you tell them?" Connolly asked.

"I asked why they were so interested in those two paintings among the hundreds that I sell each year. The agent said that, for now, it is a routine inquiry, but that it is in my interest to be cooperative."

Connolly tensed up as he spoke.

"I said that I had sold more than one Canaletto this year," Li said. "The agent was not amused. 'A view of St. Mark's with the *campanile* placed on the wrong side of the Piazza San Marco'," the agent said. 'You displayed the painting on your website for two weeks last fall.'"

Li continued. "I told him I remembered the painting and that it has been sold to a Shanghai collector. I further said that the collector was a highly placed member of the Central Committee who would not welcome inquiries from the American government."

"He then asked me how I came into possession of the painting, and I said it was offered to me by a 'finder' who was representing the heirs of the owner. I further said that the painting's provenance appeared to be genuine and that I had verified the provenance insofar as gallery records allowed me to do so."

"Did he ask who the 'finder' was?" Connolly asked.

Li nodded. "He was most insistent. He said if I did not cooperate fully that the FBI would not hesitate to close my gallery."

"And so you gave them my name," Connolly said.

"I was given little choice in the matter," Li said. "I made very clear to the agent that the paintings were represented to me as genuine and that their provenance was impeccable."

"Did he say why he was interested in those two particular paintings?"

"I asked him several times," Li said. "Each time, he said his inquiry was part of a preliminary investigation. He would give me no further details."

Connolly felt the chill in Li's response. She asked, "Did you tell the agent the current status of the Fantin-Latour?"

Li nodded. "I told him the painting has been sold, but that it is still in my possession pending the arrival of funds." Then, he said, "I think this is the last time we will talk, either in person or over the phone, until this issue is resolved."

With that, Li had gotten out of the car and walked back to his house. There had been no formal "goodbye" or wishes for a safe journey back to Boston. Li had distanced himself from her; they would almost certainly never do business again.

Left unsaid was the fate of *White Roses*. When they last spoke ten days ago, Li's excitement had been palpable when said he had three keenly interested buyers, all willing to pay more than a million dollars for the painting.

*Alice Beauchamp is to blame for this,* Connolly thought. *I am going to kill her but, before she dies, she will tell me where to find everyone else who had a hand in this.*

47.

Samantha listened and heard a mechanical "click". A moment later, the ornate steel gate began to open. She noted a green sensor on the inside of the gate. There was definitely an alarm system.

"Everyone ready?" she asked.

From the back seat of Jean's minivan came murmured voices. Jean's stood out. "It's fine. You go inside where it's warm while we get to stay out here in the cold."

"You just keep listening. And you can bet he's called his goon squad," Samantha said. "I'm just praying they're all up in Hardington, but we need to be out of here in an hour, tops."

The driveway was perhaps a hundred feet long and it led to a very large shingle-style house. Only one room in the front was illuminated. A driveway light came on and a front door opened with the outline of a man in it.

"Keep that blanket over you," Samantha whispered. "Let's just hope he isn't a gentleman and offers to help."

Samantha turned off the engine and hopped out of the minivan. She walked around to the passenger side, opened the door and picked up a large box. It was there, as much as for the convenience, to prove there was no one in the car with her.

She walked to the front door. "I have two more," she said.

Pokvovsky looked at the size of the box and judged it to weigh twenty pounds or more.

"I'd offer to help, but I'm getting to be an old man," he said.

She put the box just inside the front door and went back for the second and third. Less than two minutes later, she was inside. She glanced at the alarm panel by the door. She had not heard the gate close behind her and the panel gave no indication if the alarm had been reset.

She regarded Pokrovsky, whom she had never seen before except in photographs and video clips. He was relatively tall and wore gray sweatpants and a baggy, hooded sweatshirt. He was mostly bald, with just a thin fringe of white hair. A pair of frameless glasses with thick lenses seemed to magnify his eyes. He looked neither older nor younger than the eighty years she knew him to be. Underneath the loose clothing she detected no paunch. Had she passed him on the street, she would have simply thought, *old, retired guy'*

"You said something about coffee," she said. "It was cold out there."

Pokrovsky smiled. "It's one of those little packet systems. I never knew there could be so many kinds of coffee to choose from. First, though, let's bring the boxes into the library so I can make certain they're what you say they are."

Minutes later, they were in a library, or at least what a decorator thought a library should look like. There were shelves of books, all sets and each shelf color- and size-coordinated. The perfect rows of aligned spines made it evident these books were never moved, even to be dusted. Smilin' Al Pokrovsky was not a literary-minded man.

Pokrovsky took a vintage world atlas off a reading table in the center of the room and moved an exquisite small vase off to the side, allowing Samantha to heft the first box onto the table. He opened the box and picked up the first three sheets of paper inside it. The papers were window stickers onto which his son had added fictitious equipment or upgraded features. He satisfied himself that these were the original documents and not photocopies.

He then reached into the center of the box and pulled out a dozen sheets. These were salesmen commission sheets on which his son had changed vehicle selling prices or commission rates. Pokrovsky scowled as he read the changes. "Stupid idiot," he said under his breath.

"Let's see another box," he said to Samantha.

She placed the first box on the floor and lifted another box onto the table. At the top were receipts for gifts and payment of fees associated with the Revere condo. These Pokrovsky ignored. He reached down into the box and pulled up an inch-thick wad of papers and laid them on the table, spreading them out in a fan shape.

"Holy mother…" he muttered.

"These are the original timesheets submitted by employees," Samantha said. "You can see where your son arbitrarily changed hours worked. Nobody in the dealership ever got overtime. There are about eight hundred of those in the box covering ten dealerships."

"My son is a moron," Pokrovsky said, more to himself than to Samantha.

"For cheating his employees or for not bothering to destroy the evidence?" Samantha asked.

Pokrovsky looked up from the papers. "Does it matter?" He indicated the third box still on the floor. "What's in there?"

"Accounting records," Samantha replied. "Everything about the 'doc fees' diversion and the 'incentive account'. It's fairly dry stuff – except to an IRS auditor."

"And you got all this in two months," he said, indicating the three boxes with his chin.

Samantha nodded.

"Why did you do it?" Pokrovsky asked. "Why did you go after my son?"

"It was my job, Mr. Pokrovsky. You son filed four claims against my company in a six-month period. Over the course of a year or two, one car totaled during a test drive is plausible. Two in two months is improbable. Two cars being torched in separate incidents pushed it all into the 'definite fraud' zone."

"You could have just told him to stop," Pokrovsky said. "You could have told him you weren't going to pay any more claims."

Samantha nodded. "That's exactly what the adjuster told him after the second crash. But your son didn't stop. Instead, he just went for one more big score."

"But why all this?" Pokrovsky indicated the boxes of papers. "This couldn't have been part of your job. This had to be personal."

"It was never personal," Samantha said. "Mass Casualty could have assigned any of five investigators. I guess my name was next in the queue. I collected this evidence because I wanted to catch your son in the act. I had no idea he was doing any of these other things until I started going through his trash."

"And what do you get out of all this?" he asked. "I mean money-wise."

"I get a percentage of what Mass Casualty would have paid in claims for the eighteen cars."

"What percentage? Give me a ballpark figure."

"Five percent," Samantha replied.

Pokvovsky nodded. "So, for roughly a hundred thousand bucks, you were perfectly willing to destroy the reputation of my company."

Samantha shook her head. "All I did was catch your son in the act of defrauding my employer. Destroying your company's reputation?" She waved her arm across the three boxes. "I didn't do any of this. Your son did this to you."

Pokrovsky's voice began to show anger and tension. "You could have come to me and none of this would have happened."

"It would still have happened, Mr. Pokrovsky," Samantha said, collecting a ski parka from a chair in a corner of the library. "Your son is completely out of control, and that is something you have to deal with. My guess is that it's all related to a very serious gambling problem. Rigging the businesses' books is what lets him keep gambling."

She continued. "But I've upheld my end of the bargain. You have the originals of everything and my word that there are no copies. You agree to stay away from my people. When the preliminary hearing is held in ten days, your attorney can tear the state's case apart because there won't be any evidence."

"Don't leave yet," Pokrovsky said. "We have more to talk about. We haven't even had our coffee yet."

Samantha shook her head and put on the parka. "I'm tired. It's nasty out there. If you want to talk, we can do it another time."

From the pockets of the baggy sweatshirt, Pokrovsky extracted a small gun and pointed it at Samantha. She identified it as a .22 caliber. It was hard to kill a person with such a gun, but a well-aimed bullet would certainly incapacitate her.

"Is this where I raise my hands?" she asked. "I thought we had a deal."

Pokrovsky nodded. "We have a deal. But I want an expert to look at these before I decide if I want to go through with it."

"So, all we had was a provisional deal," Samantha said, keeping her eyes directly on Pokrovsky. "I deliver the documents as promised and, even though they're everything I said they would be, and I brought the originals, you still reserve the right to go after those four ladies."

Pokrovsky nodded and gave an almost imperceptible smile. "I believe you were the one who said 'you win'."

"I did," Samantha replied. "But I've changed my mind." With that, she reached out and, with one motion, grabbed the small vase Pokrovsky had moved ten minutes earlier and flipped it to him, chest high. Caught by surprise and following human instinct, Pokrovsky reached out with both hands to catch the object.

Samantha lunged and batted the gun out of his hands. At that same moment, from behind him, Paula pulled a black, reinforced Hefty bag over his head, shoulders and torso. A head-sized hole had been cut in the bottom seam to allow him to breathe and brought the bag further down his body, sealing him from shoulders to knees. A second later, and with Pokrovsky screaming obscenities, Jean began unrolling clear plastic strapping tape around the bag, turning the bag into a tight cocoon. The two women lowered Pokrovsky to the floor.

Samantha found a wash cloth in a half-bathroom next to the library. She knelt beside Pokrovsky and showed him the washcloth. "Are you going to keep screaming?" she asked. He continued to shout that he was going to kill them, and Samantha forced the washcloth into his mouth.

"I want you to listen very carefully, Al," Samantha said. "And, over the next few hours, I want you to think back on what you did just a few minutes ago, because the decisions you made are going to change your life, and not for the better."

She suddenly had Pokrovsky's attention. He stopped struggling and making sounds.

"I came here tonight prepared to make a deal," she said. "Had you been prepared to go through with that deal, I would be gone now, you would have your documents, and your life would have gone on as before."

"But I also had a backup plan in case you were lying to me. When you pulled that gun, and I asked if this was where I raised my hands, that backup plan went into motion. These ladies were waiting outside in the cold, and all they had for company was a cell phone. They listened and, when they heard that you had broken your word, they acted to protect me, and themselves."

"Al, you've started down that bad road, and I'm afraid there's no going back. But there's a fork in that road, and you've got one opportunity to make your future a little less bad. You said someone was coming. I assume that was Mike McDonough. We're going to call Mike, and you're going to say, 'I've taken care of everything. There's no need to come. I'll see you in the morning.' You say those three sentences, and you say them convincingly, and I guarantee you'll be alive in the morning. If you screw it up or if you won't make the call, I make no such promises. Nod if you understand."

Pokrovsky nodded.

"Nod if you're willing to make that call, and you understand the consequences of screwing up."

Pokrovsky nodded again.

Samantha pulled the washcloth from his mouth. "Which pocket is your cell phone in?"

"Sweatshirt, left side," he said.

Samantha felt through the bag and the tape and discerned the outline of the phone. She cut the plastic bag just enough to reach in for the phone, tapped it into life and looked for the last number called.

"We're going to call him now," she said. "Do you remember what you're going to say?"

"I've taken care of everything. There's no need to come. I'll see you in the morning," he said.

"Perfect," Samantha said. "Get ready." She tapped the Redial icon, heard the phone ring once and a male voice say, "I'm on the road. Forty-five minutes, max."

She held the phone in front of Pokrovsky and pointed.

"They've broken in and have me tied up!" he screamed. "Call the police!"

Samantha, however, had her finger over the End Call icon. McDonough heard, "They've bro..." and then a dead line.

"Al, over the next few hours, you're going to have a lot of time to reflect on your life. This night, among all the ones you've lived, is going to be the one you regret more than all of the others combined."

She put the washcloth back in his mouth and turned her attention to the two women.

"Ladies, we need to wipe every surface any of us might have touched. By the time we leave, there should be no evidence that we were ever in this house. Then, let's get rolling."

As they backed out of the driveway fifteen minutes later, Samantha phoned Eleanor and Alice. "We're done here," she said. "You know where to meet us. The roads are getting slick so take your time."

* * * * *

Two successive calls to the cell phone went to voicemail, and McDonough stared at his own phone. He then called his boss's house phone and that, too, went to an answering machine. It could mean only one thing: something had happened to Pokrovsky.

McDonough pressed down on the accelerator, passing eighty

miles per hour through the icy mix. Interstate 495, the expressway that looped around Boston and connected to the Bourne Bridge, had been treated, but that was hours earlier. The STC lamp glowed multiple times as he went around even the gentle curves of the highway.

Up ahead, though, he saw the blue flashing lights of a state police car and the red glow of flares. He braked lightly, bringing his speed down to seventy. He was a quarter mile from the lights, and he tapped the brake harder. The STC lamp glowed bright red.

He was still down to just fifty when he felt the rear wheels slide out. He tried to oversteer to straighten out but overcompensated. His SUV began a lazy spin on the ice-covered road. Then the tires grabbed a patch of bare pavement and the spin reversed direction, this time distinctly faster.

The SUV was slowing, which was good, McDonough thought. The bad thing was that his car was now pointed directly at the state police car.

The impact was at thirty miles an hour. The state trooper, seeing the spinning headlights coming toward him, abandoned his car for the safety of the trees along the side of the road. The driver's side of the SUV hit the blue and gray police car with a thud, and the vehicle jumped forward several feet.

The trooper raced to the SUV. Front and side airbags had deployed, saving the driver's life. But the side of the SUV was crumpled in, and it would likely take the jaws of life to extricate the driver.

The trooper went to his own, now-undriveable vehicle and radioed in. "Got another accident. We need the cavalry for this one: EMTs, ambulance, jaws of life and two more tow trucks. One of them is for my car. And I think you better tell the DOT folks to add more sanding trucks before someone gets killed…"

48.

Samantha said a silent prayer as she keyed the first code into the alarm panel. The red light blinked an angry red, as though the mere notion of someone being at the door at three in the morning was enough to cause bells to start sounding.

Instead, when she touched the last number and "enter", the red light went out and a steady green one appeared in its place. The door that had been resolutely welded in place now opened with a touch.

*Step one*, Samantha thought.

Inside the door was a wholesale showroom perhaps fifty feet long and twenty feet wide. The streetlights outside provided enough illumination to get a sense of the room. Hundreds of candles were on display in every permutation of height, diameter, color and material. Text signs proclaimed the virtues of Wellfleet Candles' natural beeswax and hand-dipped lines. Graphs demonstrated that Wellfleet's product burned longer and brighter that those from Yankee or Cape Cod. There was even a special selection of ecclesiastical candles for multiple faiths in holiday-appropriate hues.

Samantha ignored the showroom and went to the second panel, located next to a plain metal door at the rear of the showroom. She again tapped in codes. A red light was replaced by an amber one. She read off another set of codes from her phone screen. The amber light blinked.

And then turned green.

"We're in," she said.

Beyond the door there was no light and so no real sense of size or space; only an echoing of footsteps that said this space was *large*. A bank of unmarked light switches was located on the wall to her left. She flipped one at random, and a small break room became illuminated. She turned that one off and flipped another. One row of mercury-vapor lights flickered on.

As the lights brightened, they began to add dimension to the room. It was a warehouse, a hundred feet deep and two hundred feet wide. A glassed-in office area was dwarfed by the surrounding industrial shelving.

On the shelving were pallets of boxes. The higher reaches of the shelves held brown cartons four feet on a side. The lowest shelves held individual boxes. Large signs at the head of aisles indicated Toyota, Honda or other brands.

Only one row of lights had been activated, but it was enough to inspire awe in the five women. Before them was the best-hidden and most lucrative counterfeit parts operation in New England. It was a supply chain that began in factories in China, where automotive parts – correct in dimension, at least – were stamped out from the cheapest metal available and assembled by unskilled factory workers who worked from disassembled originals.

The parts were then placed in blister packs that were indistinguishable from the packaging used by each automotive company, down to reproducing bar codes and inspection stickers. The parts came in shipping containers to various ports along the East Coast and then by truck to this warehouse, ostensibly the home of the Wellfleet Candle Company.

From this warehouse, two dozen salesmen fanned out to garages across the Northeast, including to automotive dealerships eager to pad their margins by substituting these knock-off parts for factory ones. Judicious use of counterfeits could triple or quadruple the profit margin on a repair.

This warehouse and its contents were the true legacy of Smilin' Al Pokrovsky. Ten years earlier, he had started with a single shipping container of screws and bolts that one salesman sold on commission. The nearly $100,000 he netted on that first container financed two containers and three commissioned salesmen, each of whom probed their customers for other desired products. Smilin' Al found fabricators for those parts and added them to his line of counterfeit goods.

In two years it was a five million dollar enterprise with seemingly unlimited potential for growth. It was not age but, rather, the management of this enterprise and its opportunity that prompted Al Senior to turn over the reins of the Pokrovsky Motor Group to his son. Last year, the business had generated revenue of more than $30 million with profits representing more than a third of that figure.

There was a downside, of course. Parts wore more quickly and in certain cases disintegrated. People were injured and some died because brakes failed or engines seized. On those rare occasions when he thought about this downside, Al Senior rationalized that the parts that failed were not ones supplied by him; or that the breakdowns were the fault of the installing garage; or even that if Subaru or Kia priced their replacement parts more sensibly, there would be no demand for his counterfeit ones.

What Al Senior knew, and what Samantha and the others now saw, was that this was enormous. Ten forklift trucks were parked in a corner of the warehouse, ready to go back to work Monday morning. Twelve loading bays allowed for the smooth flow of incoming and outgoing products.

"We have, maybe, three hours," Samantha said. "We ought to figure on making twelve packages. Turn on every computer, print out everything that looks useful, especially bills of lading and customer invoices. Don't worry about trying to keep things in order. Just print it out, make a dozen copies of it, and then print out the next file. And, whatever you do, don't take off your gloves. As far as anyone is concerned, we were never here."

While the women went to work in the small office area, Samantha surveyed the warehouse. There was a steel column near the office. That was just what she needed. She pulled a well-padded chair from the office and placed it next to the column. She next found several rolls of plastic tape of the kind used to seal boxes. Her final find was a rolling cart.

"Eleanor, can I borrow you for a few minutes?" she asked.

Together, they went out to Samantha's car and retrieved

Pokrovsky. His feet remained tightly bound together and his hands were secured to his waist. Conscious that they were dealing with an elderly man, they gingerly lifted him out of the back seat of the car and gently placed him in the cart.

It was likely Pokrovsky's first view of where he had been taken to. His eyes widened and sounds emanated from the gag in his mouth.

They quickly wheeled him inside and set him in the chair next to the column. Pokrovsky's head swiveled and his eyes went to the activity in the office area. There was a look of panic on his distorted face.

Samantha asked, "Would you like some water? Are you thirsty?"

Pokrovsky nodded his head vigorously.

She found bottles of water in the break room and brought one back. She unscrewed the cap and then slowly removed the gag from Pokrovsky's mouth.

"I am going to personally kill you," were the first words out of his mouth.

"Do you want the water or not?" Samantha asked.

"I am going to take a knife, and I am going to slice you open from your neck down to your crotch," he said, a coldness in his voice. "It will take you an hour to die, and you will be aware of the life seeping out of you."

Samantha held the water in front of his mouth. "Either you drink this or I put the gag back in."

Pokrovsky opened his mouth and tilted his head back. Samantha slowly poured water into his mouth.

"Not too fast," she said. "You don't want to gag on this."

He drank more water.

"Is one bottle enough?" she asked.

"Remember this moment when I stick the knife into you," he said.

"It must be enough," Samantha said, and forced the gag back into his mouth.

"Mr. Pokrovsky, we're going to be a few hours," she said. "I'm sorry I can't offer you a bathroom break but that would be a little too complicated. Some people will be by in a few hours, and they'll cut you free."

Pokrovsky's brow furrowed at the words "some people". Samantha did not elaborate. Instead, she positioned his chair to face toward the vast aisles of parts and away from the office. She first taped the chair to the steel column and then Pokrovsky to the chair. With that done, she began cutting away the Hefty bag and the tape Jean had used at his home.

When she was finished, Pokrovsky was held to the chair by fewer than half a dozen strategically placed pieces of tape. The job was as escape-proof as she knew how to make it. There were no bruises or contusions on his body. Just an old man secured to a chair to keep him from falling out of it.

At seven o'clock, Samantha instructed the four women to wipe down and clean all surfaces they had come into contact with, especially keyboards and the copier, but also boxes and envelopes. When that was done, she began arranging a dozen boxes, each containing upwards of two thousand sheets of paper, in a circle around Pokrovsky. Against each box she placed a separate manila envelope containing two dozen Xeroxed pages.

"We need to leave now, Mr. Pokrovsky," Samantha said. "You should be cut free in two hours or less."

With that, the women left. They left the lights on and the doors un-alarmed.

Outside the building, Samantha gathered them together. "Al's goons are still out there," she said. "The news is going to get out sometime today but, for the next twenty-four hours, you want to stay out of sight. We've still got a little more work to do on Jillian Connelly to tie that up neatly for the police, but that's mostly on my shoulders. Paula has turned over everything on Mandy Ojumbua to Detective Hoffman, and it wouldn't surprise me if he is arrested today."

She continued. "We're almost to the finish line. Alice, we know someone's still outside your condo, so you're best off at Cavendish Woods. Eleanor, I know you want to be with your husband, and that's a safe place for you. Jean, you may or may not be on their radar, but please find someplace to stay for today. Maybe you and Paula can check into a hotel for the day because you definitely can't go home yet."

"Considering what we were up against, we've done really well," Samantha added. "I'm proud of each one of you. Now, let's lay low."

49.

John Kepple, Zone Parts Manager for Subaru of New England, heard the buzz of his phone. He glanced at the clock beside his bed and saw that it was exactly seven o'clock. Careful not to wake his still-sleeping wife, he reached across to the bedside table and picked up the phone, curious to know who would be texting him so early on a Sunday morning.

The sender was not familiar but the message said "URGENT MESSAGE RE SUBARU PARTS".

He opened the message.

AT 9:00 THIS MORNING YOU ARE INVITED TO VIEW THE LARGEST INVENTORY OF DEEPLY DISCOUNTED, FACTORY-FRESH SUBARU PARTS IN NEW ENGLAND. The message ended with an address in Norton, Massachusetts, some thirty miles from his home in Wellesley.

Kepple believed himself to be the keeper of the largest inventory of Subaru parts not only in New England, but in the country, and his principal warehouse was in Norwood, not Norton.

He re-read the message a second time. What was so special about nine o'clock? The more he thought about it, the more disturbing the message became. Kepple got out of bed and went to the closet.

"Where are you going?" his wife asked, rubbing her eyes and peering at the clock.

He showed her the message. "I don't know what this is all about and, until I do, I'm not going to be very good company."

\* \* \* \* \*

When Kepple arrived at the Wellfleet Candle Company warehouse, his was the third car to enter the parking lot. Standing by the front entrance were two men he instantly recognized: his counterparts at Toyota and Kia.

He nodded to the two. "I'm guessing you have a text message

this morning about Subaru parts?"

The Toyota manager pulled out his phone and shook his head. "Toyota," he said.

The Kia parts manager showed his own phone. "It looks like we each got individualized invitations."

Kepple pushed at the door. Surprisingly, it was not locked. Inside, the candle display appeared unmolested. "Someone seems to have left the door open," he said. "I'm taking that as an invitation."

The three men went into the showroom. As they did, a fourth car pulled into the parking lot. They recognized the regional warehouse manager for Honda as he got out of the car. The passenger door also opened, and the head of Honda's New England Region sales stepped into the chilly air.

Kepple glanced around the showroom but made straight for the metal door. It, too, was not locked and the alarm panel showed green. "I'm guessing what we're looking for is in here," he said.

He stepped into the warehouse, looked at the signage, and said, "Oh…. my….God…."

Kepple did not initially see the seated figure by the office area or the boxes surrounding the man. Instead, Kepple instinctively walked to the aisle marked Subaru and grabbed a box from the lowest shelf. He examined the packaging carefully, then took a Swiss Army knife from his pocked and slit open the box. Inside were blister packs. He examined that packaging as well before using the knife to open the cardboard backing.

Kepple held the handful of parts in his hand. Their weight – less than a third of what these parts ought to be – confirmed what the slightly blurry packaging had already told him. He had just found the source of the counterfeit parts ring that had plagued his business for more than five years.

Kepple heard a shout and he turned. Only then did he see that someone was in a chair next to a column. The Honda manager was next to the person and was still shouting to attract the attention of the others. Kepple also saw the ring of boxes and stooped to pick up a handful of papers from one of them.

He again stopped breathing. It was an invoice for parts – Hyundai parts – that had been shipped to a body shop in Connecticut. He quickly leafed through the other pages he had picked up: all were shipping invoices, including one to a Boston-area Subaru dealer dated three weeks earlier for nearly four thousand dollars of parts. He *knew* the parts manager at that dealership; they had socialized on numerous occasions. The bastard was knowingly buying counterfeit parts.

Then Kepple looked up to see the man in the chair. It was Al Pokrovsky, Senior. He was bound with what looked like sealing tape.

There were now six men gathered around him. Three of them held boxes of parts. None made a move to free Smilin' Al.

A separate manila envelope leaned against each box. Kepple opened one and took out a sheaf of two dozen pages. The topmost document was a lease for the building at this address with Wellfleet Candle named as the renter. Five documents, all with circles, arrows and underlines, traced the ownership of Wellfleet Candle through a string of dummy corporations until one name and signature appeared at the bottom of the final page.

The name: Al Pokrovsky, Senior.

Kepple stepped forward and started to remove the gag from Pokrovsky's mouth. A hand fell on his. It was the Honda regional sales manager. He, too, held a sheaf of papers in his hand.

"I think we need to discuss what we're going to do before we hear his side of the story," the Honda manager said. "I want one of those boxes of papers back in my house before we call anyone. Even if I have no idea how this happened, it's fairly clear what we've walked into."

Kepple nodded. He took his phone out of his pocket and tapped his "home" icon. A few seconds later, he said, "Honey, I need you to throw on some clothes and meet me as soon as you can. Let me give you the address...."

Hearing Kepple's conversation, the others reached for their own phones.

50.

Paula and Jean dropped Alice at the entrance to the Cavendish Woods Great Lodge. It was just eight o'clock.

"Are you sure you won't have breakfast with me?" Alice asked.

Paula shook her head. "I need about six hours' catch-up sleep more than I need breakfast. We're going to find a hotel with big, soft beds. I know that as soon as this adrenaline wears off, I am going to fall over, face first. I'd rather it be into a pillow and not a stack of hotcakes."

Alice went into the vast atrium, sensing that this might be her last day here. The receptionist on duty waved at her and smiled; Alice was known now and that was comforting. She turned left toward the elevators that would take her to the suite. She paused, though, in front of the breakfast grille, smelling the aroma of bacon.

*One final meal,* she thought.

An hour later, having enjoyed coffee, croissants, an omelet and a rasher of bacon, she rose from her table and headed toward the elevator. As she did, she paused at the darkened Cavendish Collection. Samantha had said she would collect and catalog the evidence against Jillian Connelly, then turn it over to the proper authorities. Alice's business with Connelly was now done.

As she looked into the gallery with its shapes of paintings and sculptures, Alice felt she had done very little toward solving the crime. Indeed, until yesterday afternoon, she did not even know that Connelly was the likely killer. She had not even *suspected* the woman. Rather, Jillian Connelly had seemed to Alice to be an enthusiastic and knowledgeable teacher, albeit one caught up in the sexual politics of the paintings and artists she explored.

How far back did her crimes go? How did she kill her victims? Did she have an accomplice? Alice knew the answers to none of these questions, and it made her feel quite useless. It also made her feel quite tired. *If only I had worked harder,* she thought. *If only I had asked more questions.*

She took the elevator to her floor and turned right toward her room. The two floor nurses greeted her by name. Would they forget her just as quickly when the next resident moved in?

Two-thirds the way down the winding corridor, Alice placed the key in the lock and opened the door. She felt depressed and weary. She would bathe after she slept. She ought not to have had such a large meal.

She was pondering these things when she heard a voice, part conversational, part peeved. "I was wondering if you were ever going to come up from breakfast."

It was Jillian Connelly, seated on the sofa in the suite's main room.

"How did you get in here?" Alice asked.

"Master key," Connolly replied, holding up a key ring. "I'm a trusted employee." Her voice now was mocking.

"I would thank you to leave my room," Alice said, standing as straight as possible and pushing her shoulders back. "You have no business being here." She tried not to let the weariness she felt be heard. At the same time, she thought about the two nurses by the elevator who could be summoned at the press of one of the four red buttons around this room. The nearest one was ten feet away.

"Oh, but we do have business," Connolly said. Watching Alice's eyes go to the red button on the wall, Connolly added, "And if you make one move toward that button before we're finished, I will not hesitate to break your fingers, your hand, or your arm."

Alice turned her gaze toward Connolly. "You murdered my friend, Cecelia."

Connolly nodded. "Yes, I did. I know you've been 'investigating' her death." She added a snicker to the word investigating. "And before we're done, you're going to tell me everything you know about everyone you've been working with, starting with the woman on the cleaning staff who broke into my private office Friday night."

Alice was startled by Connolly's knowledge that Jean had been posing as a member of the cleaning crew. She had tried to keep her face impassive; now her countenance slipped.

"Oh, I surprised you?" Connolly said. "I also know that a night nurse started just a day after you checked in. I'm going to assume she's in on this, too. How many others are there? How many Miss Marple wannabes?" Another snicker.

Alice was silent.

"We can do this easily, or we can do this painfully," Connolly said. "But you're going to tell me." It had not occurred to her that physical force might be required. Connelly stood up, picking up the heavy Thermos with one hand and holding it as she might a club.

Alice noted the Thermos. It was not hers, so Connolly must have brought it with her. It seemed an odd choice of weapon. "I will tell you what you want to know if you will tell me something first," Alice said. "Why?"

"Why, what?" Connolly asked, genuinely confused.

"You killed Cecelia for her painting. You made a copy of it and gave the copy back to her family. It was good enough that no one noticed. You're a gifted painter. Why not just create your own beautiful art and sell it?"

Connolly laughed. "You really don't get it, do you? Have you been listening to what I've been saying in class? Do you have any idea what it is like to be a classically trained woman artist in the twenty-first century? Or in almost any century, for that matter?"

Alice shook her head. She had asked the question in part to stall for time… to come up with a plan; any plan. Connolly's response to the question, though, was visceral. A nerve had been struck.

"The art world is soaked in testosterone," Connolly continued, anger rising in her voice. "Yes, I am a gifted artist. I have an MFA from Smith. I studied in Paris. And do you know what that gets me? Nothing. I worked three months on an exquisite landscape that everyone agreed was a masterpiece. And do you know what it sold for? Two thousand dollars. I worked three months for *two thousand* dollars. Meanwhile, men with one-tenth of my talent turn out monstrous, ugly canvasses in a week and collectors get into bidding wars."

Alice saw an opportunity. Keep her talking. Find a way to get to the red button to summon help. "Why?" Alice asked. "Why is it so unfair to women?"

"Because art is a man's world," Connolly shot back. "A woman's place is to... give seminars at nursing homes where half the 'students' sleep through the lecture. A woman's place is to use the implicit promise of sex to sell men's paintings to other men who care only that they are buying a rising artist's work."

"There is no place for a gifted woman artist unless she doesn't care that her paintings sell for a tenth – or a hundredth – of what her less talented male peers command. That's *why*." Connolly's face was red, and her nostrils flared as she finished speaking.

"You won't get away with it," Alice said. "Too many people know. The wheels are already in motion." *Play for time.*

"At this point, I'm not even sure that I care," Connolly said, her teeth gritted. "My primary business is with you. You've been quite busy these last few days. You've been speaking with the FBI. You've destroyed my relationship with my New York gallery."

Alice realized that Connolly knew nothing about Samantha or the woman in California who had contacted the FBI. "What happens after I give you this information?"

"We have a cup of tea," Connolly said. She smiled and held out the Thermos. She was in charge. She was savoring this moment of victory over an enemy. "Then, after we've had tea, I talk to your friends."

Alice sensed that Connolly had relaxed for an instant and saw what would likely be her only opportunity. Tired as she was, she lunged for the red button on the wall, diving toward it with her arm and hand extended. She was within inches when Connolly slammed down the weight of the Thermos on her hand. Alice felt bones snap in her hand and wrist and she screamed in pain. Connolly put her hand over Alice's mouth, stifling all sound.

"I told you I would hurt you," Connolly whispered. "I will hurt you even worse if you try again. Now, you will start giving me names..."

She was interrupted by the sound of sirens coming from outside. *Ambulances never use sirens when coming to Cavendish Woods*, Connolly thought. She glanced at Alice, who appeared to have blacked out from the pain.

Cautiously, Connolly rose and went to the window. She was not prepared for what she saw four floors below her. Five state police cruisers and a black SUV, all with lights flashing, pulled to the entrance of the Grand Lodge. Two troopers each got out of four of the cruisers while a man in a suit pointed to where they were to take up positions. Three more men got out of the SUV, carrying briefcases. They huddled briefly before striding into the entrance.

Connolly looked down at the scene in horror. She turned to Alice, who still appeared unconscious. "They're coming to arrest me, aren't they? You knew?" A look of fear and consternation was on her face. She pressed her face to the window. Three of the troopers were taking positions by the emergency exits. Fixated by the drama playing out below her, she did not see or hear Alice pull herself to the wall using her uninjured hand, where she held down the red button with the last ounce of strength in her body.

Connolly heard the muffled sound of the alarm emanating from the hallway. She looked at Alice, then back out the window. Color drained from her face. She had been beaten by this old, stupid woman.

"You did this," Connolly hissed at Alice. The Thermos was in her hand. She raised it, ready to throw it at Alice or, perhaps, to beat her to death with it.

Then, a vision appeared in Connolly's mind. It was the face of Jeanne Hébuterne, Amedeo Modigliani's model and mistress. An artist every bit as talented and visionary as her lover, but whose canvasses were traded for food. Days after Modigliani's death from tuberculosis  Hébuterne, nine months pregnant with their second child, had thrown herself off a fifth floor balcony.  Only in the manner of her death were her talents recognized; her fame was posthumous but enduring.  Nearly a century later, Hébuterne's name was spoken of in reverential terms within the art world.  *Yes*, she thought.  *This is the way.*

Connolly pulled at the sliding glass door onto the balcony.  It was locked and would not yield.  She looked back at Alice, who had again passed out.  Taking off the cap and then the seal.  Connolly did not pour the Thermos' contents into the cap.  Rather, she raised the Thermos and began drinking its contents directly from the vessel.  She did not stop even when the two floor nurses ran into the room.

The nurses, in any event, were concerned with Alice, who lay on the floor next to the red button, her hand already red and swollen and her breathing labored.  It did not occur to them that the director of the art gallery was the reason for this scene.

EMTs arrived a few minutes later and placed Alice on a gurney, checking her vital signs and packing her hand in instant cold packs while the nurses comforted her.

Four ounces of aconite-laden tea was sufficient, once it had been absorbed through the stomach into the body, to induce cardiac arrest within two to three hours.   In her fury upon returning from Connecticut, Connolly had cut up twenty more leaves and brewed them into the chamomile tea.  Now, she had consumed at least eight ounces of the liquid.

The EMTs and nurses were still wheeling Alice down the hall when Connolly felt the first convulsion. Her vision became blurred and her arms and legs began to feel numb.  She collapsed onto the sofa.   She tried to move her mouth, perhaps to scream, but everything felt rubbery and no sound came from her throat.

Her mind, though, was still fully functional.  She had outfoxed them.  The law is clear that dead people cannot be prosecuted.  The state police would find her here, of course, and it would be too late. They were climbing the stairs toward Alice's suite now, guns drawn, ready to make an arrest. Perhaps they had already searched her home and come up empty. Had she waited until the afternoon to confront Alice Beauchamp, she would already be in custody.

It was only in her last moments that Jillian Connolly began to wonder how Alice could have known she would be waiting in this room and alerted the police. Alice had, in point of fact, been genuinely surprised and frightened to find her here. Was it possible the police were here for some other reason? It was a puzzling thought but Connolly did not have time to reach any solution before the final blackness descended on her.

**Six Weeks Later**

On a pleasant Saturday in April, Marilyn Davis hosted a party to honor the return of *White Roses*, which rested on an easel in her living room. While the painting was the nominal reason for the gathering, her real reason for the celebration was to privately thank Paula, Jean, Eleanor, Alice and Samantha.

For her parents and for Uncle Rudy and Aunt Donna, the forthcoming sale of the painting meant a sort of financial salvation. Christie's had placed a pre-sale estimate of $800,000 to $1.5 million on it, with additional bidders possible because of the work's notoriety. And there was, of course, a wrongful death suit filed against the owners of Cavendish Woods. If the prospect of more money was supposed to be the healing salve on the marriage of Marilyn's parents, it did not show. Pete and Clarice Davis spent their time in different rooms, coming together only for a group photo.

Mounted on display boards around the living room were a series of newspaper articles published during the preceding months. The oldest were about the arrest that Sunday morning in February of Mandy Ojumbua by the Massachusetts State Police. Ojumbua had now been charged in four deaths of invalid residents of Cavendish Woods, and was implicated in the murder of as many as ten more at nursing homes in New York and Ohio.

While the management of Cavendish Woods initially attempted to portray itself as having been pro-active in the investigation and arrest, computers and papers seized by the state police at the time of Ojumbua's arrest (and subsequently leaked to the media) told a much different story. Cavendish Woods was on the brink of letting the nurse go for "lack of work", leaving him free to seek employment at other health care facilities with no stain on his record.

More recent stories in both Boston and New York newspapers linked the apparent suicide of Jillian Connelly, an "art curator" and part-time employee of Cavendish Woods to the murders by poisoning of as many as five of the nursing home's residents, including that of Cecelia Davis. The stories told of a bizarre scheme devised by Connelly to use the gallery she operated within the high-end nursing home to uncover valuable works of art held by residents. Connelly, a gifted copyist, reproduced the paintings while sending the originals to a New York gallery.

Winston Li, the owner of the Hao Ming Gallery, protested that the works were consigned to him with satisfactory documentation of ownership. Analysis by the Federal Bureau of Investigation showed both that the provenance provided was fraudulent and that sale process showed that Li was aware that he was dealing in stolen artworks. The Hao Ming Gallery had been closed and its assets seized. Of the four paintings known to have been copied by Connelly and sold through the gallery, three were in China, and efforts to get the owners to voluntarily return the works was thus far proving unsuccessful. The fourth painting, a Fantin-Latour, was recovered from the gallery and had been returned to the heirs of Cecelia Davis.

The FBI credited "independent sources on both the east and west coast" in helping it uncover the gallery's role in the fraud.

The final boards displayed the first two articles of a Boston *Globe* "spotlight" series on the use of "instant poverty" schemes concocted by law and accounting firms designed to protect the assets of the elderly from the cost of nursing home care. The first article described "scare tactic" seminars that lured retirees with the promise of a free lunch and that ended with hard-sell ploys that frightened those attendees into making life-altering financial decisions.

The second installment enumerated the array of self-dealing products that primarily ensured a continuing flow of income to the firms that held the seminars, while shifting the cost burden of nursing home care to taxpayers. The firm of Liss and Swann was prominently highlighted in the second article.

As Paula re-read Leonard Swann's vehement denial of any ethical breach on the part of his firm, she felt a tap on her arm. It was Samantha. "You didn't bring Martin today?"

Paula shook her head. "It would be too difficult to explain, especially with you here."

"You're going to have to tell him something, and he's a very smart man," Samantha said.

Paula smiled and nodded. "He *is* very smart, and some folks in the state police know they're going to owe their promotions to him."

"You're going away?" Samantha asked.

Paula nodded again. "Seven days in the British Virgin Islands. We leave tomorrow morning."

"Big step," Samantha said.

"Very big step," Paula replied. "And, sometime during the next week, I'm going to have to have to tell him enough of the truth to answer the questions I know he has about why I had all that information about Mandy Ojumbua. And I know he's smart enough to figure out that Jillian Connelly's body being found in Alice's room was no coincidence."

"He is a good man," Samantha said. "Don't lose him. And ask him if he has a younger brother who likes tall ladies of color."

Paula smiled. "I'll try to work the conversation around to that topic."

"Can I get the five of us together for a few minutes?" Samantha asked. "It's important."

\* \* \* \* \*

Eleanor was of two minds about being at this party. On the one hand she was pleased for Marilyn Davis and the other members of the Davis clan. Everyone was in high spirits.

But as she sat in the chair in the living room, an untouched glass of wine at her elbow, she felt the penetrating sense of loss. A month to the day earlier she had buried her husband. Yes, it had been a release from a terrible disease and from a non-life he would not have wanted for himself. But Phil was gone, and she would never see him again.

She had once described herself as "a widow, except that they haven't held the funeral." Now, she knew that description was wrong. For as long as Phil breathed, even with his mind irrevocably taken away, she could still feel his warmth, stroke his face, or smell his skin.

Now, Phil lived only in memory and in photographs. She would cherish those decades they had together but, inside her, she also knew that a new chapter was opening. *Thank God for friends*, she thought as she saw Paula approaching her.

\* \* \* \* \*

A few minutes later, they were assembled in Marilyn Davis's kitchen.

"I want to bring everyone up to speed at the same time," Samantha said. "The big news is that Smilin' Al's latest stroke has officially been deemed a 'permanent incapacitation'. He can't communicate with his lawyers or assist in his own defense, which is going to throw a monkey wrench into both the criminal charges and the civil litigation against him. There will probably be some kind of a public announcement tomorrow."

Samantha looked at each of the other four women in turn. "This means there's no way anyone is ever going to come looking for any of us. I was probably the only one who had to be concerned about 'revenge' but, just in case any of you were thinking that Al's goons were still interested in you, you can put that out of your mind. If Smilin' Al is hooked up to racks of machines, he isn't giving instructions any longer."

"Does anyone have any idea of what caused the stroke?" Jean asked.

Samantha laughed and started ticking off fingers. "Take your pick. He's been indicted by a federal grand jury for racketeering for his counterfeit car parts business, he has six civil suits from six car companies seeking compensation and damages, and the families of everyone who was ever injured or killed in an accident where his parts failed have filed their own suit. Everything he owns has been attached. No more house in Naples. No more spread on the Cape.

Plus, of course, he watched his son practically give away the car business."

"But we didn't have anything to do with that," Jean said.

Samantha shook her head again. "We had everything to do with that. I never told you – probably because everything moved so quickly afterwards – but on my way to the airport the day Paula and I flew to San Francisco, I paid a visit to the state Attorney General's office, and I spent two hours walking one of her assistants through the more sordid parts of Al Junior's business. They had copies of everything they needed to close down the business, but I suspected that there was so much it would take them a month or more to figure out how to prosecute it."

Samantha continued. "But when we got back from California the next morning, Al Junior's wife – Muriel – had the decency to call me and tell me that Smilin' Al was on the warpath. Maybe I already knew most of it, but it took a world of courage for her to make that call. So, at nine o'clock on Sunday morning – after I assumed that the parts people had seen what Smilin' Al had been doing to them for years – I called Muriel."

"I told her to tell her husband that if he had any offers to buy the dealerships, he should take them, because things his father had done were going to become public knowledge and that would drive down the price further. I asked her not to use my name, and I suspected she knew exactly what I was talking about."

Samantha opened her purse and pulled out four envelopes. "I've been saving these for today. This is Mass Casualty's way of saying 'thanks'. I don't think any amount of money could be enough to make up for what you went through." She looked at Alice, who still wore a cast on her hand. "None of you got into this thinking your lives could be in danger."

She passed around the envelopes. "I guess my question is whether this is the last meeting of the Garden Club Gang or, if something comes up, I could give you a call…"

They were interrupted by a knock at the kitchen entry. Marilyn

Davis stood in the doorway.

"I hoped to catch you together," Marilyn said. "I'm still not sure how you did it, but thank you. The family knows how my grandmother died, they know who was responsible for her death, and they have back the painting – the real painting. Without you, none of this would have happened."

Marilyn reached into her purse and pulled out a checkbook. "Back when this started, I asked who would be paying for Alice's stay at Cavendish Woods, and Samantha said not to worry about it, but that if I wanted to make a contribution afterward, that would be all right."

Paula laughed. "After Alice's brush with Jillian Connolly, management insisted on a full refund of her fee. We even got a letter of apology."

"They didn't apologize for wanting to charge me nine dollars for those smoothies, though," Alice added. "That would have been highway robbery."

"But you risked your life," Marilyn said to Alice. "And all of you were so involved…"

Alice held up her good hand to cut short Marilyn's words. "Don't thank us. We were Cecelia's friends. That's what friends do."

## Acknowledgments

When 'The Garden Club Gang' was published in 2011, I had no thought to it being anything other than a stand-alone story. After all, you can rob a fair only once. But the reaction to the book was immediate and vocal: "What are 'the ladies' going to do next?" is the question I have fielded ever since. It took two years to come up with a satisfactory answer to that query.

I did not set out to write a screed against nursing home care, automotive dealers, or 'protect your assets' law firms (although I find the latter's ads as annoying as do the characters in the book). Rather, the genesis of the story was attending the wake of a nonagenarian member of my garden club which, like the one for Cecelia Davis, took place in the nursing home where she and her husband resided.

That event sent me on a research mission to learn about nursing homes and then an expanding circle of eldercare-related subjects. Within a few weeks, I was certain I had a plot worthy of 'the ladies'. As to Pokrovsky Motors (alluded to in the final paragraphs of *The Garden Club Gang*), newspapers are filled with a depressing number of scams of the type being run by both 'Smilin' Al' and his son.

I pride myself on 'getting details right' and, to the best of my research abilities, what Eleanor learns about getting her husband 'Medicaid ready' in Chapter 26 is accurate, even if the fictional firm of Liss and Swann has pulled out every trick in the collective book. Jane Cronin's confession about the 'fundamental lie' of Medicaid care in Chapter 16 is also well documented as are the financial arrangements required by CCRCs such as the fictional Cavendish Woods. A Google search of Kristen Gilbert, Charles Cullen, Cathy Wood and Gwendolyn Graham will provide ample details about caregivers in nursing homes who have deliberately caused the deaths of patients under their care.

I have a circle of supporters whose efforts make my writing appear far more polished than it has any right to be. Proofreaders

Faith Clunie and Connie Stolow have my profound thanks for their keen editing eyes. My wife, Betty, is unstinting both with praise and criticism as warranted on points of plot and dialog. These stories are far better because of her diligence.

The past several months have been exhilarating ones for me. The trickle of speaking opportunities has turned into a torrent of invitations. I am deeply grateful to the garden clubs and libraries that have provided such great word of mouth. For me, such talks are immense fun and an opportunity to meet readers and convert non-readers. Please keep those invitations coming.